Freak of Nature

Also by Phil Whitaker:

The Face
Triangulation
Eclipse of the Sun

# of Freak Nature

Phil Whitaker

Atlantic Books
LONDON

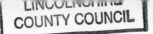
First published in Great Britain as a Paperback Original in 2007 by Atlantic Books, an imprint of Grove Atlantic Ltd.

9 8 7 6 5 4 3 2 1

A CIP catalogue record for this book is available from the British Library.

ISBN: 978 1 84354 536 1

Design by Lindsay Nash
Printed in Great Britain by Bookmarque Ltd, Croydon

Atlantic Books
An imprint of Grove Atlantic Ltd.
Ormond House
26–27 Boswell Street
London WC1N 3JZ

In memory of Derek Whitaker, who did justly,
loved mercy, and walked humbly with his God.

And, of course, for LPR, with love.

Most people in the Western world today accept some form of dualism. They believe they have both a mind, or a soul, and a body. I have even heard some people tell me they have three parts – a body, a mind, and a soul. But this is definitely not the view of the professionals.

John R. Searle, *Mind*

In Utero

It starts, as all things do, with an explosion. A sudden rush, pumped by urgent smooth muscle, propelling them pell-mell in a switchback of breakneck bends and long long straights.

Whoosh!

Whooooah!

Whee!

Then out. Away. Free-falling for an instant before touchdown. Unclip harness, throw parachute to one side. Not a moment to take stock, not a moment to lose: this is alien territory. They scatter in all directions, swimming like that is all they were ever made to do – some the right way, most the wrong, sheer weight of numbers compensating for the lack of an intelligence briefing.

In the midst of it all one sturdy fellow, tail swishing, tadpole head down. Blind to the bodies piling up all around him on the Normandy beaches, the weaker ones, those less lucky. Panicked, deformed comrades turn endless circles – one with half a head, one with a broken tail – but he pays them no heed. This is pure competition, no room for compassion, no prizes for running up. The winner takes it all.

Abba. Father. Four Swedes in sequined jumpsuits. It doesn't bear thinking about.

What shall we call him? John, let's call him John. John is going well, flickering tail thrusting him onwards through the mazy spinbarkheit strands. He steers a straight course, slotting like a tube train into the tunnel up ahead. Where it will lead he doesn't know. But he will swim, swim, swim till his energy runs dry or he hits a dead end or some calamity befalls him or – dare he dream it? – he is finally engulfed in the pillow-like membranes of the Beloved.

Part One

There is something that many find disturbing,
even revolting, about the notion of a soulless
body, a purely physical creature that acts as
though it were a person. This reaction is
worrisome given the scientific consensus…
Modern science tells us that the conscious self
arises from a purely physical brain.

Paul Bloom, *Descartes' Baby*

Ariadne

Ariadne's rooms were at the top of one of the ancient staircases off Chapel Quad. Above the archway someone had chalked the crossed blades of the women's eight, together with a list of their conquests in the recent torpids.

'Rower, do you think?'

Mick followed the direction of my gaze. 'So?'

'It would explain the glutes.'

'Behave,' he told me.

The climb up the worn stone steps was technically challenging, given the medieval narrowness of the stairwell. A muffled 'Come in' followed Mick's knock. She was in the sitting room, ensconced in an old armchair, which she didn't deign to vacate to welcome us. My mouth was dry – not from nerves, but because of the filthy anticholinergics Mick insists I take to cut down saliva production.

'Thanks for coming,' Ariadne said, indicating the other chair. From what Prof had told Mick, our agreement to participate in her research was about as thrilling a thing as could happen to a neuropsychologist. You wouldn't know it. We were being greeted like a pair of spotty freshers, come for our first tutorial on rats and mazes and lumps of cheese. That's Oxford academics for you. The more legendary the thing they're working on, the more they affect to appear slightly bored. Still, her Nordic features were as enticing as I remembered: strawberry blonde hair, lips that Julia Roberts would pay a plastic surgeon good money for. I bet myself I could make them smile.

'So,' she said, crossing her legs, the movement causing a sibilant friction between the nylon encasing either limb. Now there was a thing. I tried to encourage Mick to settle a little lower in the chair, the better to assess the situation beneath her skirt, but nothing was doing.

'This first session will consist of a basic interview. I will be exploring the generality of your relationship, nothing too threatening. I'm on new ground here, and I really want.' She frowned, and sucked the top of her pen. 'The literature on twins is full of anecdotal evidence of parapsychological rapport, but your *obligatory proximity* is essentially unique.'

I tried to work out how she'd done that, spoken in italics.

'What I'd like to do first, if I may, is get you to do a drawing for me.'

She leaned forward, giving me a glimpse of cleavage and Mick a couple of clipboards. Then two coloured pencils. The sort Ellie uses: *Tree with Five-Legged Dog*, *Portrait of the Artist as an Orange Blob*. Memories of Mick's besandalled GP training days rushed to the front of my mind, clanging little handbells as they came. Self-analysis, role play, let's all sit in a circle and hold hands. If she mentioned the word empathy, I'd leave. Mick passed me a pencil and one of the clipboards. On the sheet of A4 was a stylized outline of a naked man, like you used to get on the credits to *World in Action*, complete with Davidian genitals.

'Now, I appreciate this is an artificial exercise, but I'd like you to shade on the diagram the areas of your body you consider to be yours – either wholly or in part. And it would contribute greatly if you would refrain from looking at each other's answers, please.'

The spring sun was streaming through the stone-mullioned windows. As Mick's pencil began to scratch methodically, Ariadne turned to look out at the roof-tops of St Ablart's. Her cheekbone cast a soft shadow; the brilliant light picked out the tiny downy hairs above her upper lip. She half closed her eyes, as though on a beach somewhere. I figured if I actually moved my head she'd pounce, so I made do with a sidewards peek.

The little bugger had his arm laid across the picture. All I could see was the nearest part, which he was fastidiously colouring without trespassing outside the lines.

I turned my attention to my own paper. My pencil was red, I noticed, while Mick had taken the blue. I dutifully did my stuff.

'Thank you,' Ariadne said, collecting the finished articles. She glanced at the results, and I saw the momentary rise in her eyebrows.

'That's very helpful. Now, I also want to ask you a number of preliminary questions. I need to establish the degree to which you believe your psyches impact on each other.'

Out of the corner of my eye I sensed Mick nodding. I nodded too.

'If I could start with you, Dr McDonald?'

'Mick, please.'

Bastard. The gentlest upturn in those lips. Fudge Brownie, that's what I reckoned the lipstick was. Jules wore it sometimes. I wondered if Mick had noticed.

'OK, Mick, thanks. So, yes, tell me, how do you see your brother?'

'Using a mirror,' I said.

She fixed me with a steady gaze. 'Perhaps if I explain some ground rules? I will ask you to speak in turn. While one is talking, the other should keep his thoughts to himself, so as to allow free expression. As much as is possible, you should try to forget that the other is here. We'll get much further.'

'Sorry,' I said.

'Dr McDonald? Mick?'

As Mick began to explain his feelings about me, Ariadne made notes on her own clipboard. This involved raising her knee slightly, the thigh forming a slanting desk. A glimpse of bare flesh. Joy of joys! Nobody but nobody wears stockings any more. I looked back at her face, the dark lashes, the eyes fixed on her notepad, the delightful little concentration crease right in the centre of her forehead.

'...but mainly I tend to think of him as American.'

'American?'

Such an endearing concentration crease, deepening as she puzzled over Mick's comment.

'American?' I said.

'*Mister* McDonald.'

'John, please.'

'Yes,' said Mick. 'You know, loud and brash and full of himself. Embarrassing to be seen with.'

She made an aha-ing noise and scribbled something on her pad.

'And this makes you feel, how?'

'Well, you know, embarrassed. Not all the time. But a lot. Really.'

'So there's a lack of control? In your environment, in the company you keep?'

'Spot on, yeah.'

Mick was nervous, I could feel the acceleration in our heart rate, and the palm of my hand was becoming moist. I'd get him for this, the bastard.

'And you, John? How does that make you feel, hearing what Mick has to say?'

Whoah, blue-grey eyes, the hint of a watery glister. Was that pity I could detect there? That's first base, getting the sympathy vote.

'Well, it hurts, you know?' I thumped our chest. 'Deep down, right here.'

She nodded and added another note. 'And do you feel that pain, too, Mick? The same as John, simultaneously?'

Mick has an unattractive noise he can make by sucking air too quickly up his nose. 'He's bullshitting. He's heard all that a thousand times before.'

Ref-er-ree! There's speaking frankly, and there's fucking your brother over. Although Mick and I are genetically identical, pretty much the only hobby we have in common is our appreciation of women. And given that Mick has long since taken himself out of the transfer market, this was spoiling tactics. Any glister there might have been in Ariadne's eyes had hardened now to a glitter. I held my hand up placatingly.

'He's right, I admit it. It's just.'

She gave me a tilt of her pretty head.

'I didn't want, you know, to do the same to him.' I hurried on. 'Not that I'm embarrassed of *him*. He's my brother, I'm proud of him.'

A snort to my right. Ariadne shot a warning glance.

'But it's like living with one of those call centre people. You know, you have an entire conversation, explain yourself in fifty different ways, and they keep saying yes I see what you mean, but when you finish they still haven't got a fucking clue what you're on about. Excuse my French.'

I waited, trying to read her expression. Oxford is stuffed full of these über-chicks; I see a lot of them, sitting in surgery as I do with Mick. They're a certain breed. Brains the size of, oh, I don't know, something very large indeed, and fit as fuck. They have the same haughty, iceberg demeanour. I wonder about it; I think it's the dumb blonde thing. They are absolutely gorgeous, all of them, and I reckon they've cultivated this I-have-no-genitals look so people are forced to take them seriously for their minds. Then when they get this far – she's a post-doc, so it's Dr Ariadne; and a proper doctor, too, not like Mick – they have to appear even more asexual because everyone assumes they must have been shagging their supervisor. I've always wanted to get one in bed. See if I can make her yowl.

Ariadne was tapping her pen against those perfect white teeth. Mick, or me; I didn't know which way she was leaning. Eventually she spoke.

'What about your professional relationship?' She gave Mick a promisingly wan smile. 'I don't mean in your regular practice, Mick, but in your media work. I've watched you as part of my preliminary research. This mutual antipathy you describe is presented on television as fraternal affection. This is for the cameras, yes?'

'Media doctors are ten a penny. With John and me, they get both sides, considered professional opinion and ignorant irrational scepticism. The viewers love it.'

I nodded vigorously, figuring the sympathy vote must surely be back on.

'OK, yes, I see.'

When she was really perplexed, two other lines came to flank that central crease. The silence stretched like Lycra. I saw her slowly working it out, thinking through the implications. Jules, Mick and me. One bed. Ellie. I was intent on her eyebrows. Another slight lift and I'd know the way her thoughts had turned. Instead, she glanced at her watch.

'That's as far as I'd want to go today, gentlemen. I would like some time to consider matters further before deciding how to continue. In the meantime, perhaps you could take these away with you.' She passed across a couple of booklets. 'They're modified Boden biopsychosociometric personality inventories. We've compiled a series from sixty pairs of monozygotic twins with high concordance scores on the Alberta life trajectory index. I'd like to compare your profiles to the mean. It should be fun.'

She tossed her Timotei hair and smiled enthusiastically. 'Is there anything you'd like to ask, Mick?'

I felt Mick shake his head, and sensed his irritating, long-suffering smile.

'John?'

Her expression was depressingly neutral. I thought about asking her out for a drink. I thought about last night, Jules and Mick and me. And the sheet. And the rest of it.

'Nah,' I said. 'Maybe we'd better leave it there.'

Mick tried to get us up, but I played limp so Ariadne would have to show us out. We got to follow her to the door. I don't know about parapsychological rapport, but I could feel the heat off Mick's face on my cheek. Sheathed in the close-fitting material of her skirt, her backside was a joy to behold.

A Child is Born

My name is John Michael McDonald, son of Diane and Murray McDonald, both now deceased, god rest their souls. I am, in the words of my late father, a freak of nature. I have one brother, Michael John McDonald. He too is a freak of nature, though Dad, before he croaked, was to be heard voicing this verdict far less frequently in Mick's direction than in mine.

Our parents, by the way, were not generally noted for their sense of humour. It is inconceivable they believed the thing with the Johns and the Michaels was actually funny.

Because of our unusual physiology, Mick and I are currently not expected to make it past middle age, whenever that might be. Well before dementia and arthritis and cataracts, anyway. Some time around then it is predicted that our big baggy heart will give up our ghosts. No one can say whether our deaths will be a traumatic event for us – whether a coronary artery will suddenly block with clot, our chest crushed in a vice of pain so severe that our final acts will be to chorus 'Fuck *me*!' in perfect unison. I sincerely hope not. Mick, who ought to know, thinks it unlikely. In his opinion, it'll be an arrhythmia that gets us. One minute we'll be fine, the next our poor overworked ticker will shudder to a halt. All we'll notice is a feeble fluttering in our breast. There'll be a second of faintness, an overwhelming sense of impending doom, then that will be that. Whatever our eventual fate, we find it impossible to get life insurance.

Mick and I were born in the Royal Edinburgh Infirmary, under the watchful eyes of a whole gaggle of obstetricians and paediatricians and surgeons and god knows what. We are exactly the same age, down to the nearest split second. I am not going to mention the precise time and date of our birth – there's always the danger that someone will ascribe geopolitical symbolism to it. Suffice to say it was thirty-something years ago, and what was supposed to be a low-key delivery in the local cottage hospital ended in a mad ambulance dash for the capital, our mum transported in a head-down position with a panic-stricken midwife's hand shoved up her snatch, pushing back the umbilical cord that had prolapsed past our undiagnosed twin heads. These were, I should point out, the days before ultrasound scans; days, furthermore, when faint foetal hearts were monitored with nothing more sophisticated than an ear trumpet. In short, no one could have been expected to pick up the monstrosity lurking within our mother's womb. Nowadays we would have been detected well in advance, and if we weren't then our parents could sue the living daylights out of someone. Back then, it was just one of those things.

After a tricky couple of months on the neonatal ward, we were discharged to a council house near Biggar. It wasn't where we were supposed to have had our family home, but social services decided it would be the best place for our parents to bring us up. Nice and isolated. Cold and damp, too, which should have helped bring on a speedy resolution. We weren't supposed to make it past a year. Then certainly not to an age where we might actually talk. But at every stage the predictions have had to be revised. Like I say, currently we're looking at middle age. Time alone will tell.

Despite being Scottish through and through, Mick and I are most often referred to as Siamese. We each have a head. We each have a neck. Somewhere below the bulky fusion of our respective nearside shoulders our rib cages merge. Inside our chest is a pair of lungs, albeit unduly capacious in the upper lobes. We have one heart between us, which supplies our bizarre circulation. It has been much chopped and fiddled with, but to all intents and purposes it functions like anyone else's. I am the lucky owner of the only patent oesophagus, so I do all the eating and drinking, and Mick has to spit what saliva he produces. Each of us has one arm under our sole control. Mick is right-handed, I am left – etymologically speaking, he is dextrous whereas I am sinister. We have joint operational responsibility for everything below the nipples. Trying to coordinate walking is rather difficult – imagine your legs keep heading places you have no intention of going. It took us till we were five before we even began to master the art, but when we apply ourselves we manage. When we can't be bothered, we use a wheelchair.

Anatomical misfortune compels us to carry our heads at an angle to the vertical. Over the years this has put considerable strain on the muscles and ligaments: I am a pain in Mick's neck, he is a pain in mine. If spasm causes either of us to jerk in the opposite direction, the other gets a bang on the ear. Certain relief can be obtained by synchronized lateral flexing, but this requires cooperation and communication. We sleep on our back. Mick snores like a bastard. He says I do too. Mick's wife, Jules, refuses to be drawn.

Whenever we go places we're not well known – and we see no reason not to get out and enjoy ourselves – we attract a good deal of horrified attention. No one wants to look up from their exquisite starter to find a two-headed man shovelling food into one of his mouths while expectorating saliva into a stainless steel spittoon from the other. We're only five foot five, skeletal growth being compromised when you're eating for two. I do have a healthy appetite, though, with a weakness for refined carbohydrate and animal fat. Exercise is something of a problem, hence the weight. Being from the one egg 'n' sperm combo, we are identical. We cut our hair the same – short, to mitigate premature male-pattern baldness. We tan to a similar degree, match exactly for eye colour, have mirror-image pudgy noses, and possess equally gappy front teeth. I have been forced to grow a goatee to assert my individuality.

People like us are as rare as raw steak. We started as one – one conceptus growing in the womb. Who's to say, but I have always been convinced that the single person of the early post-fertilization period was destined to be *me*. I am quite certain that Mick should never, by rights, have existed. Before anyone even knew I was there – long before Mum suspected the duff was well and truly up – a split, a schism, occurred. It's twins, Mrs McDonald. Yet the division was incomplete, the dough never separated into individual buns. Most people like us are born dead, or expire soon after. Of those who survive, some can be surgically separated, perhaps left with nothing more dire than a peculiarly shaped arse. But for Mick and me no operation is possible – we are completely parapagus, fused at the lateral trunk, and we share our vital organs. Back when we were born, the common term for people like us was double monsters. The world has moved on, has learnt a smidgen of tact. Nowadays we are known as conjoined twins.

Jules

Our gait tends to suffer when our minds are otherwise engaged. We staggered across the billiard table lawn in Chapel Quad, looking for all the world like we'd been to the SCR for lunch.

'You have to go and fuck everything up, don't you?' Mick said, at last.

People who say smoking is no longer cool haven't witnessed me in action. I can flip a fag out, spin it round my finger like it's a Colt Peacemaker, then land it between my lips while simultaneously sparking the lighter nestled in my palm. It's wizard. I took a much-needed drag.

'What about you?' I said. 'I was in there, definitely, till you went and guffed all that stuff about not liking me.'

'I don't like you.'

'Well, I don't like you much, either, but there was no need to tell her. What ever happened to Mick 'n' John, the likely lads, the wanna-see-what's-in-our-trousers routine?'

Because we share the same lungs our arguments have a peculiarly exciting quality, as though we're perpetually being rendered speechless with rage at the other's impertinence. I waited while Mick allowed the bellows to refill.

'The whole point of *that*' – he jabbed a finger in the air – 'was to tell her the truth. How do you suppose she's to formulate valid psychometric profiles if we're lying through our teeth? I'd be surprised if she even holds another session.'

'That's what it always comes down to you with you, isn't it? You know they all laugh at you, don't you?'

'Who does?'

'That lot. The bloody academics.'

He produced an impressively cross growl. 'The point is, you agreed to take part in her research, and she expects you to be honest with her. That's all *I* was doing.'

'I agreed to take part because she's got a fantastic arse.'

'I rest my case.'

We negotiated the tunnel into the main quad in silence, our feet landing more rhythmically as we marched towards the porter's lodge. We were on our way back to the practice, where afternoon surgery awaited us. The ill-feeling wouldn't last. Now I was out of the heat of the situation, I could see how ridiculous the idea of a naked Ariadne was, sitting astride us, panting yes yes yes, her hair draped over her bouncing breasts. About as ridiculous as her avowed aim of investigating the neuropsychological apparatus of the self. Mick would come round, once he saw the ludicrousness of it all. If anyone wanted proof positive of a metaphysical basis to character, of the feathered phoenix hovering above the jellified soup of neuronal substrate that is the brain, they need look no further than us. In fact, the more I considered it, the more I regretted not entering into Ariadne's project with anything like the required sobriety. We were an awkward fact that couldn't be shoe-horned into any neurobiological theory of the soul. Genetically indistinguishable; identical nurture, such as it was; and as alike as yin and yang.

Mick was still in a huff, humming his I'm-going-to-deprive-you-of-the-oxygen-of-publicity hum. Now was not the time to share my thoughts. Humpty-hum humpty-hum. I waited till he had to take a quick breath, then interjected myself.

'So what did you put on your picture?'

'What picture?'

'The colour by numbers thing.'

'Oh, the usual.'

I took another lungful of smoke, and watched it reappear as Mick spoke again: 'How about you?'

'Nothing, really,' I told him. 'I didn't think her diagram was representative.'

'It wasn't meant to be. She said that, didn't she? The whole point was, she was trying to separate us into individual selves.'

'We are individual selves.'

'We're individual brains. The self is a construct, incorporating the physical body and much else besides.'

'Ooo, listen to you.'

'You didn't draw anything?'

'I didn't colour it in. I made it a bit more realistic.'

'You put me in as well?'

'Sort of.'

Albert was in the lodge. He called a cheerful 'Afternoon, gents!' through the hatch. We raised our hands as we passed.

'She does have a fabulous arse, though, doesn't she?'

Humpty-hum. A soft exhalation. 'Absolute peach, yes.'

Jules Jules Jules. She was over at the sink, chopping courgettes, when we arrived home.

'Hi, there.' She summoned up her sunniest smile, drying her hands on her jeans as she came to meet us. 'Good day?'

'Uncle John! Daddy!'

Little Ellie appeared from the sitting room and launched herself airborne from a full-pelt run, something she's been told a thousand times never to do. Thankfully, we made a safe catch.

'Hello, girls,' we synched, giving Ellie a combined hug. Mick took delivery of a quick kiss on the lips from Jules, I had my cheek pecked the moment after.

'Come on, you.' She prised a reluctant Ellie from our arms. 'Let Daddy and Uncle John get in.'

Jules plonked her on the floor and turned her in the direction of CBeebies. I watched her skip across the tiles. Skip! For weeks she'd been on about how the bigger girls do it, had been trying desperately to emulate them. As often as not her ungainly hops and stutters would finish with her sprawled on the floor. And now she could do it! My eyes followed her light-footed progress down the length of the kitchen, skippity skippity skip. Her blonde hair flicking. Her little skirt swishing.

'Brilliant!' I called. 'Great skipping, Ells.'

Jules helped us out of our bespoke jacket and gave our back a tender rub. I alone have sensation around the left shoulder, Mick the right. Below our scapulae, we can feel everything both sides. The soft journey of her fingers and palm. The soothing glide over the cotton of our shirt.

Supper was double helpings of chicken and mushroom pie, encased in Jules's excellent short-crust pastry. Two large jacket potatoes with oodles of melted butter. Steamed courgette, though I am not, by nature, a vegetable person. I oblige with a few of what's on offer as an example to Ellie.

'Fantastic,' I told Jules, waving my fork.

If ever I feel sorry for Mick, it is at mealtimes. A whole world of sensory delight is denied to him – he has never once relished the bloody marvel of Aberdeen Angus, the cloying sweetness of *tarte au citron*, the hoppy roundness of Timmy Taylor's Landlord, the effusive charms of a chicken jalfreizi. In the past, I have tried to persuade him to taste, to chew, to savour. The swallowing, after all, is the least interesting part of the process. He has never been convinced. There's the disposal to be thought of, of course, though he has to do something with the floods of saliva that pool in his spinster mouth, in any case. But I think there's a more deep-seated dread, a fear that if he were ever even partially to appreciate the gustatory glories never to be his, the injustice might send him mad.

Still, look on the bright side, it means he can talk uninterrupted through the meal. Moans about the new contract, problems with the PCT, yatter yatter yatter. I was well into the first baked spud before it dawned on me that tonight he wasn't. I stole a glance at Jules. She was dabbing her napkin at a smudge of white sauce at the corner of her mouth, eyes downcast. I kebabed a stack of courgette and transferred them to my eater, my movements slowed by a new caution. Out there in the big wide world I'd slipped too easily into the usual pattern of things. I'd managed to fool myself into thinking things would be similarly normal when we got home.

Jules caught my eye for a second, then looked hurriedly back at her plate.

In the way of four-year-olds, Ellie had sensed the mood without understanding the first thing about it. I fixed her with a serious stare and ever so slowly inflated my cheeks, as though my mouth was filling with vomit. She laughed.

I washed the courgette down with a purposeful swig of beer.

'So, how was your day, Jules?'

She held my gaze briefly. 'Fine, thanks. All right, yes.'

I nodded. 'How about you, Ells? Good day at nursery?'

She giggled from across the table. 'Uncle John! I was a mouse! Not a pretend mouse, a *real* mouse!'

'Yeah? That's great.'

'Mrs Bateman was com*pletely* confused. She thought: that's odd, normally there's Ellie at nursery, but today there's a *mouse!*'

'Squeak, squeak, huh?'

'Squeak, *squeak!*'

'Ellie!' Mick interrupted. 'Finish your supper. And have you thanked Mummy for making it?'

'*Thank* you, Mummy.'

'That's quite all right, darling.' Jules gave Ellie a cheerful smile. 'Thank you very much for thanking me.'

In accordance with hard-hammered compromise, we devoted the early evening to family matters. Ellie trounced me at *Buckaroo* while Mick caught up on the post; then Jules, kitchen cleared, joined us for a fun-filled game of *Don't Wake Dad*. Mick lost, as usual, but if he will insist on simultaneously watching Channel 4 news then he can't complain about being slipped the occasional duff card.

Ellie spent her entire bathtime lying on her front, kicking her legs and flapping her arms.

'I'm a dolphin! I'm a dolphin!'

'I see that,' I said. 'Splish splash splosh.'

'OK, Ellie,' Mick butted in. 'Time to get out now.'

'No!'

'Ellie!'

'NO!'

'ELLIE!'

In the end I intervened, pretending to be a nasty tuna fisherman who'd caught her by mistake in his dragnet (towel). She's very interested in matters ecological.

Down in the bedroom, Mick, tired out by his day at

the practice, continued to hurry her along. The older she gets the more she chafes against it. She spent a while haring round her room pretending to be a horse, neighing and shrieking with excitement while her pyjamas dangled limply in his hand. I love her spirit, her energetic non-cooperation – and given that I'm not her dad I'm actually expected to leave Mick to deal with it. She judged it perfectly, tipping him over the edge into fury.

'ELLIE! Will! You! Just! Come! Here!'

Once she's made him lose it the fun is over. Some nights she turns the screw by bursting into tears, but tonight she went for meek-lamb, climbing swiftly into her jammies and leaving Mick in no doubt just how helpful she could have been were he not such a grumpy old git. She sat on our lap while Mick speed-read *Ginger* and I dawdled my way through *The Gruffalo*. Then it was snuggle down beneath the duvet and time to be a snoozle-woozle.

'Night-night, Uncle John,' she said, grinning. 'Night-night, Daddy.'

We shared an hour of telly with Jules. It was one of Mick's favourites, *Second Fiddle*, that makeover show where top surgeons redo bodge jobs from those cosmetic surgery clinics that advertise in the *Sunday Times*. As he watched, he periodically tapped his fingers on the arm of the chair. Jules gazed blankly at the screen.

'Christ! Buttock implants, eh?' I said, trying to lighten the mood during the ads.

Neither of them responded.

When the final credits rolled – and I had to admit, if you wanted an arse like J-Lo's, the end result was a good 'un – I made a big deal of looking at my watch.

'So, what's it to be?'

I felt Mick turn to look at Jules.

She let out a noisy exhalation. 'Up to you.'

Mick paused for a few prickly seconds. 'Well, John-boy, I guess you get to do your book.'

Jules's only reaction was to stab the remote. We wished her goodnight, leaving her curled up in front of a Michael Flatley dance spectacular. Up in the bathroom Mick studiously avoided my eyes in the mirror. I watched as he sluiced his mouth with Dentyl pH, flossed with one of those one-handed catapult contraptions, then ran the electric toothbrush all around. Ridiculous, considering his dental redundancy but, like he says, teeth are for much more than chewing. Rinse complete, he tried out his media doc smile, the wall-mounted mirror turning for an instant into the hooded aperture of a camera.

'We could turn in, if you want,' I offered.

We listened for a moment to the muffled strains of *Riverdance*, percolating up the stairs.

His eyes held mine for an uncomfortable time. 'If you want.'

I shrugged my shoulder. We turned to go.

I brewed a pint of coffee to start the engines. Ferried through a two-litre bottle of vanilla coke, a bottle of whisky. And peeled the cellophane off a ten-pack of Marlboro Gold, my grudging concession to Mick's status as father and provider for four. I finally got to the computer at half-nine, which would give me three or four hours before being too pissed to continue. I opened the file containing the first few chapters of *Sister Sebastian's Library*, my novel-apparently-in-progress about a missionary nun in Bogotá. Mick started to flick through the latest issue of the *British Medical Journal*. Whenever my fingers tip-tapped on the keyboard I sensed his eyes move to the screen, but if he thought the book was progressing excruciatingly slowly he said nothing. At some point creaking stairs announced Jules's retirement for the night. By the time the third Famous Grouse had landed in the stomach Mick had crashed, head hanging insensibly at the edge of my field of vision. I put my earphones in, loaded the delectable Sophie Ellis-Bextor into the CD drive and set her *Groovejet* playing on perpetual repeat to drown out his snores.

Ariadne had a point. As much as is possible, you should try to forget that the other is there. I shrank

Sister Sebastian on to the task bar, ready to be expanded at the click of the mouse should he stir. Then I opened Outlook Express, clicked the Create Mail button, and dashed off a note.

To: jules@mcdonald.demon.co.uk
Re: last night

Jules
Would I be right in thinking that, after all these years of marriage, you are utterly familiar with the limits of Mick's and my sensory awareness in this body of ours?
Yours, John

After sending it, the PC downloaded mail into my inbox. A clutch of messages from coquettishly named lasses containing fake stock market tips; offers of generic Viagra; and promises that, as well as bestowing an extra three inches, VP-RX penis enlargement pills would banish premature ejaculation. Plus a couple of spams from hardcore porn sites, which are always worth opening for the promo pics.

Post attended to, I recharged my whisky glass, lit a fag, and opened a file named, with pitiable optimism, 'Income tax self assessment'. Then I settled myself down for the real work in hand.

Dr Mick

It's the seventies. Punk head-butts disco right in the gob. There are street parties for the Silver Jubilee, OPEC rules the world, strikes are a national pastime and the country has only a few years' irresponsible fun left before Thatcher comes to power. At some point, free milk ceases to be available to children at break times. Neither Mick nor I would know exactly when, because we never once set foot in a school. When we were five, our mother, having given up on the untimely curtailment of our young lives so confidently predicted by the doctors, sought to teach us to read and write. By then we were being given another ten years at the outside. Presumably, in the unthinkable event that we were to reach the age of majority, we needed to be equipped to make last wills and testaments. She also coached us in rudimentary maths so that, if we ever did, we'd be in a position to query the solicitor's bill.

We turned eleven, our prognosis was revised upwards, and the thorny question of fitting us for adult life sneaked its way on to the agenda. It was an era before PC. Mainstream education didn't appear to be on – the powers-that-be in the local authority feared it would prove too unsettling for the normal children. We would, of course, be welcome to attend the special school, housed in a low, flat-roofed building in nearby Carstairs. The council would even pay the taxi fares. Mum was keen on the idea, but our father harboured lingering misgivings.

Mum: It's for the best. I can't teach them anything more here.

Dad: How many times do I have to tell you, they're not going in with the spastics.

Dad's position on this issue could be construed as a prefiguration of the current, highly laudable determination to educate all children together wherever possible, regardless of physical or educational need. It is far more likely that he simply didn't want us to be seen by the outside world. Without wishing to speak ill of the dead, I don't think it unkind to speculate that Mick and I were an enduring source of shame to him. A taciturn, great-lump-of-granite of a man, he came from a long line of minor Scottish folk heroes. His own father lost an arm and several front teeth one storm-lashed night in an epic lone struggle to pull a stricken fishing vessel off rocks in the Firth of Forth. A jobbing farmhand, Dad had more than lived up to his forebears' legacy with three consecutive victories in the all-counties ewe-wrestling championship at the annual Lanark show. It is hard to see how any son of his could have surpassed that, and with our unique physical circumstances Mick and I certainly knew better than to try. Throughout our childhood, Dad remained a remote and unaffectionate figure, spending what little time he had away from work down the pub. In his absence he left strict instructions with our mother that we were not to be allowed out. Anyone who has spent considerable periods inside a two-bedroom Lanarkshire council house will understand the tedium.

Which is not to say that we didn't on occasions make good our escape. Mum suffered dreadfully from constipation, and if we picked our moment carefully there was very little she could do to prevent us dodging out the back door. We had no friends to visit, no specially adapted Raleigh Chopper to ride, and the mobile library came but once a fortnight. By and large we made our own entertainment. The house enjoyed unobstructed views over a landfill site, and we spent many a happy hour seeking out glass bottles with marble stoppers in the neck, and other relics of a bygone age. After the bare linoleum of home, the unevenness of the mounds of rubbish over which we scrambled brought our walking on a treat. I remember those carefree and joke-filled excursions with something akin to pleasure. Back then we were all we each had in the world.

It was rare for our presence at the dump to excite any interest. Kids our own age were away in class, and the old tramp who scratched a living scavenging among the detritus of human consumption was so meths-sozzled it must have been a good while since he'd seen a person with just the one head. However, until we learned to avoid half-terms and holidays, Mick and I did from time to time encounter other young lads. The taunts and brick throwing led to several unscheduled hospital visits. The adjustment difficulties the LEA had feared in the normal children were confirmed.

Enter a social inept called Mr McMahon. Greasy hair cut in classic pudding bowl style, and with a remarkably unpleasant body odour – no school would keep him on its permanent roll longer than one term before finding some spurious reason for redundancy. In order to avoid begging in shop doorways – an occupation at which I still believe he would have excelled – he became our home tutor.

Mr McMahon was a physicist first and foremost, but could hold his own in chemistry and maths too. Weaker subjects included everything else. Presumably we should have been given a broader education, but I imagine he was the best the local authority could get.

Mick displayed an early fascination with science, most particularly human biology. What started as a harmless interest in Jonathan Miller's *The Body in Question* soon turned personal, and before long he was trying to figure out exactly why, anatomically speaking, he couldn't eat. Once he'd got that one sorted he was hooked. To comprehend the complexities of a body like ours requires detailed knowledge. He read every text-book going. It still makes me faintly sick to say it, but he and Mr McMahon bonded. Mick did so well in his science Highers, the exam board investigated him for cheating.

Biology, chemistry and the like are OK. You wouldn't want to devote your life to them or anything, but when faced with a wet afternoon in the company of a tearful mother and a stuporous father they can help pass the time. To me, nothing is more tedious than the What Why and How. If you can do something, there's simply no need to give it a second thought. My refuge during those long adolescent years lay in a world far beyond the Scottish Borders, a land of the Lazy S, where buzzards circled, wagons rolled, and sagebrush tumbled across the range. While Mick tried to understand why when he swallowed a mouthful of something it remained lodged in his throat, I worked my way through every paperback in the mobile library's Western collection.

For all my ardent enthusiasm, my familiarity with the works of Zane Grey had no outlet in the conventional academic sense, and Mr McMahon was not the man to harness it to any constructive purpose. The years passed, our voices broke, exams loomed. Mr McMahon could see no merit in my taking any. Forced to sit idly by and watch my brother scribbling his answers with frenetic intensity – a performance that was to lead to straight 'A's in every paper – I consoled myself with surreptitious genital stimulation, lent an S&M flavour by Mick breaking off to slap my hand away between sentences.

Throughout our gap year – a necessity given the inordinate length of time it took the General Medical Council to resolve the ethical dilemmas Mick's UCCA application had thrown up – my misgivings about his determination to go to university grew. I was crippled by feelings of inadequacy: after all, I would have no right to be there. Mick was the star turn, I was merely his appendage, a fact that was hammered home to me at interviews in various medical schools around the country. Our sorties among the rubbish heaps lost their lustre, Mick and I ceased to laugh together, and even the unearthing of our two-hundredth stoneware Milk of

Magnesia jar failed to raise more than a desultory cheer. We were callow youths, but Mick at least had his academic armour-plating to protect him. Though I longed to flee the parochial world of our one-house hamlet, the route open to me filled me with deep ambivalence.

Once Mick's place was finally confirmed, and our departure date was set in stone, I increasingly sought solace out West. But the chicory coffee proved strangely bitter on my tongue, and the beef jerky had turned unaccountably chewy. Those tall, taciturn heroes of yesteryear, with their lightning draws and intriguing facial scars, weren't quite the men they once were. I flirted with the Algerian desert in the company of P. C. Wren's *Beau Geste*, but life as a foreign legionnaire held little allure. Sven Hassel looked more promising, and for a while I dallied with his platoon of adventurers as they enacted atrocities against the Red Army. Yet the Russian front was cold and inhospitable, and the novelty of automatic weapons rapidly palled. I felt directionless, floundering among the fiction shelves with no idea how to escape the destiny being mapped out for me.

I remember the day Mick and I left home as if it were yesterday. Dad was clearing up the matter of a drunk and disorderly charge that had seen him spend the previous night in the local police station. Mum was on hand, though, as she had been every single minute of our excessively house-bound lives thus far. She supervised the loading of our cases in the boot of the specially chartered taxi, ensured the driver had at least some idea where England was, then retreated to the porch of the shabby little prefab that had hosted what passed for our childhood memories.

I can still picture her, standing there on the doorstep, waving hesitantly as the car pulled away. I was looking out of the window – Mick was, too, but on his side was the landfill of our youth – and I suddenly saw her with disturbing clarity, a frail woman of abnormally short stature being left to cope as best she could with the tattered remnants of her life, a life without role or meaning now the sons she had devoted herself to raising since their first combined breath were flying the nest. As the Austin Allegro gathered momentum, the house and my mother began to slip behind us. Her face was so contorted by grief it was almost possible, at that distance, and with the bouncing of the car on the unmade-up road, to mistake her expression for one of unrestrained joy.

Throughout the two-day journey to Nottingham – the taxi blew its head gasket just outside Jedburgh – I pondered my future. I was to have none, whereas my brother was beginning an inexorable march to respectability and success, a path that would lead eventually to his partnership in an Oxford general practice.

Unlike every other wastrel sibling of a poor boy made good, I would walk each inch of that road with him, excepting the parts we travelled in the wheelchair. Little did I realize that by tagging on the heels of his achievements I would find my own modest satisfaction. Left to my own devices, it is difficult to imagine that I would have carved out the contented little domestic set-up I currently enjoy.

Happy Families

Walking is considerably easier when Mick's asleep. There are no conflicting motor outputs to reconcile, no incongruent joint-position sense to overcome. These putative advantages were more than outweighed by the minimal blood content of our alcohol stream. I lurched my way along the landing – Mick lolling insensibly against my ear – and slewed into what I thought was the bathroom. By the time I'd realized my error I was too desperate even to think about rectifying it; I only just managed to get our plonker out in time. Urine gushed through the open window in an interminable stream, spattering, with a noise like shorting electricity, on the plastic patio furniture fifteen feet below. Once Nature's call had been fully and frankly answered, I let out a satisfying belch. Ellie, bless her cottons, never stirred. I leaned over and planted a fumey kiss in the vicinity of her nose. I tucked her duvet more snugly round her. So peaceful in her dreamy child's sleep. My niece, my almost-daughter, the delight of all our lives! I smoothed the hair from her forehead, poking her accidentally in the eye, then headed off to Mick's and my bedroom.

Pyjamas were out of the question, so I contented myself with divesting us of most of our clothes before collapsing on the mattress. The darkened room spun wildly around me. I marvelled at Mick's ability to sleep the sleep of the just while being tossed on the vertiginous equivalent of a storm force ten. He tells me he has the weirdest dreams.

Jules. She roused briefly with the impact of our arrival, and landed an arm over us. I could feel it heavy on our chest, rising falling with our breathing.

'Jules?' I whispered into the blackness.

She let out a croaky 'Hmmm?'

'Jules, we've got to talk.'

I waited, blood pulsing in my throat.

'Jules?'

But she had gone, slipped back to the realm of the unconscious.

We own a Hypnos king-size, Mick's and my side sprung with extra stiff coils to support our overworked back. Once we're down, it's the devil's own job getting up to the vertical without his assistance. Our heart thumped madly. I lay as still as I could and willed myself not to puke.

Jules. When we first met I wasn't thinking straight. I wasn't thinking of anything beyond the next dose of drugs. A median sternotomy might sound innocuous, but there is something uniquely agonizing about a breast-bone that's been sawn down the middle. Every breath is pure pain, each cough an unthinkable torment. Pethidine was my friend, Opium my fiancée, Poppy the woman I would marry for her seed. Jules barely registered on the radar.

I have hazy recollections. Bobbed brown hair; generous smile; indefatigable good humour every time I tried to wangle some extra morphine. She helped Mick shave, ran a comb through my goatee. She gave us a bed bath once. I was listening to hospital radio at the time and enjoyed the consequence-free erection. I remember thinking she had nice hips, the sort you'd clasp as she ground herself on to you. And I suspected there was more to her bust than her uniform was letting on. But her calves were muscly from excessive cycling. The fingers that injected each blissful dose of Papaveretum were stubby, the nails bitten. And she moved with work-manlike efficiency, none of the wiggling wonderfulness of Charlie the locum physio, with the cascading waves of auburn hair, who came every day to assist us in expect-orating gobs of jelly from our post-operative lungs. Whose underwear was faintly visible through the white material of her uniform. Who always wore a teeny weeny thong.

I never saw what was happening till the day we were discharged.

Drummond-Smith, the consultant cardiothoracic surgeon with ongoing responsibility for sorting out the anomalies in our circulatory plumbing, came by in the morning.

'Well, that's about done it,' he said, speaking directly to our chest. 'Your aorta no longer overrides, your septal defect is closed, and I've fitted a new valve to your pulmonary artery. It's got a ten-year guarantee.' He handed Mick his card. 'You should be OK, but I've put my mobile on the back. Give us a shout if there are any problems.'

He wandered off, trailing his retinue of junior doctors and students, and left the ward without speaking to a single other patient. Several of them cast resentful glances our way, but if half of you happens to be medically qualified then that is precisely the sort of professional courtesy you can expect.

Jules peeled away from the round and sat on the edge of our bed. She made a show of smoothing the blanket.

'Well, that's good news, isn't it? I expect you're looking forward to getting home.'

'Not really,' Mick said, and I could tell he was thinking of our bachelor flat. The pokey kitchen with its stacks of empty pizza boxes, the threadbare carpet tiles, the spartan decor enlivened only by the Blu-tacked pictures culled from the previous year's Pirelli calender. We wouldn't be fit enough for him to return to work for another twelve weeks. That's one hell of a lot of daytime TV.

'Well, I for one am going to miss you,' Jules said.

I couldn't understand that. I'd hardly said two words to her during our entire ten-day stay. When I glanced up, she was looking straight at Mick.

'I expect we'll be popping back for follow-up,' Mick told her.

I couldn't see, naturally, but I felt Mick nod his head towards the swing doors through which Drummond-Smith had made his exit.

'Really?' said Jules.

'He's a decent bloke, usually sees us on the ward. Out-patients is hell.'

Jules was decidedly more chirpy by the time we were packed and ready to leave. I even persuaded her to give us a parting shot of diamorphine to cover the wheelchair ride back home. She pushed us out to the lift, and stood awkwardly in the lobby till the doors closed shut on us.

'What's going on?' I asked him, pressing the button for the ground floor.

'How do you mean?'

'With her, what's going on with her?'

'Nothing,' he said. 'She's sweet, that's all.'

The lift jolted, and started to descend.

'Pardon me for stating the blindingly obvious, but did you not notice the angel in white who daily came to relieve us of our bronchial secretions?'

'Sorry?'

'The bountiful Charlie. The physio. The one with the prominent nipples.'

'Ah, yeah, well. You ask her out, then.'

'I will. The moment's not been quite right as yet, but I will. The thing is.'

'What?'

'Are you thinking of asking Jules?'

'I might,' he said.

I gazed glumly at the LED display, counting down from 7.

'What?' he asked.

'I'm the one who does the sharking. You're hopeless.'

'That's fine, you carry on.'

'You want *me* to ask her?'

'No. You carry on with your sharking. Leave Jules to me.'

Ping! The doors slid open, unveiling the bustle of the hospital entrance foyer. Mick flicked the tiny joystick on his arm of the chair and the batteries kicked in, propelling us forward. The jolt over the uneven junction between lift and vestibule caused a stab of pain in our chest, in spite of the heroin.

'Seriously?'

'Seriously,' he told me, steering us round to the left. Passers-by gave us curious looks as we progressed, dalek-like, towards the main doors.

Jules rolled on to her other side, taking her arm with her. Its absence still pressed on our chest. Mick began to mutter in his sleep, lying between her and me. My eyes had adjusted to the gloom, and if I kept them focused on the light-shade I could tame the vertigo. Wellied as I was, release would not come.

I'd sat in a sulky silence throughout the entirety of their first date, drinks in the White Hart, a trip made several months after she'd cared for us on the cardio-thoracic ward. I listened to their gauche news-swappery: where they grew up, what music they liked, how super this pub was. I downed pint after pint and worked my way steadily through a pack of fags, from time to time catching Mick off guard and managing to squeeze out a fart.

It wasn't that I had anything against Jules. In fact, in tight leggings and a baggy man's jumper, she was trans-formed. Painfully so. Sly glances through beer glass bottoms, squint-eyed study as I pretended to follow another perfect smoke ring ceilingwards. Her faultless skin, her ready smile, her rapt attention as she listened to Mick. Hitherto I'd been responsible for the short-listing, interview and appointment of all prospective shags. Whenever we went to bed with someone, they went to bed with *me;* Mick was merely the jammy bugger who got to ride along for free.

Now, though. I couldn't remember that any girl had ever looked at me like that.

It wasn't just that he'd pulled, not simply that I was sidelined. I was worried for him. We'd never had a relationship, but from what I'd read this looked omin-ously like the start of one. I experienced the gamut of anxieties Mick should himself have been feeling: vulner-ability over opening up emotionally; the potential for rejection; the pain and bitterness that would arise should I manage to lure Charlie, say, back to our flat. As last orders was called, I steeled myself for the night to come, for the possibility that life would never hence-forth be the same.

He didn't even try to kiss her! We showed her back to the nurses' home, then told her goodnight. She took the hint, and took it with good grace. Her beaming smile hid all trace of crushing disappointment. It would have been so embarrassing if she'd tried to invite us in.

'Thank god for that,' I told him, as we weaved our way home.

'Yeah, good evening, wasn't it?'

'Great, great,' I chuckled, my thoughts already turning to how to persuade him to fly by the physiotherapy department some time on a palpable pretext. By the time we made it back to the flat, I felt positively well disposed to Jules. Hell, it wouldn't have been so bad if she had offered us coffee. I'd always fancied a threesome. Even if she and Mick had had a bit of a fling, I would soon have got my freedom again. It wasn't as if we were the sort of guys you could have anything long term with. It wasn't as if we were the kind of blokes anyone would actually think of marrying. In fact, I decided, as we made it into our cold bachelor bed, if Charlie kept up the hard-to-get routine much longer, I might just have a crack at Jules myself.

Mick had stopped muttering, had descended a level or two deeper into sleep. The room had finally ceased spinning and I felt an unaccustomed stillness, an eerie calm. Jules's breathing was quieter than his. Its obliviousness caused a physical pang. I wanted to reach across him, touch her head, stroke her hair till silently she woke. Ask her what the hell she'd done. What the hell it had meant. Whether it meant anything at all. But I was too drunk. And too tired, suddenly. And too afraid, I think, of what I might hear.

Wake Up Britain!

Only one train leaves Oxford early enough to get us to the studio on time. To catch it, Mick sets the alarm for 04:45. The bell smashed into my head, macerating my brain. I silenced it with a single, vicious, karate chop.

Next I knew, Mick was head-butting me from the side.

'Eat some breakfast, will you. I'm Hank Marvin.'

Somehow we were dressed and in the kitchen. My hand throbbed. The spotlights were piercingly bright, as though I was under interrogation. There was a bowl of mush on the table, topped with a sliced banana, standing beside a steaming mug.

'Oh, fuck,' I said. 'Oh fuck, oh fuck.'

'What time did you get to bed?'

'Four-a-fucking-clock.'

He held up a bottle, tilting it to accentuate the dribble of whisky remaining in the bottom. I nodded dumbly, head thunderclapping with the movement. The ruddy brown grouse on the label fixed me with its beady little, knowing little eye. Mick set the offending article down and tossed a couple of yellow pills into my palm.

'Get these down your neck.'

'What are they?'

'Salvation.'

I swallowed them with a scalding mouthful of tea.

'What's with the herbal shit?'

The night's fagging and boozing had laid waste to my tastebuds, and the cereal was inedible. The banana was not quite ripe, either, with a slimy texture reminiscent of okra; several times I gagged. I usually start the day with a monster fry – sausage, bacon, eggs, beans, hash browns – but when Mick's up and about before I wake he unleashes the organic muesli. I huffed and tutted my way through the whole disgusting exercise, observing that if we were to pass out and fall under the wheels of the train, it wouldn't be my fault.

'Stop fussing,' he said. 'I'm hungover, too, you know.'

'Yeah, but you don't have to eat this stuff.'

'Productive night, was it?'

'Sort of,' I said.

While I shovelled spoon after spoon of estuary silt into my gob, Mick ploughed through a couple of insurance forms from work.

'We can't keep going like this,' he told me at one point, crossing out the third mistake he'd made in transcribing the patient's personal details.

'Like what?' I said, extracting a bit of hazelnut from my teeth.

'If you're not bothered about us, at least you ought to think of Jules.'

'She's fine.'

'I assure you, at the moment she is anything but fine.'

'And whose fault is that?'

Mick took a deep breath, but before he could say anything, the taxi beeped from the street. We hurried outside, me torching a fag.

'You're not supposed to be having any before lunch,' Mick said, opening the car door.

'Technically, I haven't been to bed yet.'

'No smoking in the cab,' the driver told me.

'Fucking hell.'

Mick used his rechargeable Philishave on the way to the station. When he'd finished, I borrowed it to smarten up my cheeks and trim some protruding nasal hairs. We arrived with ten minutes to spare, and Mick told the cabbie to wait. Over the years Channel Five has had to pick up a fair few intercity taxi fares. That morning Thames Trains promised to have its act together, so we paid the driver and ducked into the gents to freshen our mouths with Listerine. Mick spat his into the sink. I swallowed mine by way of hair of the dog.

*

Lurking in the studio complex's green rooms, its airy house-planted foyers, there will be real live celebrities – it's guaranteed. The thing is, you've no idea, among the billion or so folk milling around, who they actually are. That lad you brushed past at the water cooler, that could be Michael Owen, but probably he's an apprentice carpenter. That gorgeous woman pressed against you in the lift, she could be Charli from Hi 5, or equally well a perky Aussie PR. The bloke you thought was here to service the heating ducts, as likely as not that's Alan Titchmarsh. You wander around eyeing everyone, thinking: ooh, now, who's *that*? And you can see people sizing you up, too, racking their brains, trying to work out if you're remotely important. There's glamour in the air here. Just by walking in you're dousing yourself in the possibility of fame. For the duration of his fateful few minutes in reception, that humble motorbike courier might just turn out to be Jamie Oliver.

Trouble is, no one looks like they do on telly. They're invariably considerably shorter, and, David Mellor excepted, a lot fatter too. Mick and I once had a slash standing next to Melvyn Bragg. Either that, or it was a midget with a passing facial resemblance and a post-ironic hairpiece.

The sets are the inanimate equivalent. There's the newsroom – banks of monitors, industrious people hard at it newsgathering. Only it's plonked in the middle of a cavernous space, cameramen and technicians orbiting like moons, and all manner of uninterested foot traffic passing by. A fully kitted kitchen for *Nigella Fries Good Egg*, the gaudy desks for quizmeister and contestants of *Who's Laughing Now?* Little islands of reality adrift in otherwise undifferentiated whiteness, brought to life only when cropped within the camera's frame. I love the whole glorious fakeness of it. Hubba hubba!

Mick and I were late – flooding on the line outside Didcot – so we hurried straight to make-up, passing just the one familiar figure on the way.

'Shit,' said Mick. 'Was that Robert Winston?'

I didn't disabuse him. He cares little for sport, even less for Des Lynam.

'Crack open another tub of foundation,' Jo called to Su. 'We are looking pasty this morning.'

Mick and I took our seat in front of the mirror. The monitor on the wall was showing the live output of *Wake Up Britain!* A woman who'd recently completed the first Channel crossing on an inflatable banana was promoting her new Pilates video. Jo draped a gown round our shoulders, then primed her powder puff.

'Ready... steady... go!'

She and Su set to, dabbing and brushing with deft strokes. Then a bit of lippie, then a bit of liner.

'Yey!' Jo claimed victory, in spite of Su having my bearded visage this week.

Finished in make-up, we shambled down to the green room. I downed an anticholinergic with some coffee straight from the cafetière, and we watched the screen as Davina strode purposefully along a snowy ridge, hair blustering around her, shouting into a hand-held radio mike.

'Coming up next: the robot who's set to replace the humble dog as man's best friend. Why more of *this*… might lead to more of *this*… And, thirty years after the *Clangers*, why soup is the new sushi. Plus our very own Dr Mick will be here to answer your health concerns. See you in four.'

'Miiick, Joohn.' Aldo, one of the production team, hurried in. 'Great, great,' he said, brandishing a sheet of paper.

'Thanks,' Mick said, taking it from him. Although it looks like Mick's being put on the spot, callers are screened and rehearsed by researchers during the first ninety minutes of the show. Mick needs a chance to mug up on rare syndromes, and no one wants the investigation of genital chlamydia detailed over their Pop Tarts.

'Here's your outfit,' Aldo said, unfolding a mass of

nylon and fake fur to reveal a two-hooded parka. He nodded in the direction of the adverts. 'We're in the Lakes today, up Helvellyn.'

There aren't many presenters who can get away with breastfeeding on national TV. None, in fact. Davina unzipped her Berghaus to give the bairn some air during the ads.

'Hi, guys!' She smiled as we came over.

We kissed her, one on each cheek, and she patted us affectionately on the chest.

'How's it going?' I asked, tickling the wee mite's feet.

'Great. She's sleeping through now, you know!'

'No! *How* old?'

'Three months!' She grinned delightedly.

'Bitch! Ellie didn't do that till she was one and a half. Nearly killed us.'

'So we're supposed to do this like we're on a mountain, are we?'

Davina looked at Mick. 'Yeah, they've made your desk up to look like a cairn.'

'Thirty seconds!' Aldo shouted.

'Off you come, sweetie.' Davina gently unplugged boob from sleeping baby, and handed the pink 'n' white bundle to Aldo, who gazed lovingly at it snuggled into the crook of his elbow. We headed across to the vast expanse of blue sheeting covering the walls and floor at the end of the studio. Davina fastened her 'Little Mutha Sucka' jacket, Mick and I flipped up our hoods. We took our seat behind a mound of grey polystyrene boulders, and watched as the crew formed up on Davina.

'Three, two, one,' the producer's voice came in our earpieces. Aldo mimed along, doing the old Ted Rogers thing with his fingers.

Davina minced determinedly towards the camera-man, who back-pedalled furiously. 'It's Tuesday, it's eight-twenty, and that can mean only one thing –'

A crew member shouldering an enormous fan blew wind in her face. Another production assistant threw handfuls of fake snow in the air.

'This is ridiculous,' Mick muttered.

'On air!' hissed the producer in our ears.

'– It's Dr Mick and his conjoined sidekick! Morning, fellas.'

'Morning, Davina!' we chorused.

Mick's a pro, all right. As soon as the camera was on us I felt him sit us up. His tone was bright, faintly amused, just the sort of voice for a doctor who finds himself conducting a surgery three thousand feet above sea level in the middle of the Lake District national park.

'It's been a busy week in the world of medicine. We've seen a fresh scare over HRT and breast cancer, another scare over breast cancer and alcohol consumption, and

new findings from researchers in the Netherlands suggesting that scares about HRT are driving women to
problem drinking.'

A handful of white powder hit me square in the face.

'I'll be unravelling the conflicting evidence surround-
ing the use of this increasingly controversial therapy.'

I blew the polystyrene granules off my lips. 'And I'll
be giving out a recipe for a seed cake that can relieve
unpleasant symptoms of the menopause entirely naturally.'

'First, though, your calls.'

The guy with the fan turned it full on me. The hood
blew off my head.

A disembodied voice boomed into the studio.

'Hello? Hello?'

'Hello, you're through to Dr Mick.'

'Hello? Is that Dr Mick?'

'Yes, you're through to Dr Mick. Who's calling,
please?'

'Right, yes. Dr Mick, it's Elsie. Elsie from Chelmsford.
My question is, my doctor has recently diagnosed
Alzheimer's disease, and I've been started on some
tablets called Aricept. What I wanted to know is –'

'Elsie, can I interrupt? Elsie, do you remember calling
in last week with the exact same question?'

'Did I? No, I don't think so.'

'You did, Elsie. Didn't she, John?'

I nodded solemnly. The guy with the bucket of snow sprinkled a handful directly into the airstream blowing in my face. Moving that fast, the stuff actually stung.

'Did I really? Well, I never.'

Across the studio, Aldo was making frantic cut-throat signs. Davina's daughter started to cry.

'It's a fucking joke,' Mick told me.

The cooked breakfast looked like being the perfect antidote to both the organic muesli and the traumas of the show. I couldn't get the side of the fork to cleave the sausage, so I pronged it and shoved it all in in one go.

'It's not her fault, though, is it?' My voice was muffled by the mouthful of pork. 'What did you reckon?'

'Akathisia,' he said.

We looked across the studio canteen to where Davina, infant slung in a BabyBjörn, was pacing restlessly back and forth eating a croissant. I swallowed my own massive bolus of food.

'Anyway, I'm the one the production guys keep picking on.'

'How do you mean?' he asked.

'Snow in the face, gale force winds in the chops? They know I can't do anything, not while we're on air. I'm going to nut them one of these days, I swear.'

I dunked a couple of chips in ketchup and surveyed them mournfully. 'You're not thinking of giving up, are you?'

Mick was silent, as if seriously contemplating the idea.

'Listen, this new book's going to be a cracker. You only need hang on till it gets published, then you can tell them where to stick it. My agent reckons a hundred grand for the UK rights, not counting serialization. Academia beckons you, Mick, my boy!'

'When did you get an agent?'

'A few months back. I told you.'

OK, I was only trying to boost his spirits. What I *had* got from the mailshot of sample chapters from *Sister Sebastian* was my very first personalized rejection letter. A handwritten note from a woman called Candida Lucas-Montefiori, saying she liked bits of it, but thought I'd do better if I wrote about what I knew. Set against the stacks of photocopied rejection slips in my enormous collection, her two-line pen 'n' inker was a veritable jewel, progress indeed.

Mick pushed the pepper aimlessly across the tabletop. 'You say that every time, and it's always the same.'

'Yeah, but this one's different. I tell you, it's rocking and rolling.'

'It doesn't look much cop to me.'

'Virgin nun comes of age in the cocaine capital of the world? Are you kidding?'

Candida Lucas-Montefiori clearly had no idea quite how spectacularly dull my life was. All I knew about was the Wild West, plus what it's like to be Mick's conjoined twin. Nevertheless, I was following her advice in my new work-in-progress. If Mick got wind of what I was really writing, he was not going to like it. Not one little bit.

He inverted the salt cellar, pouring a white hillock on to the Formica. Tiny grains tumbled down the side as it spread and grew. When he laughed, the salt scattered.

'Elsie from Chelmsford!'

'Yeah, bless her.'

'Aldo!'

'Aldo!' I agreed.

We fell into a companionable silence. Moments like this I feel close to Mick, just like when we were lads clambering over the landfill. Us united against the world. With every passing month the production team on *Wake Up Britain!* treated us with increasing frivolity. What had started out as fascinated respect had deteriorated into frank piss-taking. We might as well be working with Chris Moyles. It was a miserable dilemma: salvage our self-respect and quit in a strop, or swallow everything they could throw at us and keep pocketing the dosh. A few years back we'd have lined those snow 'n' wind merchants up and simultaneously broken their noses with our foreheads. Now there was Jules and Ellie to think of. And a dodgy ticker. And no life insurance. And a rented house in a sought-after neighbourhood, plus exorbitant school fees they'd be unable to keep up when we were gone.

The cabbie taking us back to Paddington kept glancing in his mirror. I'd seen the signs a thousand times. When we turned into the station approach he came out with it.

'Here, are you that Claire Rayner?'

I leaned my head slightly, touching Mick's temple. 'Dr Mick, from *Wake Up Britain!*'

The driver slapped his bald pate. 'Gotcha! Well, fancy that. *Fucking idiot!*'

He swerved to avoid a motorcycle courier; gave him a blast of horn.

'My daughter's a big fan of yours. You too,' he said, catching my eye in the rearview.

'Thanks,' we both murmured.

'That thing you did, about how to check your what-sits, that was top class.'

'Thanks.'

It's a bastard when this happens, it means you've got to give a big tip. It's a bastard any time Channel Five isn't picking up the tab, anyway.

'Fifty? You sure?'

'No problem.'

'Here, sign this will you?'

He handed over a jumbo marker together with his disability living allowance book. Mick and I scrawled our autographs on the inside cover.

'Smashing,' he said, admiring our signatures. 'I write poetry, you know.'

'Yeah? That's great.'

'Wait till I tell the daughter.'

We got a table seat on the train back to Oxford. I was seriously hanging, and was preparing myself for a big snooze: we still had an afternoon's work ahead of us once we'd made it home. Mick fetched some more paperwork out of his briefcase.

'Have you done yours?'

'My what?'

'This questionnaire. That Ariadne gave us?'

I shook my head. I couldn't even think where I'd put the pigging thing. 'Are we going back, then?'

'That rather depends on whether she wants us to.'

I looked at the booklet on Mick's half of the table. Must be a dozen sheets in all. Close-packed questions about our intimate details. Mick sucking up to Prof: yes yes of course we'll help out. His tongue practically hanging out with the idea that this might be it, his chance to weasel his way into the academic world.

Being reminded of it soured my mood, brought back all our disputes and differences after the brief camaraderie between us.

'Do you want to?'

'I thought you fancied her,' he said.

'I did. I do.' The thought of the sheet, of Jules's hand stealthing beneath it.

'Well, then.'

'I've got more important things on at the moment.'

'What, like your novel?'

I forced myself into a smile. 'Actually, perhaps it would be good to go back.'

Mick chuckled, and unclipped his pen from our shirt pocket. 'That's more like it. Ahoy ahoy, John, my boy!'

Baby Father

One of the oddities of Mick and Jules's marriage is the lengths they have to go to in order to have a private chat. It wasn't a problem before Ellie, back in the days when they used to go out: plays at the Burton Taylor, concerts at the Holywell music rooms, taking the Booster for a spin around Christchurch Meadows – any time they announced they actually wanted to spend an evening at home I would put my earphones in, pop a CD on, and leave them to it. Nowadays, though, I only know to do so when asked. If they're not careful about the timing, it's pretty obvious which particular issue they're about to thrash out. It's early days with the lip reading, but Jules's body language usually lets me know who's winning the day.

We made it back from London at half eleven. Jules was in the sitting room, in tears, the remnants of the alarm clock on the coffee table in front of her. Its casing was dented, the bell clapper bent, the springs and cogs and internal workings spilling out. Mick and I stood stock still; I was astonished by the mess of metal and the fragmented glass of its face. I became acutely conscious of the dull throb I'd been carrying round in my hand all morning. Sometimes I don't know my own strength. Sometimes I don't know I'm Bruce Lee.

Jules turned her wet cheeks towards us and tried a feeble smile. Instinct started to nag at me. Something was not right; Jules is not a materialistic person. Anyway, you can get that exact same clock from Argos for £11.99. It had no particular significance to her – it was a present from Mick to me last Christmas, and how I laughed. There was no earthly reason for her to be this upset over its demise.

The *Oxford English Dictionary* defines a symbol as a microscopically trivial thing that a woman will resurrect in an argument years after everyone else has forgotten it ever existed. It could be a material object, a throwaway remark, or a glance at another woman's chest. The unifying characteristic is that, in objective terms, it means diddly squat, but psychologically speaking it embodies every fault there has ever been with the relationship in question.

The realization evidently dawned on Mick at precisely the same moment. The trashed clock had become a symbol. Of something.

We rushed to her side.

'What's wrong?' Mick asked.

'Nothing,' said Jules, wiping her eyes with the heels of her hands. 'I'm tired, that's all.'

'I'll get the Discman,' I said.

I tend to buy albums on the strength of crackingly good singles, a purchasing strategy that frequently leads to disappointment. I've lost count of the times I've returned from HMV with a new CD, only to discover that the uplifting dance track that's been entrancing me all summer is a stylistic aberration from the artiste's long-standing commitment to dub techno. To make matters worse, the single that's been electrifying the airwaves invariably turns out to be an Oakenfold remix that doesn't appear on the album, and is irreconcilable with the pedestrian original version that does. In this respect, Dina Carroll is a goddess. *So Close*, her 1993 release, features no fewer than six pukka club anthems, and even the filler tracks are passably good.

Even so, I barely registered the songs. Mick had sat next to Jules, so the only thing I had to look at was the clock. Of her voice I could hear nothing; Mick's was but a vague vibration beneath the chirpy intro to 'Special Kind of Love'. I regarded the mangled timepiece warily, wondering what compact it had entered into with Jules's mind. She would have got my email some time during the morning. Could it be she was consumed by guilt, was even now blurting a pleading confession to Mick? I wanted to rip the earphones out, defend myself against any suggestion of impropriety on my part.

And yet, and yet. The shards of glass, the plain white face, the luminescent numerals. The motionless hands accusingly indicating quarter to five, the time of death. Time. Halted time. Time run out.

I began to develop an inkling. One with which I wasn't entirely comfortable.

When Ellie was four months old, Mick and Jules's entire NCT group had a reunion at Dan and Daniella's house. Eight variously patterned McLaren buggies parked in the hall. Eight mewling little angels, six of the pink variety, two of the blue. Sixteen fucked parents. Thirty-four black holdalls bunched beneath our eyes. Midway through the afternoon, Dan went and stood in front of the fireplace, and tapped a spoon against his glass of Red Bull.

'Attention, everyone!'

The room fell as quiet as a gathering of babies ever does.

'Um.' Dan laughed nervously. 'Danni and I have a little announcement to make.'

Five minutes later I was out on the patio, having a comforting bifta. Col, one of the three smoking dads, voiced our collective thoughts.

'How the fuck did they manage that?'

His tone was a mix of reverence and horror. We shook our heads, stared at the paving stones, and puffed harder on the nicotine sticks.

Mick did the self-conscious chuckle he imagines disarms people whenever he's about to pronounce on matters in his professional domain. 'Breastfeeding isn't particularly effective as a contraceptive.'

'No,' said Col. 'I mean, how the fuck did they actually *need* contraception?'

I nodded silently, the way one does in the presence of perspicacity incarnate. I wasn't even a father and I'd forgotten the last time I'd had a shag. Ellie arrived in our house like a mini-terrorist, and the other seven babies currently sprawled beneath activity arches in Dan and Daniella's lounge were members of her cell, ideologically opposed to adult sleep and prepared to use any means to bring about its downfall. They employed sophisticated techniques to infiltrate normal society and evade detection – gurgling, chortling, and gazing adoringly at any grown-up faces that entered their visual fields. Even going down for a nap in the middle of the day without a hint of protest. But in the evenings and at night time, when their sworn enemy was at its weakest, ground down to the verge of submission, they unleashed their fearsome arsenal. Ellie, unquestionably the Bin Laden of the group, was capable of screaming for two hours forty minutes for no apparent reason. Jules shhed, shuggled, paced, and lullabied, yet there would be no respite. Mick brought home Calpol, Infacol, Woodward's Gripe Water, but they proved puny weapons. We are a spineless society; our liberal democratic values leave us defenceless in the face of determined attack. Gin is the only thing these people understand, but our regard for civil liberties and due legal process have made a slug of Gordon's in the eight o'clock bottle something one can only contemplate under conditions of absolute secrecy.

Col was shaping up nicely as leader of the resistance. 'Personally, I've never thought there's much wrong with being an only child.'

Yeah! Right! Absolutely! – The others murmured their assent.

'I fought tooth and nail with my sister,' James chipped in.

'I still hate my brother,' said Simon. 'He was always allowed to stay up later, and I only ever got his hand-me-downs.'

Yeah! Right! Hand-me-downs!

'We're not having another,' said Col.

'No, nor us,' said James.

'I'd rather have a vasectomy,' said Simon.

I waited for Mick to contribute. He was as buggered as the rest of them, snappy with the receptionists, impatient with his patients, furious at his inability to alleviate Jules's frequent tearfulness and despair. Even I – only an uncle, for god's sake – was tetchy and irritable. I was short on sleep but, more distressingly, Hurricane Ellie had rent our carefully crafted lifestyle in twain. No more nocturnal writing for me, not while both Jules and Mick were on the verge of breakdowns and the only thing staving off compulsory admission under the Mental Health Act was the few hours' sleep they managed to scrape between them every night. The novel I was working on at the time – a promising yarn called *The Singer*, inspired by a chance meeting with the last of a dying breed of specialist sewing machine retailers – had been suspended in aspic. By the time I'd get an opportunity to finish it, it looked like no one still alive would remember what a Singer was. My dreams of publication and a life of literary notability were becoming intractably frustrated.

Col, James and Simon were regarding Mick strangely. He'd said nothing. Could it be they had a double-agent in their midst? Col slid a hand into his trouser pocket, reaching perhaps for a cosh with which to silence Mick before he could report back.

'How about you, Mick?' I intervened. 'You on for another?'

He laughed, bitterly. 'I'm as likely to father a sibling for Ellie as you lot are to give up smoking.'

Simultaneously, Col, Simon, James and I dropped our butts, and ground them into the patio with determined soles. A flurry of handshakes sealed the brotherhood. Then we returned to the lounge, to the wives and partners and the clutch of unsuspectingly only-children awaiting us there.

A year later, Col and Cath were the next to announce their re-impregnation. Slowly and surely, the others have followed suit. Up till Ellie was three, her status as an only child could be passed off as deliberate planning, but now she's well past her fourth birthday it's becoming increasingly apparent that there is, in fact, trouble at t'mill.

I never quite understood Jules, not till she had Ellie. She doesn't own a single pair of heels, and is rarely to be found in anything other than comfort-fit jeans. Her bobbed hairstyle suits her heart-shaped face, but she never does anything different with it, anything that might take longer than two minutes to fix in the mornings. Sure, I'd seen hints of resolve during their courtship – Mick was such a wuss when it came to making the first move I doubt they'd ever have got it on had Jules not eventually taken matters in hand herself – but I mistook her casualness over her outward appearance as evidence of a lack of inner drive. How wrong a man can be. Since she's become a mum, I've seen her in a new light: her complete focus on the little scrap in her arms, feeding at her breast; her inexhaustible patience with the terrible twos; her total care. She knows exactly what she wants, exactly how to achieve it, and usually does so without even raising her voice. Take Ellie's schooling. Mick was all for the state system – it is free, after all – but Jules had deep misgivings. He wouldn't listen to her, of course. So, she didn't argue. All she did was wait a few days before making some comment – seemingly at random, though in reality it must have been targeted with the precision of a smart bomb – about Mick's own decidedly singular education. That was it. If you'd blinked, you'd have missed it. But it set Mick contemplating the considerable advantages of the pupil-teacher ratios to be found in the private sector. Plus, conversely, the enormous difficulty in trying to learn anything while perpetually seated next to an attentionally deficient oik. State schools were never mentioned again.

Seeing her cuddling her friends' newborns. The pang in her eyes when she had to hand the infant back to its owners.

They sat me down one evening, a wee while ago. I'd long since abandoned *The Singer*, and was wrestling instead with the bewimpled Sister Sebastian.

'Look, John, there's something we need to tell you,' Mick said.

Jules's hazel eyes were intent on him. She gave him the slightest of nods.

'We're going to expand the family. Just the one, but, you know, a brother or sister would be nice for Ells.'

'Uh huh. Well, congratulations.'

'No, we haven't. I mean, we're just at the planning stage.'

I saw Jules flush with embarrassment.

'The thing is.'

'Go on,' I told him.

'The thing is, we're going to need your help.' He hesitated; Jules nodded again. 'We know you're in the thick of this nun novel. We, um, we realize how important your writing is to you. And that stuff about consistency, the need to keep chiselling – we're completely on board with it all. All it is, is. Well, you know about menstrual cycles and everything.'

I nodded sagely. 'There's some kit you can get from the chemist's. I've seen it advertised.'

'Sorry?'

'I don't know, it's called Predictor or something.'

'No, we're perfectly capable of –'

'What, then?'

'It's just. Well, when it's *that time*, we'd appreciate it if you could take a night or two off from writing. To give us a chance. You know. To.'

'Ah, I see what you're saying.' I jutted my jaw and nodded, to let Jules know I was giving the matter serious consideration. 'Well, that's fine by me. Just say the word and I'll call it an early night.'

She smiled. I think he smiled too. I never like to be thought a spoilsport, so I grinned along with the pair of them. The three of us, smirking inanely at each other. I may even have slapped my thigh with false bonhomie. I wondered if they'd thought this thing through.

You read any women's mag and you'll find an article telling you the secret of a happy marriage is to mix it up a bit. You know. Let him come home one night to find you cooking in the scud. Invest in a tripod for the camcorder. Do creative things with root vegetables. Mick never reads *Cosmo*, he's way too busy with the *New England Journal of Medicine*. But Jules does. Every time Ellie goes off to grandma's.

Jules: I didn't know, maybe, if you fancied christening the shower?

Mick: No, no way.

Jules: I knew what I was getting into when I married you.

Mick: I'm not having him feasting his eyes all over you.

Jules: He wouldn't.

Mick: He's a lecherous old tart.

Me: (nods.)

So they're stuck with the bed, the sheet, the same unvarying position. A recipe for disaster, as any *Cosmo* girl knows.

Time. Halted time. Time run out. Jules's hand sneaking beneath the white cotton, her finger, wet with saliva, running round and round my nipple. The sheer electric shock of it. How I waited, breath bated, for Mick to explode. The unnerving, puzzling silence. Replaced eventually with the basso vibrato of his snores.

Dina Carroll was halfway through the outstanding club classic 'Express' when Jules appeared in my line of sight. She paused to gather the shattered alarm, scooped up a stray spring. Maybe she sensed my gaze. Our eyes engaged. Not even the faintest of smiles. She headed through to the kitchen.

I killed the CD, removed my earphones in time to hear the thud as the clock hit the bottom of the swing bin. The bell gave a farewell ting. I'd been used. For a different purpose, sure, but she was just like the rest. I'd never minded with any of the others, it was an unspoken understanding, one I'd wholeheartedly endorsed: this is for fun, this is for kicks, if I pass you in the street tomorrow I'll blank you to kingdom come. But Jules! For Jules to have done this.

What right did I have to be upset? Who was I kidding, this flat anticlimax? Pull yourself together, John-boy, that's how life is. I could recommence pursuit of Ariadne with a clear conscience. I should be thankful.

The back door slammed. Jules's footsteps faded. Mick and I sat together, staring at the empty coffee table, with its fine layer of partly disturbed dust.

The wheelchair is all right for short distances on the flat, but for major runs Mick and I rely on the altogether sturdier Booster. Pneumatic-tyred wheels, comfy padded seat, eight-mile range, and a battery that recharges in twelve hours when connected to the domestic mains. Ours is metallic red, with smart black trim and a handy plastic shopping basket slung on the handlebars, which takes Mick's briefcase and my packed lunch with ease. Our cruising speed is four miles an hour; six at top whack, downhill with a tail wind.

We churned up the ramp to the footbridge over the Thames, the motor whining between our thighs. The sky was cloudlessly blue, the sunlight played fractals on the water. A flotilla of swans processed serenely downstream. A gaudily painted narrow boat was chugging from the direction of Iffley Lock, trailing a lazy V of wake. Across the river, the council flats of Preacher's Lane stood in shabby contrast to the bijou Victorian terraces of the Grandpont we had left behind. Down at the foot of the stairwell, a smackhead was scoring from a crusty dealer. It was a lovely Oxford spring day.

'Jules all right, then?' I asked.

'Yeah, tired, that's all. She had a crap night. Ellie had one of her nightmares.'

I thought about that for a second. 'I told you, you shouldn't let her watch that *Dinosaur* video.'

'No, it was something about a bloke pissing out of her window then trying to gouge her eyes out.'

I pursed my lips. 'The imagination she's got, that kid.'

'They all go through it. It's just a phase.'

'You're the doc.'

'Ready about!'

The ramp dog-legs halfway up. I have to pull back hard on my handlebar; Mick simultaneously pushes his to the full extent of its arc. We rounded the corner, the Booster's turning circle barely adequate to clear the railings, and straightened up for the rest of the climb.

'She wasn't upset about the alarm, then?'

'Er, no.'

'It's just. Well, it was on the table. I assumed.'

Mick laughed. 'It's only a crappy clock, John!'

'Sure. I just thought, that's all.'

We completed our ascent, and trundled across the bridge, thence to make our way through St Ebbe's, past

Gloucester Green, coming out on Beaumont Street just along from Mick's practice. The town centre is a nightmare from May to September. Hordes of teenage Frogs, knapsacks on their backs, being herded by harassed teachers. Coachloads of middle-aged Americans modelling the latest fashions from the links. Mobs of designer-dressed Italian students, sultrily hanging out in front of McDonald's. They come for the architecture: it's a beautiful city in parts. They come to improve their English, especially the Yanks. They love the sense of history. Oxford was home to J. R. R. Tolkien and C. S. Lewis, Boyle formulated his famous law of gases among its fabled spires, a geeky Maggie Thatcher was a Somerville gal. And there's Morse, of course. It's easy to become dumbstruck at the sheer intellectual and cultural milestones being reached all around you. Barely a week goes by without Mick and me being flagged down by a company of Japanese tourists, wanting to know if we're that Stephen Hawking. Generally I croak out a 'Yes' and we submit ourselves to a volley of shutters and popping flashes. Presumably they'll be off to Cambridge the following week.

We parked the Booster at the rear of the practice. The other GPs were out on their midday house calls, so Mick caught up with the gossip from Muriel Redknap, who has been head receptionist from time immemorial.

'And how was your little show?' she asked, simpering the way people do when talking to TV personalities.

'Good, thanks, yeah,' Mick said.

It seemed incredible that *Wake Up Britain!* had been only this morning: so much had happened since we set off before dawn. We closeted ourselves in Mick's consulting room, where he launched into yet more administration. I snatched forty winks before surgery. Mick woke me at five to, and I tried to get my head clear while he called up the afternoon's appointments on his PC.

'Listen,' I said. 'I've been meaning to say.'

He moved the mouse to click on the first patient. 'What?'

'Well, if you wanted to get hold of some Viagra or something, I'll pop it for you.'

His hand hesitated for the briefest of moments, then carried on its journey to the phone. His forefinger danced on the buttons. The intercom crackled.

'Mrs Murgatroyd to Dr McDonald in room six, please.'

There are a number of professional tasks Mick finds difficult, taking blood pressure being as good an example as any. Attaching the cuff is a two-handed job, and he can't operate the deflation valve while simultaneously holding his stethoscope to the front of the patient's elbow. There are machines that do the whole thing automatically, but when you've got as capable an assistant as me why would you go to the expense?

I caught Mrs Murgatroyd's eye as air began to hiss from the sphyg. Mick was concentrating on the Korotkov sounds, his ears occluded by his tubes, his gaze focused on the steadily descending column of mercury. Mrs Murgatroyd winked. I winked back. Mick's been trying to control her hypertension for eight months. She's had diuretics, beta-blockers, ACE inhibitors, calcium channel blockers, ARBs. None of them have made the blindest bit of difference. He's on to centrally acting alpha-blockers now, but I know the outcome already. The Murgatroyd BP will be as immutable as ever.

The trouble with Mick is, he never thinks to listen. Way back, when he first picked up her high blood pressure, she mentioned in passing her tried and trusted remedy, the cocktail that had seen her through seventy-eight years thus far. I made a note, in case I ever wanted to use it on *Wake Up Britain!* The juice of one orange, one grapefruit, one lemon, a teaspoon of Epsom salts, a dollop of cream of tartar, one pint of water, steep and strain, drink a glass a day. Mick chuckled and patted her on the hand, then dashed off a prescription for bendrofluazide. If you had to choose between a tiny tasteless pill and a tumbler full of drain cleaner, which would you trust to keep your arteries from furring up?

'A hundred and eighty over a hundred,' Mick said, unhooking his stethoscope from his lugholes. 'It hasn't budged an inch.'

'Oh, doctor, I am an awkward patient, aren't I?'

Mick made reassuring noises while he typed something into his computer. 'It's not you, Ethel. But your blood pressure is proving remarkably resistant. We'll give Physiotens a bash, but if that's no good then it might be time to refer you to a specialist.'

'Oh!' She looked thrilled at the prospect. 'It's that serious, is it?'

'Well, not in itself.' Mick's tone was grave, much as I imagine his expression must have been. 'But it is a risk factor for stroke and heart disease, and we don't want you to fall foul of one of those, do we?'

'Well, I am nearly eighty, doctor. None of us can live for ever.'

Mick passed her the new prescription.

'No, Ethel. But I for one would like to see you around for a few years yet.'

I don't know if she screws up the FP10s, or whether she collects the tablets from the chemist and flushes them down the loo. Either way, not in a million years is Mrs Murgatroyd swallowing any of the shit Mick is peddling.

That's where his professional dissatisfactions arise. He's been educated to a highly technical specification, he understands human physiology, biochemistry, anatomy and pathology to an extraordinary degree. But Mick is from Mars, and his patients all have Venus postcodes. No wonder he's demoralized. No wonder he wants out. No wonder the academic life holds such allure.

At the end of surgery his phone rang. I could hear Muriel's voice, squawking in his ear.

'Message from Ariadne,' he said, replacing the receiver a touch clumsily. 'She's been talking things over with Prof. She'd like to see us straight away.'

I've done my fair share of dissembling in my time. I listened while Mick called Jules to tell her he had to go to college, to meet with the warden to discuss procedures for ensuring blanket vaccination against meningitis C in next year's freshers. We'd be late in, she wasn't to worry about feeding us, there was bound to be an invitation to dine in afterwards. And if she wanted to get an early night, he'd quite understand. He loved her. Give a kiss to Ells. And a kiss from Uncle John, too.

'Have you done your questionnaire?' he asked, nestling the phone back in its rest. His tone was defiant.

'Not since the last time I told you I hadn't, no.'

Mick sighed. 'You're a fuckwit, John. Women like

Ariadne, they don't get where they've got by pissing around. You'll only stand a chance if you're sharp as a pin.'

He shut down his computer and got us to our feet. 'Never mind. It's not as if we were expecting to be invited back so soon.' I felt him shake his head. 'What do you think it means?'

'I think it means I'm a fuckwit.'

'I'll think of something.' He picked up his briefcase.

'To St Ablart's?' I said.

'St Ablart's.'

'Ahoy,' I said, staring down at his desk, at the clock, the calender, the framed photo of Jules and Ellie on the beach in Devon last summer. Thought about the two of them back at home, going through the evening rituals alone, resigned to the way Daddy's job kept him and Uncle John out at such unsociable hours. 'Ahoy, there, Mick, my boy.'

Funk Star

In his rooms at college Prof has a collection of brains, each in its own bell jar. He displays them on a long shelf mounted on the wall above his fish tank. They look identical, floating in their formaldehyde: convoluted cortices, frontal lobes overarching, cerebella like miniature cauliflowers. Guppies and electras switch and shoal in the tropical waters below. The jars are arranged neatly, labelled with the names of the people these once were. First time we came here Prof gave us a guided tour, telling us, with evident pride, about the long-dead artists, composers, politicians, and scientists to whom they supposedly once belonged. Bernatelli, Balhatchet, Chevreaux. I nodded politely as he whittered on, but in truth I was embarrassed for him. I'd never heard of any of them. This was a distinctly C-list collection.

Ariadne reappeared, leather case in hand.

'Ready?' she said.

'He's got some new additions,' I said, indicating the shelf.

Ariadne came over to join us, rested her bag on the sofa. 'Yes, he's really excited. Won't even let me guess how much he paid for that one.'

She nodded at the as yet unlabelled jar occupying pride of place directly above the filter pump. There was no actual brain, just a cube of greyish tissue, about an inch across, suspended in the clear preservative.

'Is that Einstein?' Mick asked, his tone bizarrely reverential.

Ariadne was surprised. 'Absolutely. Yes.'

I looked again at the specimen. 'That's *it*?'

'He got chopped into chunks,' Mick explained. 'Some enterprising pathologist. I didn't think anybody knew where any of them were any more.'

Ariadne smiled. 'Prof has his contacts.'

'So who's that?' I said, glancing at the other new exhibit, also awaiting labelling. A whole brain, this one. Flimsy frills of membrane wafting in the formaldehyde. Tortuous blood vessels snaking over its surface.

'That's Judy Garland.'

I stared at the jar. I loved *The Wizard of Oz*. Judy Garland was Dorothy, she was somewhere over the rainbow, she was vulnerability and strength: her voice captured emotions beyond expression in words. Off screen she was a troubled soul who died of an overdose in a London hotel at the fag end of the sixties. The brain looked greasy, friable. Little specks of tissue were floating free of its surface. Whatever it was that Prof had in that bell jar, it sure as hell wasn't Judy Garland.

'Where is Prof, anyway?' Mick asked.

'Oh, he was sorry to miss you. He had to go to a faculty board.' Ariadne retrieved her case, transferred it to her other hand. 'He managed to wangle the scanner session before he left.'

I was distracted by Judy, fascinated yet appalled that she should have ended up here. At the same time curiously comforted that she hadn't.

'What scanner session?' I asked.

'In the Institute. At seven.' Ariadne checked the time. 'If we miss it we'll be waiting weeks for another slot.'

The circular magnet, powered by a liquid helium superconductor, was shiny and grey and massive. Towering above head height. Two million quid's worth of high tech. And in the centre was a small opening, leading into the narrow tunnel that burrowed to the heart of the machine. This was Big Science, no doubt about it, hardnosed, impassively rational, implacably disinterested. It was something of a surprise to realize its gender. The rail-mounted slab that would slide us into the scanner's orifice, drawing us deep inside – we were merely the puny, passive phallus, quaking at the prospect of scientific engulfment.

'Are you sure we'll fit?' Mick said.

'Prof thought it would be fine.' Ariadne sounded doubtful.

The scanner was on the other side of the room, separated from us by a thick Perspex screen. Ariadne punched a button on the console and we watched the trolley slide out from the narrow aperture, compressed air hissing.

'Never mind, we can always shove up,' Mick said, shaking his watch off his wrist.

Ariadne nodded. 'Have you got any metalwork? Aneurysm clips, prosthetic valves, artificial joints?'

'No.'

'What about the heart?' I said. A sudden vision of Mick and me lying on the trolley, a ragged hole erupting *Alien*-like in our chest, our falsie pulmonary valve clanging against the wall of the MRI, our life blood oozing down its shiny surface.

Mick tutted. 'It's porcine.'

Ariadne raised her eyebrows in what was clearly a mirror of Mick's own expression.

'Right. Silly me.'

'OK, boys, let's get you loaded.' Ariadne indicated a mike headset. 'I'll be able to talk you through things once you're inside.'

She came round to help us aboard, knee-length leather boots squeaking on the lino. We eased ourselves horizontal and I caught a noseful of her musky perfume as she draped a strap across our foreheads. Her hair brushed my face as she leaned over to tighten the plastic buckle, the pressure clamping my head firmly in place.

'The important thing is to keep absolutely still,' she explained, absent-mindedly unbuttoning her white lab coat.

She returned to the console; I stared at the poly-styrene ceiling tiles. I imagined her swaying hips, her swishing thighs. Quips came to mind, how I should be enjoying this, her strapping us to a bed. None of them seemed especially funny.

'I'm really not sure about this,' I whispered.

'Don't worry,' Mick said.

He'd been strangely unquestioning when Ariadne told us she planned to scan our brains. Which made me think he already knew. Which implied she'd mentioned it in her message. Which meant he'd decided not to tell me. Which worried me. Like anyone who's had half a dozen major operations, four of them before the age of ten, I have a deep and highly rational distrust of medical pro-cedures. They tend to hurt like hell. These days, a doctor would be lucky to get a look at my throat. Mick would know what an MRI entailed, but just because he was prepared to submit himself to it didn't mean it was harmless. He was so eager to get his tongue between the Prof's bum cheeks he would feed his head to a lion if he thought it was in the interests of neuropsychological research.

'What about the wires in our sternum!' A mental flash of all our chest x-rays, metal loops lacing the breastbone in every one.

'*I* don't know.'

'What do you mean you don't know?'

'I'm not a radiologist, am I?'

'Fucking hell, Mick!'

'They're anchored pretty tight. In bone. It'll be fine.'

'Holy shit. Don't you think we ought to *ask* or something?'

The trolley jolted, started to slide us, heads first, towards the huge magnet with its awe-inspiring power.

'Hey!' I shouted.

'Do you want her to think you're a total wimp?' Mick hissed.

'Everything all right?' Ariadne called. If I peered right down, over our toes, I could just see her, behind the Perspex screen. Smiling directly at me, the living image of wholesome Scandinavian enthusiasm. She was invigorating saunas, she was health and efficiency, she was a naked roll in the snow. She was the blonde from Abba; I was the beardie on the keyboards, stuck with the brassy brunette but dreaming, dreaming.

'Fuck it,' I said. 'Never mind.'

The magnet edged closer, gradually enclosing us. Mick's ear squashed against mine. The tunnel wall was hard and unyielding on my other side, its roof just a few centimetres above my nose. It was dark in there, oppressive. The trolley stopped, the scanner hummed. I strained my senses, trying to detect the telltale ping! as the first metal clip wrenched free from our sternum to rip through our chest wall. There was the faintest prickling sensation deep to the skin, nothing more.

'You OK?' Mick said.

'Yeah, you?'

'Yeah.' He laughed. 'I guess it's all right, then.'

A volley of static startled me, then Ariadne's amplified voice came from somewhere.

'OK, Mick and John, everything's ready. Um, now, if you don't mind, I'd like you to think sexy thoughts.'

'Sorry?' My response was involuntary; only after I'd spoken did I wonder whether she could hear us.

Evidently she could. 'It's functional MRI. Brain areas active in any given mental process light up in the pictures. I'd like you both to think sexy thoughts.'

I stared at the grey magnet above. Mick adjusted his position, easing the pressure on my ear slightly.

'Did she say what I think she said?' he whispered.

'I think so.'

'What the hell did you draw?'

Ariadne told us she'd had a supervision session with Prof, that she'd shown him the body maps she'd had us colour in. He'd become tremendously excited, had got on the phone to the Institute straight away.

'Um, Ariadne?' I called into the gloom.

'Yes?'

'It's kind of cramped in here. And hot. And a little scary. It's going to be difficult to think anything, sexy or otherwise.'

The scanner hummed, the speaker hissed sibilantly. Then Ariadne came back on the line.

'That's it, boys, you're starting to feel really hot now. Really horny.'

I thought about it for a moment. 'No, not that sort of hot. Sweaty hot. We're like sardines in here.'

'Oh. OK.' There was a few seconds' silence. 'OK. Try to think of the sexiest woman you know. Imagine she's sliding her hand inside her panties. She's wet, wet at the thought of you, hard as iron, pushing into her, pushing her apart. Is that any good?'

'Yeah,' I said, surprised. The disparity between what she was saying and the way in which she'd said it – cool, professional, entirely unembarrassed, as though she was reading out the instructions for assembling an Ikea coffee table. 'Is that good for you, Mick?'

'She's mad, isn't she?'

I raised my voice. 'Ariadne, that is good, actually.'

'OK, so she's feeling really horny now. She's rubbing herself. She's pulling her panties aside. You can see her, the whole of her, gaping for you. Her hand is reaching inside your boxer shorts, feeling the length of you.'

'Ariadne? Do you think you could do that, the thing with the boxers?'

'Um, no, I don't think so.'

'Never mind. Go on.'

'Hang on, I'll just take a picture.'

We waited while she got the computer to capture a real-time image of our tentatively turned on brains. And I do mean our: Mick had a stiffy, too. Don't ask me the neurophysiology, but I can tell who's having the erection. Generally, I think of our penis as mine: I'm the one who does the hauling out for a waz, the soaping in the shower, the scratching of the itch. On the rare occasions Mick takes charge of urination it's the oddest feeling, exactly like your brother's just reached inside your flies and pulled your plonker out for you to have a slash. I count myself fortunate that he's not much given to masturbation. I've tried to find out if he experiences the same thing, if he has the sense that I'm constantly interfering with him. He professes not to understand what I mean.

And there we were, feet poking out of a ton of buzzing magnet, and I was well aware that I had a hard-on. But I was also aware that Mick had one too.

'I take it back,' I told him. 'About the Viagra.'

The speaker crackled. 'OK, boys, I think that's got it. Now, where were we?'

The Turf is my favourite pub in town. Tucked away at the end of St Helen's Passage it's a haven from the tourist hordes, few of whom have any idea there's anything down here. It also happens to be an ancient low building, one furthermore in which the floor level has risen with successive reflaggings over the centuries. Mick and I can stand unbowed, but most people have to stoop to approach the bar.

'You all right?' I asked Ariadne.

'It's OK,' she said, rubbing the top of her head. 'What can I get you?'

'I'll have a pint of Landlord, please.'

'Mick?'

'I don't drink.'

She nodded, and turned to the barman. Who had bypassed two other customers to dance attendance on her every whim.

We took our drinks over to a table and I sparked up.

'You got some good pictures, then?'

She shrugged. 'We'll have to wait. They're stored as digital files at the moment.'

'What was with all the sex talk?' Mick asked.

'That was Prof,' Ariadne said, sighing. 'He's so brilliant. He took one look at your body maps and *instantly* saw the possibilities.'

She took a sip of white wine, her eyes far away for a moment, presumably as she tried to conceive of a day when her intelligence would be honed to a comparable rapier-sharpness.

'The brain circuitry of male arousal is well defined – the medial preoptic area, the paraventricular nucleus, the caudate, the putamen, the hypothalamus, the hippocampus, need I go on?'

Mick shook his head energetically.

'But the distinctions between cognitive processing, and the neurological orchestration of peripheral physiological modulation are obscure. Hamann and Wallen had a stab – that study with the blurred porno pictures, yes? – but the differentiation is far from clear.'

'Come again?'

'I'm sorry,' she smiled gently. 'I forget you're not a doctor like Mick. We know the areas of the brain involved in getting turned on, but no one's entirely clear which bits are responsible for interpreting a situation as sexy, and which merely translate that sexiness into an erection.'

'Right,' I said, nodding. 'And you knew that, Mick, did you?'

'Sure,' he said.

The Landlord was tasting mighty fine so I took a couple of lengthy draughts, draining the glass. My evening dose of anticholinergic was waiting for me at home, and Mick would soon have to figure out what to do with his saliva.

'What I don't understand,' he said, 'is how the comparative fMRIs will help elucidate that?'

Ariadne smiled again. 'I think you, like me, are a little way behind Prof, yes?' She took more wine. 'When you and John were listening to my dirty talk, imagining what you would like to be doing, your areas of conscious processing should have been identically stimulated. But only John's brain would also show activation in the nuclei responsible for the erectile response. Brilliant, no?'

I had to admit, it did seem pretty fantastic. I'd really enjoyed it, I told her.

Mick, though, announced that he wanted to take a look at the body maps.

'Sure,' Ariadne said, a faint line etched in the centre of her forehead. She bent down, ferreting in her bag. Mick took his opportunity and deposited a gobful of saliva in my pint glass. Ariadne resurfaced, holding a file from which she extracted the artwork from our previous session.

And you had to admit, in contrast to the blue shading elsewhere, the genitalia on Mick's diagram had remained strikingly white. The phallus on mine – jutting skywards, blocked in stark raving red – was bigger than I'd remembered drawing. I felt my cheeks warm at the boastful implication. I glanced furtively at Ariadne, her eyes intent on the sheets of paper.

After a moment's contemplation she gathered the drawings and returned them to her file. Gave us a quiet smile. Picked up her case.

'I won't be a minute.'

We watched as she made her way in the direction of the ladies. Most of the men in the bar were watching her, too.

'What the fuck did you do that for?' Mick wanted to know.

'What?'

'Making me out to be some sort of impotent. It's hideously embarrassing.'

'You coloured your own body map,' I pointed out. 'Anyway, what do you care what she thinks?'

'If you've fucked this up, John.'

'Relax,' I told him. 'If anything, it's made them more interested. Prof rustled up that scanner session pretty quick, didn't he?'

I glanced at Ariadne's empty glass, my own pint with its puddle of saliva in the bottom. I hadn't intended asking her out for a drink. But her manner towards us had palpably thawed from the aloofness of the first session. Plus there was the effect of all the sex talk in the scanner. It had certainly put me in the mood. I could have been wrong, but my every instinct told me it had done something to Ariadne as well. Quite what, and how much, remained to be seen.

'Have you got any cash?' I asked Mick.

In the end we didn't need to buy a round. Ariadne returned from the loo, and stood behind her chair. She shook her cascading tresses as though casting off a second skin. Her cheeks, I noticed, were suffused with the faintest of pink glows, and the academic disinterest in her eyes had given way to a semblance of mischief, a hint of fun.

'So, boys,' she said. 'Are you on for a club? I really feel like dancing.'

You'd think it would be next to impossible for Mick and me to get a shag. This was certainly what we believed during the lonely adolescent years in our mildewed bedroom, when the outpourings of our rapidly enlarging testicles played havoc with our moods, skin, and sheets. We had little experience of the fairer sex, our mother and the mobile librarian being the only representatives with whom we had any regular contact. Tatty magazines found fluttering atop mounds of household rubbish served up tantalizing glimpses. From what we could see, most women went around on all fours, cared little for clothes, and subsisted on a diet rich in bananas. Without exception they looked as though they wouldn't give boys like us the time of day. They often entwined in pairs, perhaps for warmth, but we failed to find any who were conjoined. I took it far harder than Mick, but the conclusion was bitter for us both: we were almost certainly going to have to pay for sex.

How wrong we were. Consider the evidence. Some women write letters to convicted murderers in jail. One thing leads to another, and the next they know they've married them. I mean, why? In the early days there's the obvious technical difficulty involved in consummation on a trestle table in the middle of the prison visiting room. But even once he's out on parole they've got to live with the constant necessity not to rub him up the wrong way lest they get an adjustable spanner in the head. Maybe it's the sense of danger. Perhaps they're simply dim. Against such a background, the prospects for a couple of law-abiding, if parapagus, twins look distinctly rosy. There are plenty of girls who will actively hunt down and bed a bloke – with complete disregard for looks, personality, oral hygiene – purely on grounds of curiosity about the donkey-size dong he's supposed to be hanging. It takes not a great leap of faith to realize that, out in the broad church that is womankind, there will be those whose enduring desire it is firstly to discover what lurks within Mick's and my pants, then secondly to see if they can straddle it. Ours is not to reason why, ours is merely to take full advantage of every opportunity that comes our way.

And come they do. Absolutely essential is the presence of copious quantities of alcohol. You have to face facts, there is simply no way you are going to tempt the bespectacled fox in the next booth in the university library to break off from revision and slip into the rare documents room for a quick turn on the photocopier. Take the same girl, plant her in a club, prime with, say, a quart of vodka, and you may be in business. The other thing is to set your sights correctly. If a girl bears more than a passing resemblance to the back end of a sumo wrestler they're an absolute no no: they've no more desire to appear desperate than you. I am not entirely ruling out women rugby players – indeed, as a breed, they're exactly the sort you are hoping to run into – but the type you're after are the passably fit ones who are only in the team for a laugh. Pointers to success include: drinking real ale in pints; dancing on the table; even more promisingly, dancing on the bar. If at any stage they drop their kecks and flash a moonie at the crowd, I guarantee you're in with a shout. I wasn't born with this repository of knowledge. It is the hard-won fruit of innumerable outings to Nottingham's premier night-spots during Mick's days as a student.

Ariadne proved, unpromisingly, to be a mineral water drinker, and she confined her dancing to the intended area of floor. Mick and I remained by the bar while she shook her tail-feather along with the best of the Coven II crowd.

'Christ, will you look at that!' Mick shouted.

I nodded my agreement. Watching her flick her hips, vogue her arms, shimmer her hair. The asexual post-doc had been transformed into a glorious goddess of funky house.

He let out a long sigh. 'She's intelligent. She's sexy. She's everything you could possibly want. What a woman!'

Our heart was laying down a furious bpm, but it was all Mick's adrenaline, not mine. I regarded Ariadne with cool eyes. She was a practised operator, I could tell, expertly flirting with a succession of circling wolves – then a bevested white boy, now a sunshaded mini-dreaded black guy – arms raised in abandon, taut arse metronoming.

'Come on,' Mick bellowed in my ear. 'Don't you fancy a pop?'

I took a slow drink of whisky and Coke.

'She's Premiership,' I told him.

'So?'

'We're Conference these days.'

'What's wrong with you?

'I don't know. Maybe I'm rusty. It's been a long time.'

Mick's hand grasped my glass. I resisted for a second, then let him take it from me. Mixing into the current, unknown track was the unmistakable brassy piano chords of the intro to Juliet Roberts's 'Caught in the Middle (of Love)'. Not heard since Nottingham Barracuda days.

'OK, OK,' I said. 'We'll see how we get on.'

Ariadne smiled warmly as we joined her at precisely the spot where the blast from the speaker stacks converged. The noise was pure vibration, jangling the atoms of our being. Lights of every colour flashed in my eyes. Bodies bounced against us, the impacts coming in the main from the pack of Coven boys she'd drawn into her ambit. Sweat rose in a humid fug. My ears were concussed, my mind raced, my senses were overloaded. The heave and swell seemed to pick us up, tossing us about as though on a wave. An unhealthy boyhood preoccupation with Pan's People had bequeathed my favourite moves, and I tried out a pelvic gyration. But the conflicting outputs from our respective motor cortices set up unsustainable confusion in our glutes. Years away from the club scene had made me forget: Mick has no rhythm. Just as I was about to beat it back to the bar, the bobbling synth of Robin S's 'Luv 4 Luv' burst gasping through the surface of the mix. I threw my head back, raised my arm, and began to trace elaborate patterns with my hand, the strobe segmenting the fluidity of the motion. As I found my groove, the crush and press seemed suddenly to drop away. Fragmented impressions of startled jocks, edging back, their faces frozen in the moment of awestruck recognition of the presence of a true funkmaster. Ariadne swam into my field of vision, her expression intent now, serious, as she worked it worked it. She fixed her eyes on mine, shimmied her way teasingly, seductively towards me, parting dancers like they were the Red Sea. Came to halt a millimetre away, started to bump and grind, our hips describing rhythmic circles, never moving apart. A deep groan of animal pleasure thundered through me; the world was a perfect place. Our monstrous heart swelled fit to burst. I gave myself up to the music and danced.

We slotted the Booster between a couple of the cars lining the street outside the house, and fetched the tarp from the front garden. Mick remained tight-lipped as we tugged the cover over the scooter.

I delved a hand in my pocket, reaching for my door keys. The hallway was darkened; when Mick put the light on we found a note on the floor. Jules, hoping our evening with the warden hadn't been too deathly and wishing us a goodnight. Ellie's outlandish signature and a Daddy Longlegs kiss scrawled at the bottom of the old envelope.

Mick tried to head us straight for the stairs, but I resisted.

'What are you doing?'

'I've got work to do.'

'Come *on*, John! Can't you give it a rest? I'm exhausted.'

'Books don't write themselves.'

Mick did one of his snorts, but was semi-cooperative as I went through to the kitchen. I spooned instant coffee and sugar into my pint-sized mug, and we stood waiting for the water to boil.

'Fucking hell,' Mick said, at length.

'OK, OK,' I said.

'What's *wrong* with you?'

'Nothing.'

'She was totally up for it. Totally.'

'It didn't feel right.'

'It didn't feel *right*?'

The kettle clicked off, steam pluming from its spout. I filled my mug, adding a dollop of milk.

'Are you going to have another crack?'

'It always causes problems, every time I have a shag.'

Mick pulled off an entirely humourless laugh. 'Don't worry about that, tiger. I'll square it with Jules.'

I stirred the coffee, setting up a little whirlpool in the centre of the cup.

'Look, Mick, we should forget her, yeah? It wouldn't be worth it.'

He drew a deep breath. 'I'm only thinking of you. You haven't been out with anyone since Ellie was born. Jules would understand. She'd be happy for you.'

'I don't think so. We're a family now. What would Ellie think?'

'*We're* a family. You're still young, free and single. It'd do you good.'

I handed him the bottle of vanilla Coke. Tucked the Famous Grouse under my arm before picking up the still swirling coffee.

'Do you think she ever worked in the premium rate phone industry?'

He missed a beat. 'Jules?'

'Ariadne.'

His chuckle suggested a thaw. 'Almost certainly. Scandinavians, eh?'

'"You're starting to feel really hot now, boys!"'

'Ow!'

We doused the kitchen light and made our way as quietly as possible upstairs. Mick declared himself indifferent to dental hygiene for one night so we settled straight down at the desk. I booted the PC into life.

'I've had agents fighting over this one, you know,' I told him.

'Yeah?'

'If Prof does offer you a research post, take it. I'm set to make a mint.'

'We'll see, John.'

I was typing my Windows password when Mick suddenly reached forward and picked up a sheaf of paperwork lurking at the back of the desk.

'Top tip,' he said, depositing it on the keyboard. 'Fill this in, yeah. You don't want to keep the lady waiting.'

I glanced at Ariadne's Boden questionnaire. Mick had given her his; he'd made excuses for me, saying we'd left mine at home. I moved it to one side, returning my hand to the mouse and clicking on the word processor icon.

'Night, then.'

'Night,' I told him, opening *Sister Sebastian's Library*. I hadn't even finished pretending to re-read the first page before the treacherous little bastard had fallen sound asleep.

I put *The Very Best of Aretha Franklin* in the CD drive. Wiggled the mouse, landed the cursor on the email icon. Left my finger hovering over the button.

There would be something from Jules, I was sure of it. How she was sorry, how she hoped I wasn't too hurt, how her biological clock was ticking, how Mick was running on lead-free these days and she'd had to do something, anything.

My finger rapped out a double click. Hurt! I was John McDonald! Lover of legions and chattel of none! What did I want with complication, attachment, commitment? I needed love like I needed a hole in the head!

Dear John

What can I say, apart from sorry? I know what you must be thinking, but it wasn't like that. I'm genuinely fond of you, you silly great lump of contradictions.

What a mess I've made. I don't know if you've said anything to Mick. I hope not. I'd like a chance to explain.

There you go, I'm so confused all I can do is fall back on cliches. It's difficult to write things down. It would be so much easier to talk – words just disappear into thin air.

The way things are with Mick and me. I see you with Ellie, how you are with her. Always laughing and joking, never taking yourself seriously.

I've been beating myself up all day, wishing I hadn't made such a mess of everything. Quite what I think I'm expecting you to do I don't know.

I don't know how to sort it all out, I don't even know where to start. Can you forgive me?

With love, Jules/x

The Boden Questionnaire

*T*his questionnaire is a statistically validated, bimodally distributed biopsychosociometric personality inventory developed by the Department of Comparative Psychology, University of Oxford. It has been extensively piloted against random samples drawn from the mailing list of a successful mid-market mail order clothing company. Normative values were derived from a population of over 400,000 respondents recruited according to the internet chain-email methodology of Waldinski et al (2001). Its strength over traditional inventories lies in its subjective bias: each datum is scored according to a semi-qualitative analogue algorithm and mapped over an n-dimensional Eysenkian array.

1. Full name: *John Michael McDonald*
2. Young, old or middle-aged: *Young at heart*
3. What colour pants are you wearing right now: *Purple*

4.What are you listening to right now: *Respect*

5.What was the last thing you ate: *Pork scratchings*

6.If you were a crayon what colour would you be: *Red*

7.Last person you emailed: *My sister in law*

8.First thing you notice about the opposite sex: *They're the opposite sex*

9.First thing you notice about the same sex: *They're not*

10.How are you today: *Fucked*

11.Favourite drink: ~~*Whisky*~~ *Coffee*

12.Favourite alcoholic drink: *Whisky*

13.Favourite sport: *Smoking*

14.Hair: *Brown, balding*

15.Eyes: *Blue, two*

16.Siblings, and their ages: *Brother, same*

17.Sun or snow: *Sun*

18.Comfort food: *Twiglets*

19.Are you too shy to ask someone out: *Nope*

20.Relationships or one night stands: *Whatever*

21.What book are you reading: *My own*

22.What's on your mouse pad: *My mouse*

23.Favourite board game: *Don't Wake Dad*

24.What are you doing tonight: *This questionnaire*

25.Favourite smell: *Gusset*

26.Can you touch your nose with your tongue: *Yes, I can.*

27.Can you juggle: *No*

28.What do you think when you wake in the morning:
Oh fuck

29.What impresses you: *The female orgasm*

30.Hypochondriac or stoic: *Hypochondriac*

31.What's your cure for the common cold: *Whisky*

32.Who would play you in a film of your life: *Robbie Coltrane*

33.Best friend: *Cigarette*

34.Last person you had sex with: *I'd rather not say*

35.Good, bad or indifferent: *Certainly not indifferent*

/cont

Last Sunday. To keep up the semblance of research for *Sister Sebastian*, I'd brought my copy of *Unveiled: Nuns Talking* to bed. Jules rigged up the sheet. I switched on my bedside lamp and settled down to read.

I won't pretend concentration was easy. Mick and Jules are as quiet as possible. Even so, you tend to have half an ear on the rate of her breathing, half a mind on the rhythm of her strokes. And a tinsy-winsy bit of you is wondering if this time they'll get it on. C'mon, Mick. Giddy up there, boy.

Still, for all the distractions, I managed to become engrossed in the interview with Felicity, a member of the Community of Poor Clares in Arundel, West Sussex. The subjects of the book fascinated me; I'd assumed they would have been emotional refugees, finding in the convent a sanctuary from heartbreak and failure. Yet most had led outwardly successful lives – they'd had jobs and cars, flats and houses, sex, and pets, and chocolate. Each had experienced a profound calling to the religious life, a sense of vocation oft fought against but ultimately irresistible. Virtually all of them experienced periods of torment: were they doing the right thing, giving up all personal possessions; forgoing the pleasures of this world, the possibility of intimacy with another person? The way they talked about their dilemmas showed the temptations to be oh so real and strong. Their self-sacrifice was both appalling and magnificent. They had suffered great loss and in the process gained an even greater liberation.

A ticklish tracery of fingertips down our stomach, along our inner thigh. Jules's bare leg sliding across ours. A hand cupping our balls.

There are those, of course, whose ultimate fantasy would involve being on one side of a vertically slung sheet while a scantily clad woman meanders teasingly around their nether regions on the other. Believe me, in the earliest days the mere thought used to give me an erection. Then the cares of life began to accrue: worries over money, sleepless nights with the first baby, to say nothing of the toll taken trying to write 70,000-word novels while simultaneously observing the working hours of the harried GP. Soon all I wanted was to turn in early with a good book.

But Mick was a father, and he and Jules had determined to go round a second time. Duty calls. There was a faint stirring. Jules moved up from our scrotum, trying to coax him into life. I found myself reading the same sentence over and over. Would he do it, could he do it, did the boy have it in him?

Yes. Yes.

No.

The crowd go oh.

I turned back to the Poor Clares of Arundel. How Felicity had met the author in a special interview room, a mesh screen between them. Like a prison. The question as to which of them was the inmate was left open.

The sheet rippled, Jules's hand snaked under it. And made its way to my nipple, which it proceeded to circle. There was saliva, lubricating the motion, allowing skin to slide slippily over skin. My areola hardened, our heart raced, my attention was wrenched from my reading. Volts volleyed through me.

It stopped me being able to breathe.

It was intensely thrilling.

I jumped to attention. Twanged like a diving board.

It was utterly awful, waiting for Mick's hurt and angry interjection.

Jules's hand suddenly whipped away, disappeared into purdah.

Mick had started to snore.

I should have said something. Something to stop her. But I didn't want to. If I let a single word pass my lips the spell would break, the moment would be over, the magic would be gone.

I lay completely still, book held open in front of my face, every ounce of my being focused on the round and round and round of her fingertips. No longer on my nipple. The merest hint of a scratch from her nail. The lightest of squeezes. The storm gathering force in my loin. Then the wet butterfly of her labia, suddenly alighting.

Email checked, Boden questionnaire completed, I opened the 'Income tax self assessment' file and knocked out a couple of pages of my novel. As much to give me something to do while drinking and chain smoking as anything. Mick rarely mentions the mountains of money I convert to peaty firewater and acrid tobacco. Once we cop it he reckons Jules will have an incontestable case: widowed by passive smoking. She'll get it all back from Philip Morris, with interest.

Guilty, guilty, boy did I feel guilty.

I shut down the computer and made my way softly to Ellie's room. Her Winnie the Pooh nightlight. Her

Animal Ark stickers. Stood looking at her peaceful, perfect face. Stroked the roundness of her cheek. Snagged the tangles in her hair.

What would happen to her, if Mick and Jules were to split? Her world fractured irrevocably. Her sense of trust, security, evermore tarnished. Every other Sunday at the Cotswold wildlife park with Daddy and Uncle John. I loved her as keenly as if she was my own. I couldn't let anything happen to her.

And what if, some crazy how, her mum were to make the leap across the king-size, shack up with her Uncle John? A life of hand-to-mouth, clothes from charity shops, weekly trips to the toy library. Free vitamins. Uncle John was a waster, a soak, a good-for-nothing who'd never earned a penny in all his born days.

Unless, unless.

Unless nothing. Mick was right, I said it every time, about every pigging useless, ultimately rejected book. I kissed her imperceptibly on the forehead, unconscious Mick head-butting her shoulder a moment later. I brought us back to standing. He might be an incurable sourpuss, but he did bring home shedloads of moollah. She could do a lot worse for a dad.

Jules was sleeping soundly. I eased us into bed and lay, straining to hear a change in her breathing, to feel her start to stir.

'Jules?' I whispered. 'Jules?'

I simply wouldn't mention it, would never raise the subject again. Would return her email accompanied by a counterfeit server error message. Would ignore her totally, to the point of rudeness. I could be hard, I could be cold as glass. I was a pillar of salt, a statue of stone, my heart was made of iron, thawing for no one. Yeah. My life would be different from here on in, would never be the same. No more gladhanding, no more philandering, no more running round town. I'd become a model of sobriety, the image of righteousness. I'd devote myself to a scholarly work on the role of mapping in the expansion of the British Empire. I had come to a crossroads, but only one path was open to me.

My fervent tub thumping was interrupted by a strange sensation. The realization that I was thickening fast. No, that Mick was thickening fast. That somewhere inside his head the neurological orchestra of male arousal was frantically tuning up, ready for the first movement. Jules was still curled on her side, facing away.

And Mick's voice, blurry with sleep, muttering something incomprehensible. But which sounded uncannily like 'Has he had any?'

I lay, physically shrinking, while my brother dreamed his filthy dreams. Of Abba. Of invigorating saunas. Of health and efficiency. Of naked rolls in the snow.

Income tax self assessment

Once upon a Time in the West

In the beginning there was John.

In the beginning there was Mick.

No, in the beginning there was John. And John was good, and John was busy being made flesh, and John was just fine on his lonesome, thanks. Then some fucking thing happened and, lo and behold, there was Mick as well.

In the beginning there was John, and John was a cluster of omnipotent stem cells. A conceptus in search of an endometrium. The blastocyst with no name. He rolled down the Fallopian tube like a microscopic ball of sagebrush, and tumbled helter-skelter into the cavity of the womb.

No, he kicked open the swing doors and menaced the suddenly silent saloon.

John was broke out of jail, an outlaw with a bounty on his head, a gunslinger, a train robber, a stagecoach upholder. He sauntered over to the waistcoated bartender, now anxiously polishing a shot glass. Ignoring the stares of the nervy townsfolk, John rested his dusty boot on the foot rail, slapped a dollar on the bar and demanded a bottle of whisky. With a surreptitious thumb, he eased the leather retaining-strap off the hammer of his Colt Peacemaker.

There was a licking of dry lips. The mopping of beady perspiration. The straying of hands in the vicinity of gun belts. The townsfolk, to a man, thought: where the fuck's the sheriff? And the piano man resumed his jingle jangle on the keys.

John had a long curved scar on his forehead. Unsightly. Intimidating. Enviable.

The barman sloshed whisky in and around the glass. John tossed it back in one, slammed the empty vessel down for a refill, causing splashes from the puddle of liquor to bloom like blood stains on his denim shirt.

John was in possession of a pile of loot. A genetic legacy. A stack of notes liberated from a railroad company safe not two days before. It was in his saddle-bags even now. The wherewithal to start a new life, free from the need to graft or grind or tread on the wrong side of the law. He would buy a cattle ranch, marry that doll up there hanging off the bannister in wonder, and surrender himself to creative branding.

John, oh John, oh John.

Down at the jailhouse, Deputy Mick was fixing his tin star to his shirt. The pin jabbed the sensitive skin of his breast, causing his eyes to water and his nerves to fail. Where was the sheriff when he needed him?

He rose from behind his desk and drew himself to his full height. Five foot five. On the far wall was the 'Wanted' poster, the same ugly face, with its weird goat's beard, gloating at him. The face he'd seen jolting past atop a briskly cantering mare not ten minutes before. He searched the desk, his rummaging becoming increasingly fevered as successive drawers failed to yield his handcuffs.

Fuck, oh fuck, oh fuck. Where was the sheriff when he needed him?

Out on one of his harebrained posses, that's where. Every morning he set off, with a whoop and a holler and a slap of the reins, in hot pursuit of some felon or other. The rest of the posse bunched behind, eating the dust spurting from under his horse's thundering hooves. And now a genuine quarry had ridden in, bold as you like, in broad daylight. To their town! Where he, Deputy Mick, was the sole remaining representative of law and order!

He checked his revolver, spun the chamber, six fat slugs, the click-click-click sounding like the roulette wheel of doom. He looked warily at the glass-fronted cabinet on the wall. The sheriff's sprawling writing: *In extremis smash glass*. Mick brought the butt of his Colt down hard against the pane. Which shattered with an appalling crash, showering shards over his hand-tooled boots. Gingerly he reached inside and removed the cuffs, the metal painted bright red, the warning stencilled in white letters around the rim: EMERGENCY USE ONLY. Then he rammed his pistol in its holster, wedged his stetson on his head, and left the jailhouse, his hands tremulous and his anal sphincter tightly clenched.

Deputy Mick strode down the main street, his spurs jangling with eerie regularity as he trod the horse-pounded red dirt. On either side, lily-livered shopkeepers were bolting doors and fastening shutters as fast as their frantic hands could manage.

Opposite the haberdasher's his step faltered. Emerging from the store, a roll of material tucked under her arm, was his beloved wife. And trustfully clutching her free hand, his equally beloved daughter.

'Julia! Get Fenella back inside, quick!' he hollered.

'Darling! Whatever's the matter?' Julia sounded bemused, to say the least, by the manly turn to her husband's tone.

'John McDonald's in town,' he called, quietening his voice to little more than a yelp.

'*Mad* John McDonald? Oh, darling! Be careful!'

Fenella, her cascade of blonde curls held back by a pretty gingham hair-band, began to wail.

'It's all right, sweetheart, Daddy's off to work, that's all. I'll be back in time for supper.'

Mick's eyes implored Julia: get her out of here.

'But, darling,' Julia cried. 'Where's the sheriff?'

Mick squared his shoulders, rested his hand on the butt of his gun, assuming a confident stance even he didn't believe in. 'This is between me and Mad John. This time, I'm bringing him in.'

'But, darling! Remember what he did to your papa! And your dear mama!'

Mick swallowed hard, and nodded. 'That's exactly what I'm remembering, honey.'

Deputy Mick hesitated outside the slatted saloon doors, listening to the fumbled notes tinkling out into the street. The piano man was nervous, that was for sure. Could he be playing with a gun to his head? Mad John was said to loathe honky-tonk above everything.

A snicker behind him made the lawman flinch. But it was only Mad John's sweat-flecked steed, shifting apprehensively, tugging at the reins looped casually over the hitching rail. The mare's doleful eyes regarded Mick; they seemed filled with ineffable sadness.

'Easy, there.'

Mick brushed fingertips down her soft muzzle, felt her warm exhalation. Tried to fight off the thought that this could be the last horse he'd ever pet. The saddlebags were bulging, crumpled banknotes poking out from under the flaps. The gall of the man! Leaving a fortune like that out here, unguarded! An image came unbidden:

Mick, spurs frantically raking flanks, galloping the mare hell for leather out of town, dipping to scoop a terrified Julia and Fenella in the crook of an arm, swinging them up over the pommel, a figure in the street behind them loosing off ineffectual rounds at their rapidly retreating backs. A ranch up in the New Mexico hills. A hideaway far from civilization. Home education for the kids. But each day lived with an ear straining for the sound of hooves, the plume of dust on the horizon that would herald the inevitable showdown.

No, that was not his way. Not his star. He was a lawman, he would live as a lawman, die as a lawman if needs be. He was incorruptible.

Patting the mare's neck, horseflesh rippling in an involuntary shiver beneath his palm, he narrowed his eyes. Then he turned and straight-armed his way into the saloon, the distressed doors flapping in his wake.

His eyes darted this way and that, sizing up the occupants of the room. Velasquez the barman, Malloy the prospector, Douglas the card sharp, Little Big Nose from the reservation. The piano man and his jerky upper limbs. And a solitary shot glass and half-empty bottle standing on the bar.

'Where is he?'

Imploring silent looks. A flurry of mistimed tremolos. And Velasquez's eyes rising heavenwards, following the staircase that rose above the bar room.

Mick started to climb. The piano man's chords came louder, masking the creak of the treads beneath Mick's feet. These people! Decent, god-fearing folk. Mick felt pride and duty and protectiveness swell in his chest. His to serve them. His to see them right. His to rid this town of bad ass Mad John McDonald.

A shrill giggle reached his ears. Rhythmic squeaks from bed springs. Emanating from Doll's room. Dolores, abandoned by her fink of a husband without so much as a nickel to her name. Dolores, saving every last cent to pay her passage back to Spain to nurse her ailing mother. Doll, who would surely catch it in the crossfire should he burst, gun blazing, into the boudoir beyond the closed door.

What would the sheriff do?

The sheriff would send Mick in, gun blazing, say it was too bad, Dolores had had it coming ever since she ratted on him to his wife.

The frame splintered under the force of his boot. The door slammed against the wall. Crouched in the corridor, Mick drew a bead on the figures locked in a passionate tryst on the bed.

No, he drew a bead on the near-naked figure bouncing desperately on her bottom, wide eyes fixed on the open window, the billowing curtains.

Mick dived into the room, executing a perfect forward roll, just as the sheriff had taught him. Reached the window just in time to see...the main street deserted, Mad John's horse still standing dispiritedly directly below.

'Well, lookee here, if it isn't Deputy Mick.'

Mick felt the cold barrel press against the nape of his neck. Heard the thick click as the hammer engaged. Closed his eyes and offered up a silent curse. The hooker bouncing on the bed, the open window, the billowing curtains. The second oldest trick in the book, and he'd gone and fallen for it. What would the sheriff say?

'Lose the piece, lawman. Nice and slow.'

Mick let his .45 fall from his fingers. Inched his hands above his head, neck muscles spasmodic with anticipation of the slam of the slug.

'Now, give me one good reason why I shouldn't do to you what I did to your good-for-nothing pappy?'

A second metallic click cut the silence.

'How about: if you drop him, I'll drop you?'

Dolores! Blessed Dolores! Mick struggled not to laugh out loud. The whore with the Derringer tucked in her garter! The oldest trick in the book, and Mad John had fallen for it!

'So how about you lose *your* piece?' enquired Doll.

An interminable pause, Mad John weighing up the options.

'I can take a fly off a hoss's nose at fifty paces,' Doll added.

Mad John was a serial jailbreaker, a slippery eel no bars could hold. He would live to fight another day. A second or two later, his Peacemaker hit the boards with a fatalistic thud.

Mick let out a long breath and turned round. Mad John, eyes downcast in ignominious defeat. Dolores poised magnificently across the other side of the bed, stockinged legs splayed either side of her dark hairy triangle, bare breasts dangling between outstretched arms, left hand steadying right, in which nestled the glinting silver of her single-shot Derringer.

'Doll!' Mick bent and retrieved the two discarded shooters, stealing another admiring glance at her from under his eyebrows. 'Am I glad to see you.'

'Cut the crap, Deputy.' She spoke without shifting her eyes from her target. 'Just cuff him.'

As they walked down the main street the townsfolk, peeking first from behind protective shutters, began to spill out on to the sidewalks. Deputy Mick heard the muttered comments: 'Well I'll be darned! He's only gone and got the fella!' Spontaneous applause started to break out, everywhere Mick looked he saw happy, smiling, admiring faces. He raised his free hand tentatively, essayed a modest wave in acknowledgement of the adulation. The telegraph operator, his green visor pushed back on his forehead, rushed out of his office, hurriedly distributing bags of used tickertape for the citizens to throw. The church bells struck up a joyous peal. Some wag called out, 'Three cheers for Deputy Mick!' and ragged voices swelled on either side.

'Go ahead and enjoy it, lawman. While you can.'

Deputy Mick jerked his other arm, yanking the cuffs that bound Mad John securely to the custody of the Law. 'You don't scare me, McDonald. Never have, never will.'

'Oh, Mick!' Julia rushed down the steps from the haberdasher's, dropping her roll of chintz in her haste, Fenella skipping excitedly at her side. 'Mick, *darling!*'

She was laughing, her cheeks shiny with tears. She pressed against his chest, and Mick wrapped a strong arm round her shoulders.

'It's all right, honey. I told you I'd bring him in.'

Fenella kept a little ahead of them, skipping backwards now, staring amazed at the sight of her triumphant Pa and the wretched felon cuffed to his wrist. 'Bad man, bad man, Daddy's caught the bad man!'

Over the heap of auburn curls atop Julia's head, Mick caught Doll's eye. She smirked at him, lifted her palmed Derringer to her red-painted lips and blew a kiss across its barrel. He gave her a broad wink, and hugged Julia just that little bit tighter.

The hubbub diminished once they were inside the jailhouse.

'Right, you.' Mick led Mad John into the cell and clanged the door behind them. He handed his ring of keys through the bars to Julia. 'Lock it, honey.'

There was a confused silence. Julia looked at him, Doll looked at him, Julia looked at Doll, everyone looked at Mad John.

Who chuckled. 'You're on the *inside*, lawman.'

'I know.' Mick flicked the cuffs that bound them. 'I haven't got the key to these.'

'Darling! You can't stay in *there*.'

'It's all right, honey –'

'Where is it?' Mad John demanded, staring at the bunch of keys dangling from Julia's hand.

'Sheriff keeps the only one.'

'Well, go get the freakin sheriff,' said Mad John. 'It's bad enough being banged up. I'm not having you in here.'

'Oh, *darling*.'

'It's all *right*, honey –'

Fenella, her elation dashed, began to sob.

'Hey, don't cry, sweetheart. You and Ma can bring my supper here.'

'You!' Mad John pointed at Dolores. 'Quit smirking and go get the freakin sheriff.'

'He's out on a posse,' Mick told him. 'Won't be back till late. That's if he gets back tonight at all.'

*

The mournful howl of a coyote filtered in from away off on the range. The weak moonlight caused the bars to cast long shadows across the floor of the cell. Mad John rolled against Deputy Mick, almost pushing him off the edge of the bench.

'Hey!'

'Sorry.' John sounded groggy. He let out a groan. 'Sheriff back?'

'Nope.' Mick sighed. Fucking posses.

'Can't you shoot the lock?' John lifted his shackled arm, dragging Mick's up with it.

'State property.'

'Fucking hell.'

The two men lay in silence for a while, each staring at the darkened adobe ceiling.

'She's got the hots for you,' John said, eventually.

'Who?'

'The whore. Dolores.'

Mick chuckled. 'Yeah, yeah.'

'Yeah. I had a screaming fortune in my saddlebags. She was coming with me, we were going to buy a ranch some place, have ten kids and a thousand head of cattle. Till you came clod-hopping up the stairs.'

'Right,' said Mick.

'No, really.' John struggled on to his side, propping himself up on a elbow, obliging Mick to twist his arm for the sake of his circulation. 'It was her idea. The open window, the billowing curtains. She thought it was the sheriff. We were going to drop him, then head for the hills.' He gave a bitter laugh. 'When she saw it was you, she turned the gun on me.'

'Yeah, bollocks.' Even so, Mick was disturbed to feel the stiffening in his pants. Legs splayed either side of her dark triangle. Breasts with their smudged brown nipples, swelled together by the press of her Derringer-training arms. The way she turned round and bent right over to pick up her drawers, knowing he was watching.

The kiss she blew over the barrel of her gun. Her red-painted lips.

He was a married man! He forced himself to think of Julia. Her sweet nature, her homemaking skills, her baking, her darning, the layers of frilly petticoats he'd never ventured inside since the birth of their daughter four years ago.

John sighed, ruefully. 'I was about to tup her when you kicked the freakin' door in.'

'Shut it!' He couldn't bear to think of Doll with this outlaw, his coarse language, his calloused hands, his animalistic beard.

'Or what?' Mad John chuckled madly, tugging repeatedly at the handcuff chain. 'You're stuck with me, least till your goddamn boss decides to put in an appearance.'

His laugh became a cackle, demonic, nauseating. 'You didn't think of that, did you, lawman!'

Part Two

In the lab we can all aspire to objectivity,
examining the workings of other brains – or
even imaging our own – yet we go home in the
evening to our subjective, autobiographical
world, and aspire to make personal sense of our
lives and loves.

Steven Rose, *The 21st-Century Brain*

Blue Lines

St Mark's is just down the road from our house, next to the luxury retirement complex they built on the old Oxford City ground. We arrived at the same time as a brace of other families-of-the-young. Jules swapped greetings with the mums outside the entrance porch, her demeanour breezy and smiley now she was out in public. Ellie eyed the offspring shyly. Both dads, hanging back, gave me the same look: a barely perceptible, blank-faced nod that could, if necessary, be passed off as a nervous twitch. Nothing to do with Mick's and my singular appearance. Just the bewilderment of the commuting breadwinner back from the five-day week in the London flat, finding to his astonishment that his homemaker wife seems actually to know some people in the neighbourhood.

We generally sit in the third pew on the right. It's the kidzone. Most of Ellie's little mates from the local play-groups cluster hereabouts. It wouldn't be long before they were roaming the aisles, heading off to check out the toys and games they put at the back of churches in these enlightened times. Ahead of us was the music group – bass, rhythm guitar, synth, drums, vocals various – giving it praise and worship while the faithful gathered.

I am constantly surprised to find myself in church. Nay, astounded. When Mick and I were growing up, the Sunday outing was our only legitimate foray into the outside world. Our father was a Celtic fan, so we went to the local RC establishment. Not that he came with us too often. Its close proximity to Saturday night meant the 10.30 service was an unattainable goal. Mum used to take us along in the wheelchair, to keep up appearances. There was an elderly nun who kept house for the priest. She had a tuft of grey hairs sprouting from a mole on her chin. Some weeks she would lay a small posy of flowers on our lap, the stems bound in silver foil with some wet tissue inside, then she'd plant a tickly kiss on each of our foreheads. Mum said she was trying to raise enough money to send us to Lords. Cricket is a Sassenach game so I wasn't much interested. The actual services were excruciatingly boring, long tracts of incomprehensible cant interspersed with deathly hymns accompanied on the organ by an old boy whose Parkinson's precluded anything more lively than a dirge. Mick and I lapsed some five minutes after arriving at university.

We came to St Mark's the Christmas after Ellie was born. Jules's idea. She'd had a moderately more spiritual upbringing in the C of E. She said she wanted Ellie to grow up knowing the true meaning of Christmas. Ells slept through that service, but it's snowballed from there. Unless Mick is on call we now come every week, as do most of the formerly agnostic, thirtysomething middle-class parents Jules has got to know through the kids network. I was resistant to start with. Much as it pains me to recognize something of my father in me, when Sunday is your only chance of a decent lie-in you don't give it up without a fight.

Me: You don't believe in all that stuff, do you?

Jules: I don't know. Maybe. I think there's something, isn't there?

Me: Mick?

Mick: Well, no. I'm a scientist. It's a load of bollocks, obviously.

Me: So we're dragging ourselves out of bed for what, exactly?

Jules: Just look at her, John. [Brief pause to regard baby Ellie, babbling beneath jungle gym activity arch.] What's she going to grow up *for*? Just to learn things, go to college, have a good time, work too hard, drink too much, meet the wrong guy, fall pregnant, have her heart broken, bring her kid into the world on her own? For what, exactly? There's got to be more to it than that. Surely.

I could see her point. The unbearable rapture of Ellie's podgy little face, gazing up at the grinning monkey dangling above her, batting away with her tiny hand trying to make him swing some more. Her touching trust. Her untarnished innocence. Her unblemished soul.

Mick: She might become a doctor.

Me: Or a writer. Or an actress. Or something.

I could hear the hollowness in our words.

And the more I come here to St Mark's, the more I think there *must* be more to it than that. I don't know about afterlives and stuff, but that Jesus was wise with a capital Why. And a fantastic storyteller, too – it's the stories, the shape and meaning they offer, the absolutes, the points to anchor to. I don't know what's wrong with me. These Sundays I'm right there with Jules, hustling Ellie to get herself ready in time. I *want* her to have that. I want her to grow up having something in which to believe.

The vicar's a nice man called Clive. Hasn't yet got to grips with the radio mike that in the hands of a Billy Graham would allow him to roam the congregation whipping up a storm, but he gives good sermon. Gets stuck into the meat of it, how the Bible remains relevant. That day he was discoursing about the Jezebel spirit.

You had to have been there. It's the thing that tempts you to do all the things you know you shouldn't, and makes all the things you know you should do seem so utterly dull.

Jules. Oh, Jules. Oh, Jules.

The weeks since the scanner 'n' club session with Ariadne had been sticky, to say the least. I wasted no time in erasing all trace of my sister-in-law's infidelity, whacking her plaintive email straight back to her inbox with a stunningly authentic 'Mail delivery failed' header. I've never thought of myself as a computer nerd, but I even worked out how to get Outlook Express to change the display name so the returned message appeared to come not from John McDonald but from the 'Mail Delivery System' instead. If I ever give up on getting a book published, I may retrain as an IT consultant.

Jules hasn't spoken a word to me in a month. Mealtimes I keep my head down, chewing my chowder, entertaining Ellie, and otherwise staring with renewed interest at the collection of miniature jugs and teapots from fishing villages and other tourist hot spots around Devon and Cornwall that grace the shelves of our Welsh dresser. For her part, Jules remains solemn, withdrawn, snappy. On occasion I sneak a look. Her pink-tinged eyes, the fine crow's feet etched more deeply, the sallowness of her complexion. It rips me apart. I long to go to her, tell her it's all right, say something stupid like I love you, I want you too. Instead, I gaze dully at those teapots and jugs. What else am I supposed to do?

Even Mick has begun dimly to appreciate that something's seriously awry.

'Listen, John,' he told me a couple of weeks back, when we were alone on the bog. 'Jules is feeling a bit flat at the moment. Best not mention anything about Ariadne or anything.'

'Course not,' I said. 'Why? What did you tell her?'

'Nothing. Really. But I think she sussed we weren't with the warden that night.'

'Fuck.' I tore off a length of loo roll, quartered it neatly along the perforations. 'How do they do that? Women's intuition, I mean.'

He waited till I'd finished my wipe.

'I don't think rolling in at two in the morning was such a smart idea.'

'No, I guess not.'

'And you left the Coven tickets in your pocket.'

'Shit.'

'All three of them.'

Mick and I always get charged for two. No matter that we take up no more seat room than your averagely obese citizen, ticket sales executives throughout the British transport system, to say nothing of front of house staff in innumerable cinemas and theatres, take one look at us and promptly sting us for two full adult fees. The lass on the desk at the Coven was similarly unmoved by my appeals. No, it was of no consequence that we had just the one pair of dancing feet, to say nothing of a single patent oesophagus. If we wanted into the club – and at that point she'd cast a look of frank incomprehension towards Ariadne – it was three tickets we needed.

'You didn't try telling her it was the warden who came clubbing with us?'

I felt Mick shake his head. The warden of St Ablart's is a septuagenarian economist who sits on the monetary policy committee of the Bank of England.

'It'll blow over,' he told me. 'She can't expect you not to have a social life. She's just a bit fragile at the moment.'

We stood.

'One, two, three.'

We bent our knees, grasped the waistband of our boxers, and pulled them into position as we straightened our legs. And again for the trews.

'It doesn't matter, anyway,' I said, once we were over at the sink. 'Ariadne's history. I'm not interested any more.'

Our eyes met in the mirror.

'Sure you are, John-boy.'

'No, honestly. I guess I'm getting older.'

He gave a brief laugh. 'Don't be stupid. You're John McDonald. Shagtastic John McDonald. You're rusty is all. What's it been? You haven't been on the pull in ages. You're bound to need to ease back into it. But your life's not *over*. Not by a long chalk.'

He held my gaze, seemed almost to doubt himself.

'Looks like it's an academic question, anyway, doesn't it?'

We hadn't heard a squeak from Ariadne since club night. Mick's expression clouded over. 'Maybe you should call her?'

I shook my head. 'Phone her now and she'll know exactly what's what.'

'What's wrong with that?'

'Mick, you know jack all about women. Trust me. The only way she's going to bed with us is if she thinks it's her idea.'

'But what if she's waiting for you to ring? What if she thinks *you're* not interested?'

'That's precisely what we need her to think.'

I turned the cold tap on, dipped my fingers into the water.

'You don't want to lose her,' he said. 'You'll wait a long time to meet a woman like that again. Maybe never. She's so smart, so beautiful. Perfect, really.'

He held the towel up for me.

'They'll have the results of the brain scans soon. She'll have to call then, for her research if nothing else. Don't fuck it up, John.'

I wiped my hand front and back against the soft towelling, drying it in silence.

Clive wrapped up his sermon with a howl of feedback and a passionate exhortation to repel the Jezebel spirit at every turn. I stole a glance at Jules, sitting hunched forward, her hands clasped as though in prayer. The band struck up a stirring gospel number, 'My Help', by a guy named Mark Beswick, according to the blue screen above the altar where the words to all the songs are projected in these hymn-bookless days. And they are songs. Hymns are irredeemably gender-biased.

And what do I do, Clive? I wanted to jump to my feet, call my question out loud, send it ringing round this church. I've slept with my brother's wife, they stoned them for that in Old Testament days, didn't they? Far worse, I have no desire to sleep with Ariadne. And if you'd met her you'd know how serious that is. What has happened to me? I don't want to sleep with her because. Because it would fuck up my little family. And I love my little family, even though it's not my little family at all. Because that's what I want now. I want a little family, but I'm never going to have that because I'm a good for nothing waster who's shagged a lot but never loved and now I think I love someone and I can't have her because she's married to my schmuck of a brother and if I repel the Jezebel spirit and never shag another woman then I'll keep this little family that isn't mine and live the rest of my days so fucking close to what I never had for myself it hurts. And my schmuck of a brother *wants* me to shag Ariadne because he wants her and that way he'll have her and he can't see what he's got already and he's a fucking arsehole who doesn't deserve what he's got and won't get what he deserves, always the one with the brains, always the one with the money, always the one with the girl who loves him, always the one doing the right thing but now that doesn't seem to count for fuck all. I don't want to have a good time any more, don't want to work too hard, drink too much, meet the wrong gal, get her pregnant, break her heart, leave her to bring her kid into the world. I want there to be more to it than that. There *must* be more to it than that.

But I didn't stand up. I didn't send my question ringing round that church. How could I? I couldn't even speak with the one person I really needed to talk to.

Mick had fallen asleep. Jules had a hell of a job waking him to get him to put some dosh in the collection basket. Ellie was cantering up and down the aisle with her chum Charlie, the pair of them being unicorns, whinnying and neighing like horses because if you've never seen or heard a unicorn you have to pick on the nearest approximation you have in your experience. And if, like me, you've got the LeapPad of the Lion King, you'll know a zebra sounds absolutely nothing like a horse. Which probably means a unicorn doesn't either. But how the fuck are we supposed to know?

So on our way out I shook Clive's hand and told him it was a terrific sermon. And Mick did too, because that's what you do, even if you slept through most of it. And Clive looked at me carefully, searching for irony but finding none. And I still wanted to ask him, but I didn't. And now it is so much more complicated.

So very much more complicated.

Monday morning. Breakfast. I'm having a BLT phase, rashers crispy-fried, light on the lettuce and tomato, lashings of mayonnaise. How on earth do vegetarians do it?

For some reason we've been left in charge of Ellie. Ellie. Nutella on hot-buttered toast, closely followed by chocolate ice cream. Mick leaves me to it. He's an incompetent when it comes to food, has no idea how to send his daughter out into the world with any sustenance in her stomach. He tried to insist on a sliced-up apple with a cornflake-milk-no-sugar chaser, but he doesn't know the glint in the eye. The twinkle that says: Mum's nowhere to be seen, I'm going to get away with murder.

Time's ticking on. I cajole her into her uniform. Nursery kids don't wear uniforms, not unless they go to a £2,000-a-term private nursery that feeds one of the most sought-after public schools Oxfordshire has to offer, that is. Thankfully, Ellie is accomplished in dressing herself. Neither Mick nor I has much idea about tights.

'Do you think Jules is OK?' I ask, Ellie safely docked in front of CBeebies.

'Sure. Why?'

'Where is she?'

Mick and I do the look-round-the-kitchen thing, as if Jules will suddenly pop out from behind the fridge and start counting, 'One! Two! Three!...'

'No idea,' he says.

I suffer a sudden qualm. Think back to when the replacement alarm went off. Six-thirty, so much more civilized on a regular GP morning. Up we got, a-groaning and a-moaning. Staggered as far as the door, unhitched the dressing gown from the hook, slipped our feet into our slippers, and made the gummy-eyed descent of the stairs.

Was she in the bed beside us? Or had she gone, flown in the night?

'We'd better check,' I say.

'Fucking hell,' says Mick.

Up the stairs, as fast as our little legs will carry us.

The bed is empty.

Her side has been slept in. But, from a cursory brush of the hand, is cold.

'Shit,' says Mick.

Now you're talking.

Back to the kitchen. How to get Ellie to nursery. Whether to get Ellie to nursery. How to ring Mick in sick without alerting the outside world to the situation.

The upstairs loo flushes, water gurgling in the down-pipe.

Ha, stupid us. In the bathroom, all this time.

And the tread of her feet coming down the stairs. The tread of her feet coming into the kitchen. Fully dressed, but un-made-up. And the silence that greets Mick's, 'You all right, Jules?'

And the tiny thwack as she slaps something on the kitchen table.

And how, after she has left with Ellie, to all intents and purposes setting out on the normal nursery run, like she does every ordinary day, Mick and I stand staring at the white plastic oblong she left on the Sanderson-print tablecloth.

And how, for clarification, I ask: 'And two blue lines means what, exactly?'

Toilet Talk

Mick's surgery is housed in a rather fine Grade 2 listed building of Georgian origin, just down the road from the Randolph. It doesn't matter if you don't know Oxford, just think big blocks of yellow sandstone, golden sunlight, traffic snarled up behind an appallingly parked tourist coach and you've got the gist. It's a pleasant enough place to work: the partners and staff are friendly, the money good, and the patient profile relatively benign. The practice has its share of deprivation, but the population is skewed by the middle classes up the Banbury and Woodstock Roads. There are half a dozen colleges on the books and, I have to say, that has been the greatest surprise. I would have thought those fusty old dons would have shrunk in horror at the sight of their new GP. Quite the opposite; Mick and I regularly get invited to dine-ins in the great halls. There appears to be a certain cachet in having a bicephaloid college doctor. Our appearance is, in any case, assumed to be typical of those educated in the state sector.

That said, even in these enlightened times – with the Paralympics on prime time, and with people generally bending over backwards to be jolly nice to the different-ly abled – you do still run into the odd soul who finds the idea of a conjoined twin pursuing a medical career hard to get their head around. I'm right with them. I mean, can you believe it? I'm not knocking the disabled – you won't find a stauncher campaigner for our right to live life to the full. In the hospital where Mick did one of his house jobs they had a congenital dwarf as a radiologist. He used to get about on leg calipers and crutches, and they solved the necessity for him actually to be able to see the x-rays by mounting viewing boxes lower down the walls. Neither do I think Mick's salivation problems, nor the fact that he has in essence just the one arm, to be insurmountable in themselves. Christ knows there are plenty of drooling single-handed GPs out there. No, what I'm talking about is me.

I am not going to run myself down unnecessarily, but I ask you. Would you want to go and spill the embar-rassing details of your changed bowel habit, your malodorous discharge, your menstrual irregularities, to say nothing of your over-reliance on binge-drinking, to a doctor who not only spends the entire consultation listing alarmingly to starboard but whose identical twin brother occupies the other half of their specially widened swivel chair? I certainly wouldn't. But no one else seems to mind.

OK, there were complaints in the early days. Several patients objected to the tinny chunter coming out of my headphones, claiming that it put them off their train of thought, particularly if I was humming along. I soon found that reading a novel was interpreted as insolence, not lack of interest. And as for some of my other strategies, well, let's just say it's been a good few years since I've allowed myself to nod off part-way through a busy morning. We went through a sticky patch, not long after Mick joined the practice, averaging roughly a complaint a week, and Mick's surgeries rapidly became half-booked at best. The other doctors started to wonder out loud whether they'd been entirely wise to give him the chance. None of which came as any surprise to me, who had thought them quite mad in the first place.

It took the senior partner, a merry old soul called Dr Day – who, incidentally, impresses me no end by his use of hypnosis as a way of managing his most difficult patients – to put his finger on the source of Mick's woes. He drew us aside one evening, requesting a quiet word. Once we were alone in the photocopying room, he inhaled deeply, a breath which seemed to summon up all his thirty years' experience. 'What you need to do,' he told us, 'is stop trying to pretend John's not there. None of the patients minds when one of the medical students sits in on their consultation, do they? I take it you've met the students? I really don't think there's going to be much of a problem with a Siamese twin.'

As soon as I started to join in, to play my part, the moans and green-ink letters dried up. And in a funny kind of way it helped Mick. I have become adept at assisting in practical procedures. I tend to take a bit of a back seat when it comes to rectal examinations, but in numerous other tasks I have carved out a role.

I am not going to pretend I don't find a certain satis-faction. I almost enjoy it, day in day out, watching what goes on. Despite my natural antipathy to the field, I know a heck of a lot of medicine. After years of being forced to sit on Mick's shoulder – going through medical school, suffering sleep-deprivation in the torture camps that pass for hospitals, getting all psychoanalytical during GP training – I could probably do the job myself. The problem is, and it is only one of our many problems, I wouldn't do it anything like he does. We have diamet-rically opposed views on questions as diverse as the merits of the pharmaceutical industry, the necessity for depressed people to be doped up to the eyeballs with psychotropics, and the disconcerting similarities between the proponents of lifestyle medicine and the members of the National Socialist Party in 1930s Germany. Such is the irreconcilable nature of our differing opinions, I have been banned from contributing verbally to all but the most trivial of consultations. I am allowed to chip in my tuppence worth to the social chitchat which tops and tails the meat of the matter, but I am not to say a single word when there's anything of import to be discussed. Not only is this wholly unacceptable, it puts me on the spot when a patient – as so many do – turns to me after being on the receiving end of one of Mick's 'counselling' sessions, and asks me what I think. It's all I can do to shrug my shoulder and point out that he's the doc.

Don't think I haven't tried to broker a compromise.

Me: So it's all right for me to skivvy around pulling on people's lugholes so you can get a decent look at their eardrums, but if I've got anything remotely helpful to say I'm to keep my trap shut, is that right?

Mick: It's not that I don't appreciate what you do. It's just I don't think anything you've got to say would be remotely helpful.

Me: And how would you know *what* I'd say?

Mick: (sighing) Look, remember –

Me: Remember what?

Mick: Forget it.

Me: What?

Mick: Nothing.

Me: *What?*

At which juncture he usually rakes up the past. He's never forgiven me for lighting up once during a particularly harrowing 'I'm afraid I've got some bad news for you' consultation. That infuriates me, because it's years since I had a fag during surgery. And anyway, it was bloody upsetting. I counter by pointing out that his thing of gobbing in my coffee mug isn't exactly empathic. Cruel, I know, but it never fails to hit the mark. The discussion tends to go downhill from there.

I should point out that Mick and I have great difficulty seeing eye to eye. It's just not possible. We used to conduct those sorts of arguments with both of us glaring across the room at the Snellen chart on the back of his consulting room door. That's fine when you go into a sulk, because staring off into space refusing to make eye contact is exactly what you want to be doing. But you tend not to get the facial nuances that let you know all the non-verbals. These days, when there's something important to talk about, one or other of us calls a sort of time-out in front of the nearest mirror.

All of which is by way of an explanation – and, to the poor person who kept rattling the door handle with increasing desperation, an apology – for the length of time we spent locked in the staff loo that fateful morning.

'When was she doing it? Hm! While I'm working my arse off here! While Ellie's at nursery!'

'Look, Mick…'

'It's that smarmy bastard on Cobden Crescent, I know it. What is he? A poet or something? Never does a day's work.'

'Mick…'

'I cannot fucking believe it.'

'Exactly! You don't know. She could have…'

'Oh, what, it's an immaculate conception, is it?'

'No. But it doesn't mean…'

'It most certainly does. Babies don't just pop out of thin air, John. Even you know that.'

I held his gaze for a moment, let the provocation slide.

'What about that lass? Kimberley what's-her-name.'

'What about her?'

'She hadn't had sex.'

'She bloody had.'

I shook my head. 'She was a virgin, wasn't she? Bit of heavy petting, bit of pre-cum on the fingers?'

Mick showed me his media-doc teeth, in what in different circumstances might have passed for a smile. 'People say anything.'

'You believed her.'

'I did not.'

'Did too.'

'John! There's no point challenging people, is there? What about all those morning-after pills? You're not seriously suggesting condoms actually burst that often, are you?'

'All I'm saying is, maybe that's how it happened. I don't know, maybe Jules was trying to rev you up one time, got some stuff on her hand, then you couldn't, so she got a bit frustrated… It's at least possible, isn't it?'

His features seemed to sag a little, as though a notch of anger had slipped away. Footsteps in the corridor, someone tried the door. Again.

'Just a minute!' I called.

'Maybe you're right,' he said.

I pressed home the advantage.

'Come on, you can sort it. What's that thing, paternity testing? After the baby's born, get its DNA checked. That'll settle it.'

He frowned. 'I should just ask her.'

I rested my hand on the sink, let it take some weight.

'Look. Things haven't been good lately. You accuse her of having an affair and I guarantee they'll get a damn sight worse. Trust me.'

'But that's just it! If it *is* mine, why the hell was she like that? What about all the darling-I've-got-wonderful-news-for-you stuff? You remember how she was with Ells.'

I shrugged. 'Maybe it's Ariadne.'

'What's that supposed to mean?'

'She's been in a foul mood ever since we went clubbing with her. Maybe she thinks *you're* having an affair!'

'You're full of shit, John.'

'*I'm* not saying it. Obviously. But what if that's what Jules thinks? She's not going to give a monkeys if *I'm* after someone, is she? But if you were. It makes sense.'

Mick thought about that one for a bit. So did I. I'm a fucking genius. Really.

'Don't you think you ought to make a start?'

'What's the time?'

'Ten to.'

Mick tutted. 'I don't know, John. I hear what you're saying. It just seems so unlikely.'

'But not impossible. Think about it. I don't know, do a literature search or something. Find out how often babies get conceived without actual intercourse. I'm sure the *British Journal of Obstetrics and Gynaecology* will have something on it.'

That seemed to cheer him up. 'You're right. I'll do that. Straight after surgery. Come on, we're late. Keeping me in here gassing.'

*

It was as much as I could do to stop myself bursting into song. All morning I sat there, itching to be out of the chair, to be out of the surgery, so I could think, so I could bask, so I could laugh out loud, long and hard and joyful. Every patient, I kept thinking I'd tell them. Listen to this! This'll cheer you up! The last appointment was Mrs Murgatroyd, back to see what if any difference Physiotens had made to her immutable blood pressure. When Mick was safely out of earshot under his tubes, attention directed to the falling column of mercury on his sphyg, I gave her a stage wink and mouthed: Guess what? I'm going to be a father! Surprise registered, quickly to be replaced by unabashed delight on her wrinkled features. She adjusted the dial on her hearing aid, touched a hand to her blouse. Nineteen ninety-nine from Top Shop, she mouthed back at me. I nodded and gave her a grin.

A father! One shag and I am going to be a father! Fecundity is my middle name! I was filled with undiluted thrill. You hear someone's having a baby, you think: ah, that's nice. Even when it was Jules with Ellie at most I felt a semi-detached affection. But when it's your own! When one tiny microscopic bit of you has somehow against improbable odds found the needle in the haystack, has set the life of another human being in train, you think: holy fucking cow. How the fuck does it happen? *What* is it that's happening? The enormousness of it, the juggernautically unstoppable momentum of life. Humility and herohood, Clark Kent and Superman.

My mind was skipping feverishly, already nine months from the here and now. Cradling the wee one in the crook of my arm. Feeding her puréed goo. Watching as she grew into a delightful little sister for Ellie, as she matured into a wondrous young woman, full of intellect and vitality, ready to get out there and seize life by the scruff of the neck and give it her merry best. A little version of me! Me and Jules! How my chest would tighten with pride at her doughty performance in her GCSEs. The sheer excitement of watching her tear home in first place in the 800m at sports day. How I would tenderly steer her through A-levels towards a career in the arts. How would I feel, at her eighteenth birthday party, gazing at her across the hall as she swayed and twirled to Abba's 'Dancing Queen'? The pang as she slow-danced with her first boyfriend, while Robbie Williams belted out 'Angels'. The surrender to the inevitable joy 'n' pain as she left the nest, struck out on her own, taking up her place at an unfussy redbrick university, the next step to becoming the youngest and most iconoclastically brilliant presenter *Newsnight* has ever seen.

And she would be a she. I was sure of it. The boys among Ellie's nursery friends were monsters, the lot of them. Girls set up tea parties, practise feeding and changing their dolls, they play at the same gentle game for hours on end. Boys charge up to the toy cupboard of life and proceed to yank out the entire contents, dashing each thing on the floor as soon as their five-second attention span has been exhausted. In some societies it's still boys everyone wants. But in twenty-first-century Britain, the land of equal opportunity and in-vitro fertilization by donor sperm, it's girls we prize. We've had it with the antics of the ASBO generation, aggression and impulsivity are utterly passé. We value caring and compassion, nature and nurture, love and respect. We are the pink fluffy people.

How I needed to see Jules. How I needed to let her know – somehow, anyhow – my feelings. Fuck Mick. What I would give for five minutes – just five minutes! – without that miserable grouchy git hovering by my ear. I couldn't begin to think how to work it all out. Would we sit tight, maintain the status quo, resign ourselves to late-night, slow-motion lovemaking while he snored obliviously, all in the name of stability and a continuing income? Would I have to endure the fizzing anguish of seeing my own daughter growing up believing herself to be someone else's child? Would I have to bite my lip, never speak the truth, content myself with wordless delight as she galloped past her developmental milestones? Or would Jules be unable to live the lie? Would she confess the truth, take her chances, trust her children to council housing and state education? Could I do it, could I earn a meagre wage, enough at least to keep them in fish 'n' chip suppers and charity shop presents every Christmas?

The sense of responsibility was beginning to send me wobbly. I was a pressure cooker, seething with untellable news and unanswerable questions. I needed relief, release, but the pent-up steam would scald every one of us. One thousand, two thousand, three thousand. I forced myself to slow down, cool it, quiet the thoughts churning in my head. I had coped these thirtysomething years with suffocated ambition, institutional inferiority, unadulterated second-fiddledom. It had given me ulcers, but I had done it. I could do it now. Play my cards close to my chest. Keep wise counsel. Make the best of this intolerable situation.

Mrs Murgatroyd left with a referral to get her blood pressure sorted at the hypertension clinic up at the John Radcliffe. I looked forward to letters from the consultant as she continued to defy medical science. Mick typed his notes into the computer, his index finger tripping clumsily over the keyboard. He was just about to close her record when the phone rang.

'Shit,' he said, after listening for a moment. 'Muriel's got Ariadne holding on one. Says she wants an urgent word.'

'Well, have a word, then, Mick, my boy.'

Mick held the handset in front of us.

'You speak to her.'

'I'm not speaking to her. You're the one who wanted to help with her research.'

'You're the one who wanted to get into her pants.'

I waved him away. 'I'm having nothing more to do with it.'

'You can't. You said you would. What's she going to think?'

'I don't care. I'm too busy. I couldn't care less.'

'Please, John. For me.'

The handset waggled. I sighed.

'They're never going to give you a job. They're only interested in you as a research subject. Once they've done with you they'll drop you, I guarantee.'

'Right now it's the only chance I've got.'

He tapped the phone against the monitor, with its display of the last eight months' identically hypertensive Murgatroyd BP readings.

I shook my head slowly. 'Put her on the speaker.'

Mick pressed the broadcast button.

'Hi,' I said.

'Hello? Mick? It's Ariadne.'

'No, it's John. Mick's tied up just now. Can I help?'

'Sure. Look, sorry it's taken a while to get back to you. Those scan results are very interesting. Very interesting. Prof's set up a symposium. He thought we should get some experts in to help interpret them.'

'Great. I'm pleased for you. Terrific.'

'Would you be able to come?'

'Sorry?'

'To the symposium.'

'I don't know.' I felt Mick nodding, violently. 'When is it?'

'Tomorrow. We've got some people flying in. Should be able to start at three.'

'It's very short notice. Mick's got patients all afternoon.' Violent shaking of the head on my right. 'No, actually, now I look at it, that'll be fine.'

'Are you sure?'

'Yep, no problem. We'll see you then.'

I opened the door and stepped us inside. Expecting the scamper of Ellie's feet. The call of greeting from Jules. The house was silent. Unlit.

We made our way to the kitchen, flicked on the multiple spots. The table was tidy, the morning's post in a neat pile in the exact same place where earlier we'd left the pregnancy test with its two blue lines, never having dared touch it. No cutlery laid out for supper. No steam and smells and warmth.

Jules had left a note. No appellation, just a bald statement directed at Mick, or me, or us both. She'd taken Ellie to grandma's. She needed time to think. She'd call to let us know when they'd be back.

Aw, shit.

'I told you! She's having an affair!'

'You don't know that,' I said.

But it did look uncannily like it. I redoubled my earlier efforts.

'Look, give her a bit of breathing space. I'm sure there's a simple explanation.'

Mick thumped the table-top. 'Fucking hell!'

In any situation, no matter how grave, there is always a silver lining. Some way of looking at things in a positive light. Some crumb of comfort. I divested us of our jacket and tie, and rang for a pizza. Ham, mushroom, jalapeño peppers. Fourteen-inch. Since Mick married Jules it's been home-cooking, salads, wholemeal bread. My mouth watered at the prospect of reliving, for however brief a time, our takeaway bachelor days. Before hanging up, I added a side-order of garlic bread, in case this was for one night only.

'Should I ring her?'

His voice had lost all trace of bullish arrogance. He sounded so uncertain. I felt an eddy of pity. Of guilt. An inkling of the humanity behind the shrivelled heart. Of what it might mean to him to lose his family. The family he so often treated with ill-temper and contempt, like they were an encumbrance, like they sucked him dry, like he'd be better off without them. Something cold washed through my veins, something emanating from him, something that felt like fear.

'I don't know, Mick. Leave her to sleep on it. Maybe call her tomorrow.'

He nodded dumbly. We went through to the sitting room, flicked through the channels, killing time till the delivery boy belled. I was shocked, I had to admit. The air was saturated with Jules and Ellie's absence. I missed Ellie's skippity skipping, her proud presentation of the art 'n' craft she'd done at nursery, the puffing of her chest as I told her what a great job she'd made of it. And Jules's sunny smile, her hand brushing my back, the smell of Dove soap, the soft tingle as her lips touched lightly on my cheek. The house felt cavernous without them. Dead. There had to be a way of squaring this. Had to be a way of pulling us all back from the brink.

'I don't know about you,' I told Mick, 'but I could do with a drink.'

*

It took near enough a whole bottle to knock him out.
That and the blood-sucking effect of half a pound of
melted mozzarella in the stomach.

'How you can think of working?' he slurred, shortly
before sliding into an alcoholic coma.

'Adversity. The writer's friend.'

I kept fiddling with the scene where Sister Sebastian
snorts her first line till I was sure he was gone. Then I
closed the file down. For a while I gazed blankly at the
active desktop, with its picture of Jules, Ellie, Mick and
me on holiday at Arne. The lot of us grinning at the
digital camera, which was perched on a chair, its auto-
timer light blinking till suddenly Flash! we were
captured for all time. Thinking through the impossible.
A tiny piece of me, tadpole head and swishing tail,
ploughing onwards, energy failing, movements slowing,
becoming progressively mired in the gloop. Keep going,
John! You're almost there! And then, without warning,
colliding with a wall of jelly, an immovable obstacle. The
end.

But no. A sudden rupture, acrosome unleashing a
shotgun blast of hydrolases. Jelly digested, bindin meets
bindin and membranes become one. Microtubules tug
exhausted John in. Drawing him helplessly through the
cytoplasm, ferried on an irresistible conveyor, till he
feels himself begin to dissolve, painlessly, progressively,

enzymes dismantling his phospholipids, his glyco-proteins. Releasing his twenty-three chromosomes, the demi-blueprint randomly chosen to pass down the gen-eration, their coils condensing even as they are clamped to the mitotic array. Across which are ranged their twenty-three blind dates for this waltz of life, this barn dance of new beginnings. Do-si-do your partner! The entwining, the intermingling, the intimate exchange of bodily informatics. The emergence from the soup. The start of life. The touch of god.

I launched Outlook Express. I half hoped for an email from Jules, some inkling of her thinking. But after the way I'd treated her I could hardly expect it. Still, her mum had been bitten by the net bug at a library-spon-sored course the previous year. Grandma was now on broadband, and scattered terms like router and ethernet around with gay abandon. If Jules was feeling anything like I was, she'd be checking her webmail at every avail-able opportunity.

To: jules@mcdonald.demon.co.uk
Re: you n me

Jules
I'm a shit. I didn't know how to deal with it. So I didn't.
I'm sorry I ignored you. I'm sorry I sent your email back.

I can't think about anything else but you, me, and our
baby. And Ellie, of course. I don't know how we can do it,
but I want us to be a family.

I know you know I went out clubbing. And, yes, it was
with another woman. But it's not what you think. I'm a
changed man. I've put all that behind me. You've got to
believe me. It's you I want. Only you.

You've got to speak to Mick. He thinks you've been having
an affair. I told him you probably thought he was. You've
got to play along with it, it's the only way out of this mess.
One of his patients got pregnant without having sex, I
convinced him that's what must have happened. I told him
to get a paternity test. He's such a chump, he thought it
was a good idea.

Jules, I think I love you.

No, I do love you.

I don't know how you feel about me, but I love you.

Please.

John

The barn dance done, they pull apart, opening themselves to the intimate attentions of the polymerases and
their nucleotide building blocks. And so it goes on. One
becomes two, two become four. Eight. Sixteen. Thirty-
two. Doubling and redoubling. An undifferentiated ball
of omnipotent stem cells, the blastocyst with no name.

Tumbling like a microscopic ball of sagebrush down the Fallopian tube, bursting like a shooting star into the cathedral of the womb. Oh star of wonder, star of light!

John, oh John, oh John.

They are my genes. They are his genes. But they carry something with them, I'm sure of it. Something invisible to the most powerful electron microscope, something no x-ray crystallographer can divine, an essence irreducible by all the polymerase chain reactors the world has ever seen.

Something of me.

Of me.

Something of *me*.

Message sent, a couple of porn spams popped into my inbox. I deleted them both. I was a reformed character, a family man. I lit up a bedtime cigarette, aware that these, too, would have to go. Whisky? Only in moderation. What of the writing, the dream, the way I had determined to make my own mark on the world? Fuck, it was confusing. I was getting ahead of myself. I could still get an email back saying sorry, you've got me wrong, I only shagged you because I was desperate for another baby and Mick is a saggy bastard who couldn't sire a piece of wet tissue. I had exposed myself, left myself exquisitely vulnerable. Fleetingly I wished I could recall the email, pull it back by magnetic attraction, return it to my outbox and delete it from all but the most expert forensic examination. But it was gone, zinging through the ether to clang, like a limpet mine, to the Demon server. Thence to be prised off by Jules. And be opened. And my fate be decided.

I tried to get into her email account. The password dialogue box sat, arms impassively folded, in the middle of the screen.

Mick?

Ellie?

MicknEllie?

Your sister-in-law chooses a password for her email account. What would it be?

I powered down and took us on our staggering way to our cold bachelor bed.

I'd get nowhere on *Mr and Mrs*.

Two Heads are Better Than One

Mick kept us hovering behind Muriel Redknap while she made her calls.

'Mrs Morgani? It's the surgery here. I'm afraid I'm going to have to cancel your appointment with Dr McDonald this afternoon... Yes, he's been invited to attend an international scientific symposium being held at the University of Oxford... Well, yes, he is, isn't he?... Yes, I'll make sure I tell him.'

'Excellent,' Mick chirped once she'd put the phone down. If he'd possessed a second hand he'd have been rubbing it with glee.

'You don't think a simple "Dr Mick's got to go to a meeting" would have done?' I asked.

'Thanks, Muriel,' he said, by way of reply. 'See you tomorrow.'

She gave us one of her over-the-top-of-the-specs looks.

Aboard the Booster, Mick kept the throttle-grip twisted full on. We bumped our way along Cornmarket, toots of the horn parting the shoals of shoppers and tourists in our way. A discarded Dr Pepper can was flattened by our front wheel. The metallic squack! was like a rifle shot. Mick was craning his neck forward, muscles taut, an excitable puppy on a leash. I sat resignedly, fingers limp around the handlebar, the breeze causing my eyes to smart.

The despondent soon-to-be-divorcé of the previous evening had done a bunk at some point during the night. Mick had bounded us out of bed, dressed us in our smartest grey suit, whipped up a banana 'n' kiwi smoothie as an apology for a breakfast, and was ready to leave for work before the pips.

'Weren't you going to call Jules?' I reminded him.

'I thought about it, John. You were right. Best let her stew for a bit.'

I let it go at that. The more time she had to pick up my email before speaking to him the better.

St Ablart's is one of Oxford's oldest and most venerable colleges. Its founder was a thirteenth-century monk famed for his illuminated manuscript, *The Rites and Orders of Holy Dying*, the only extant copy of which is housed in the rare books room of the college library. I've seen it, or at least two pages of it, splayed open in its UV protective glass display case. All in Latin, of course, but with some fantastically colourful calligraphy and enough gold leaf to canopy a medium-sized oak. Beautiful. St Ablart's mortal remains are interred beneath the chapel transept, with the exception of the three bones of his right index finger – the Holy Quill – which are threaded end to end over a thin wire of solid gold and kept in a velvet-lined relic case in the warden's safe. In the event of a gross misdemeanour on the part of an undergraduate, tradition dictates that the warden calls the offending student into his study and wags the Holy Quill in their face while sending them down.

It's pronounced Ab-lair, by the way, St Ablair. The Ablart thing is to catch out tourists, and other people without the benefit of an Oxbridge education.

We parked the Booster outside the lodge. Mick pocketed the keys with a purposeful jingle. We strode through the archway. On the lawn, some students were playing football with a galia melon. There was an A-board, positioned strategically at the ingress to the main quad. McDONALD SYMPOSIUM it read, with a bold black arrow directing us left towards the Old Library.

'Will you look at that,' said Mick, *sotto voce*, bringing us to a halt in front of the sign. 'McDonald Symposium. Boy, oh fucking boy.'

'Mick! John!'

Ariadne was hurrying towards us. Her brilliant white blouse. Her beige linen skirt slit to mid-thigh, opening-closing as she walked, peek-a-booing her bare legs. Her very long bare legs.

'Hi!' Mick breezed. 'Not too early are we?'

'It's perfect. We need to get some x-rays done before we start. Follow me, please.'

'X-rays?' Mick said.

'Don't worry.' She gave us a smile. 'Prof got a portable machine brought down from the Institute. It's in the Hatchery.'

'No, why x-rays?'

Ariadne laughed. 'We don't want someone trying to blame this on a defective scanner, do we!'

There was a rather bemused Institute radiographer waiting for us in the small octagonal chamber of the Hatchery. She had a neat brown bob, frank hazel eyes. She reminded me of Jules. A pang lanced my stomach, wondering how she was, what she was thinking right now. I felt suddenly and irrationally fearful. Was everything all right with the baby? The pregnancy was in its earliest stages, miscarriage was a real possibility. A bloody and bitter end to my dream. And what if the baby were to be deformed? What if it were to be a double monster, just like us? What would we do, seeing the lurid heads sprouting from its frail body on the 20 week anomaly scan? Terminate the pregnancy, the prospect of another pair of conjoined twins in the family too much to contemplate? Or smile serenely at the grainy grey image on the ultrasound screen and say, Oh, look, she's got her daddy's noses.

Ariadne was regarding us with a disconcerting expression, one I'd never seen on her face before, a cross between barely suppressed excitement and wide-eyed incredulity. Like she was expecting us to do some stupendously amazing thing, but wasn't entirely sure we'd manage it.

'You all right?' I asked.

'Sure,' she said, conjuring an artificial smile.

'Here you go,' the radiographer said, taking my elbow gently, steering us in the direction of the stand on which was mounted the unexposed x-ray plate. Once she was satisfied we were lined up correctly, she collected her lead apron and pulled it on over her head.

'You better wait outside,' she told Ariadne. 'I didn't bring a spare.'

'Good luck,' Ariadne said to us. She gave a bizarre thumbs-up before leaving the room.

'OK,' the radiographer said, crossing over to her machine. 'I'd like you to keep perfectly still. You'll hear a short beep, and that will be that.'

'What's your name?' I asked.

'Sandy.'

'Sandy, would you mind telling us what the fuck's going on?'

She bobbed up from behind her apparatus. 'I'm sorry, I thought you knew. I'm to take a skull x-ray.'

'Yes. But why?'

Her neatly plucked brows dipped. 'To get an x-ray picture of your skull?'

Charming as she was, Sandy was not going to get offered a research fellowship any time soon.

'Can it, John,' Mick muttered in my ear. 'The symposium's starting in a few minutes.'

'Did you know this was going to happen?'

'No,' he said. 'Why are you fussing?'

'I just don't like being exposed to radiation without good reason.'

'Right. Like that's going to make any difference, the amount you smoke.'

I shook my head in resignation.

'Keep it nice and still, please.'

Sandy stayed looking at us for a half-second too long. What was it with these girls? First Ariadne, now her. I gave my nose a wipe with the back of my hand, in case there was a bogey or something.

'*Please.*'

'Sorry.'

She ducked down behind the white box again. The tracer light came on, with its crosshairs overlay. Her disembodied hand appeared, adjusted the angle of the beam, centring it to get our heads in the frame. I began to feel a little like de Gaulle in *The Day of the Jackal*.

'You've never seen anything like it,' Ariadne told us as we struggled to keep pace on the way to the Old Library. 'Some of the biggest names in neuroscience, philosophy, psychology, from across the world. Prof's got such amazing pulling power.'

She cast a glance our way, as if to gauge how impressed we were.

'It seems a lot of fuss over two blokes having an erection,' I told her.

'Oh, that.' She tossed her hair, and hitched the x-ray folder more tightly beneath her arm. 'No, we've moved on a long way from that.'

Prof was lurking like a guilty schoolboy outside the studded oak door to the Old Library.

'Gentlemen,' he greeted us, drawling the word extravagantly. Prof is about six foot eight, and thin as a washboard. He carries his greying head, with its clipped David Niven moustache, in a permanent stoop, as if it got stuck that way during a long career of bending down to listen to lesser mortals.

'No need to be intimidated,' he smiled thinly. 'Yes, all right, in that room we've assembled the intellectual equivalent of the Himalayas, but they're all perfectly nice. Well, most of them, anyway.

'I'll introduce you, you take a seat, then let me run the show. Try not to say anything, but if you do have to say something… Well. Perhaps you would let me say it for you.'

'I'm going,' I announced.

'John,' Mick said.

'No, I don't like this. I'm off.'

The little fucker wouldn't let me move. Try as I might.

'It's all right,' Mick insisted. 'This is academia, that's all. You might as well get used to it.'

I saw Prof look long and hard at Mick.

'Yes, quite,' he agreed. He laid a hand on the door handle and pursed his lips. 'Extraordinary.'

As we came round the door the room swam into view. It smelt of beeswax and yellowing paper. The huge old tables ranged in a rough U, an array of a dozen or more people sitting at neat intervals. Blotters, tumblers and Evian bottles at each place. Sensing our entrance, the oval faces swung in unison, swivelling like missile defence radars. All conversation ceased.

'Ladies and gentlemen,' said Prof. 'May I introduce the McDonald twins.'

*

The Anatomy Act is strict in its stipulation of who is allowed access to cadavers. Before Mick was allowed even to start as a student at Nottingham the medical school had to commission a special balaclava for me, fabricated without the benefit of eye holes, which was deemed sufficient to ensure the university would not be in breach of its licence.

The pair of us, in the dissection room for the first time, struggling to pull it on over my head: 'How does it feel?'

I tugged it to align the single aperture with my mouth. 'Prickly.'

Inside my woolly cocoon I listened while the assembled students were briefed about their forthcoming dismemberment of a real dead person, a genuine stiff. During the ensuing three terms, Mick and his fellows would systematically carve up an entire body, tracing the routes and branches of the major vessels, exposing the nerves, muscles, bones and viscera that together constituted a once-living human being – someone's dad, someone's hubby, someone's gramps. By no stretch of the imagination could this be considered a normal activity for nineteen-year-olds to indulge in, outside of the inner cities. I was thankful I'd see none of it.

Not that the initial solution to the-problem-of-John was entirely satisfactory. Within minutes I was forced to distract Mick's attention from the introductory talk.

'It's fucking hot under here, you know.'

'Shhh.'

'I'm sweating like a pig.'

'Look, shut up. It's only three hours. We'll get them to sort something else out for next week.'

'Three *hours*? I'm starting to hallucinate. I can't see a fucking thing.'

'That's the whole idea.'

By the time we returned for Mick's second session, the balaclava had been replaced by a loose-fitting black cotton hood of the sort favoured by condemned men on the scaffold. So began a year-long experiment in sensory deprivation. It's true what they say about blind people: in the absence of sight, the other senses ramp up to compensate. Whilst Mick declared himself insensible to all but the overpowering formaldehyde in which the cadavers had been pickled, I quickly became a connoisseur of the subtle biological bass-notes. The ferrous tang of muscle, the faecal whiff from bowel, the acridity of the gall bladder, the rancid rind of fat. And insomuch as taste is largely smell, I suppose I also became a vicarious cannibal. My ears developed exquisite acuity for the slice of a scalpel through gristle, the snip of scissors nipping at fascia, the suck of a gloved hand delving deep inside the abdominal cavity.

As for touch, I didn't. Not till the last session of the final term, at the very end of head and neck. When Mick

– motivated, he insisted, by uncontainable scientific awe as opposed to any premeditated desire to make me vomit over the inside of my cotton hood – suddenly broke off from his work and commanded me to hold out my hand.

A heavy weight landed on my palm. Wet. Subtly yielding, like workable clay. Rugated.

'What the fuck's that?' I asked, panicking in the blackness.

'That, John,' he said softly, his tone reminiscent of Dimbleby at a royal wedding, 'is the crux of a person. The arena of character, personality, thought, language, memory. The place of desire and dreams. The seat of the soul.'

Mick was cleaning it off our suede desert boots for an hour, and spent twice that time pleading with the Dean for clemency. I didn't see, of course, but apparently the brain splattered everywhere when it hit the floor.

I was looking at one now, as were the assembled academics at Prof's symposium. Not a real brain – a multicoloured picture of a slice through one. Taken by Ariadne's fMRI scanner. Projected on a screen at one end of the Old Library. Mine, I presumed, though how I'd know the difference between mine and Mick's I've really no idea. Prof was pacing to and fro, setting out the cir-cumstances of the experiment: how they'd hoped to gain, through a process of digital subtraction, the world's first

ever neurological localization of the conscious compo-
nents of male sexual arousal.

'Imagine our surprise,' he said, 'when *that* came back.'

He had a nifty little laser pointer. He circled its red
dot round and round the brain. I squinted, trying to
make head or tail of what might be causing the muttered
puzzlement around the room. Different areas were lit up
in a variety of colours – reds, whites, greens, oranges,
blues. It made me think of those thermal images taken
from the air. Ariadne had said the different hues repre-
sented differing metabolic activity in the various brain
loci. Presumably one had to know the first thing about
neuroanatomy in order to appreciate it.

'Pardon me, Donald,' one of the male delegates piped
up. His oversize lapel badge indicated he was Todd E.
Feinberg, from the Albert Einstein College of Medicine
and the Beth Israel Medical Center.

'Todd?' Prof said.

'I feel embarrassed to even ask.' Feinberg gave a
forced laugh, and pushed his glasses up his nose. 'I
mean, I know you'll have considered this. But why isn't
that just a technical artefact?'

Prof smiled beatifically. 'That's exactly what we
thought to start with. But we've been through the data a
dozen times. All the delimiters are present and correct.'
He turned to glance at the screen. 'That, ladies and gentlemen, is a complete MRI field.'

There was a swell of surprise from the gathering, surprise verging on consternation.

'What the hell's going on?' I asked Mick, whispering under my breath.

Prof spoke over the hubbub. 'I didn't expect you to take this on trust.'

He nodded to Ariadne, who clipped an x-ray up on a portable viewing box erected next to the table where the caterers had laid out the cling-filmed plates of biscuits, and the tea 'n' coffee-making gear.

'We obtained these radiographs this afternoon, immediately before bringing the McDonalds to meet you.'

Prof and Ariadne should be on the stage. The impeccable timing with which she flicked the switch, illuminating the viewing box.

'Well, I'll be!' That was Feinberg, his voice distinct across the clamour.

'*Mick*!' I hissed.

I followed Prof's red laser as it flickered over the white bones of the skull x-ray. I'm no expert, obviously, but it looked all right to my untutored eye.

'*Mick*?'

Someone started laughing. 'Well, that's one in the eye for the substance dualists!'

Appreciative chuckles came from various points round the room.

Feinberg called out, 'Donald, this is dynamite!'

'*Mick*!' I said, more loudly, feeling like I might be about to explode. 'What the *fuck* are they talking about?'

'There's just the one head, John,' he said. His voice had a catch in it. 'There's just the one head.'

As soon as he said it, the scales fell from my eyes. Up on the screen, a single brain. On the x-ray, a single skull. They weren't images of one or other of us. They were images of us both. There was just the one head.

I can affirm that, as a group, professional academics, whose lives might be considered altogether cushy, have surprisingly rough hands. And sweaty. And shaky. The following ten minutes of the symposium were spent with Mick and me surrounded by a press of bodies, as the assembled philosophers, neuroscientists and psychologists reached out to touch us. On the scalps. On the ears. On the cheeks, the chins, the noses. Eventually Prof called order, and the delegates returned reluctantly to their seats. While the last couple were getting themselves comfy, Ariadne came over.

'May I?' she asked.

'Be my guest,' said Mick.

She spent a few seconds doing something to him, then I felt her touching me lightly on the back of my head. Running her fingertips over my extensive bald patch.

Down over my brow, my eyes, my face, sweeping finally to stroke the line of my jaw, the bristles of my goatee. If I hadn't been so indescribably frightened, it would have been the most erotic thing to have happened to me all day.

'Thank you,' she said.

I watched her walk back to rejoin Prof. The sleek motion of her hips. The mounds of her buttocks. The perfect, fantastic arse that had got us into all this in the first place.

Prof spread his hands wide. 'That is why we've asked you here today. Frankly, we haven't the first idea how to proceed. Ladies and gentlemen, we are open to any and all suggestions.'

A woman, dressed in a snappy Chanel trouser suit, got to her feet.

'Donald, I think I speak for all of us when I say how thrilled and excited we are. How *grateful* we are to you for inviting us to share this, this *extraordinary* finding. It seems to me, on the face of it, that what you have here will *revolutionize* our conceptualization of every facet of our world.'

There were murmurs of assent. She was standing obliquely to us so I could only just make out her badge: Letitia Badinou from the Institut Philosophique de Paris. She had an American accent.

'Hold on, Lettie.' A hulk of a man rose across the room. John R. Searle, University of California, Berkeley. He looked like he probably played quarterback forty years ago when he was at college. 'I'm no scientist, but before we get ahead of ourselves, I think we ought to try to define what we're looking at.' He stared directly at Mick and me. Waved a hand in our direction. 'I mean. Just what *is* that?'

'Hey!' I shouted back at him. '*That* is two thinking feeling human beings, who don't much appreciate being talked about like an exhibit in a freak show. Come on, Mick.'

The bastard! I couldn't believe he wouldn't let me up. We had a brief wriggling battle, but I couldn't get even one buttock more than a few centimetres clear of the chair. I slumped back.

'What are you doing?'

'I'm listening,' he told me. 'It's interesting.'

'You're an arsehole. I'm not going to sit here and be insulted.'

'Look, I'm sorry, all right?' This from Searle.

'Just because. Just because you want *him* to give you a job' – I jabbed a finger in the direction of Prof – 'doesn't mean I have take this crap.'

'Calm down,' Mick said. 'Let's hear them out. Don't you think it's fascinating?'

I decided on a sulky glare at our shoes. There was an embarrassed silence in the room. Eventually, Searle spoke again.

'I didn't mean to be rude. I guess, like everybody, I'm just trying to get a handle on the situation. We can all *see* the two of you, but if the science is right then we've got to believe there's actually only one of you there.' He shook his head. 'You have to admit, it's a bit of a head fuck.'

'What do you think, John?' Prof asked him. 'Do you think this is material, or metaphysical?'

Searle shrugged. 'Things I can touch with my hands I tend to think of as material.'

The man next to him cleared his throat. 'I couldn't disagree more.'

I'd seen him somewhere before. Maybe a dine-in at one college or other. The badge said he was Richard Dawkins, University of Oxford.

'The human mind is notoriously susceptible. That's the whole history of science, isn't it, dispelling illusion? You might *think* you can touch them, you might *think* you can see them, it doesn't mean they're real. I'd go with the physics. If they don't stop x-rays, if their hydrogen nuclei don't align, I'd say they're metaphysical.' He gave a huff. 'Whatever that is.'

'One of them exists, though, doesn't he, Dawko?' This from Prof.

Everyone looked back at the x-ray, the scan.

'OK, OK.' Dawkins sounded cross. '*One* of them's material. The other's an illusion.'

'I don't see how you can make the distinction,' Searle said. 'They look and feel equally solid to me. Warm, even.'

'Dawko's got a point, though, hasn't he?' Gerald M. Edelman, from the Neurosciences Institute. 'What you're talking about, that's simply sense-data. Last time I read up on it, no one had ever made a watertight case for sense-data necessarily corresponding with physical reality. I see a table, I touch a table, but who's to say there's really a table there?'

There were a few sage nods from around the room.

'Isn't our perception of radiographs just sense-data too, though?' said Searle.

'We're getting sidetracked,' Prof interjected. 'We haven't managed to sort that one out in a couple of millennia, I don't suppose we'll do so this afternoon. I think we should focus on how this phenomenon might be occurring.'

'I'm more interested in *why*,' said Searle.

My fear and anger were beginning to be replaced by a more familiar and urgent need for the comfort of uncomplicated physical gratification. I held up my hand.

'Um, excuse me? I hate to interrupt. Is there any chance of a coffee?'

'Sure, sure.' Ariadne bustled over to do the necessary. A few of the delegates took the opportunity to fetch themselves some caffeine, too. The others watched with undisguised amazement as I did my thing with the lighter and the fag, twirling it round my finger, sparking it as it hit my mouth. Like I said, it is wizard.

'Thanks,' I said, as Ariadne popped a cup and saucer on the table next to me. I took a deep drag on my cigarette.

'Tea? Coffee?' she asked Mick.

'I don't drink, remember?'

'Of course not. Sorry.'

The astonished stares continued unabated. It is quite freaky, the first time you see smoke coming out of Mick's mouth when he speaks.

'Todd?' The French woman with the US accent was speaking again. 'Could this be some type of autoscopy?'

Feinberg nodded slowly, as if weighing the idea.

'Um, sorry. Me again.' I waved to attract attention. 'As it appears I've got to sit here listening to this, can we lay down some ground rules? I'm not going to be talked about over my head. Try to think of me as an ignorant layman. Anything you even suspect I might not understand, you'd better explain. OK?'

'OK, that's reasonable,' said Feinberg. 'Lettie's talking about autoscopic hallucinations. They're quite common, where someone has an exact replica of themselves following them around all the time. They can evolve into quite concretized delusional systems.'

'It's a good thought,' said Prof. 'But we've been over that MRI with a fine-toothed comb. There are no anatomical lesions whatsoever.'

'Autoscopy doesn't have to be pathological, Donald. Some folks think they're an extreme variant of the imaginary friend. How long have you guys been like this?'

'Since we were born,' I told him, with just the right amount of pithiness.

'Since you were born, or ever since you can remember? Imaginary friends typically form around age three.'

'Pardon me,' I said. 'I don't actually remember being born. I'm simply going on what we've been told.'

'What about your baby photos? Are you double-headed in those?'

Diane and Murray McDonald. God rest their souls.

'Our parents weren't much interested in family snaps.'

'You've got absolutely no photos from your childhood?' Feinberg looked incredulous.

'You never met our parents.'

The room fell silent, save for the hum from Prof's slide projector.

'But surely the point of autoscopy is that it's *subjective*?' This was a newcomer to the debate, a bushy-bearded chap, whose name badge was obscured by his exuberant facial hair. 'I've never heard of a single instance of anyone seeing anybody *else*'s doppelgänger. Of the twenty or so people in this room, every one of us can see two heads. How do you explain that?'

'Actually,' Dawkins spoke again, scowling at us. 'The longer I sit here, the more convinced I am that there is, in fact, only one man sitting there.'

He glanced left and right, but no one responded.

'What if he/they/it *want* us to perceive two of them?' another woman chirped up. 'There's a whole industry sprung up around that, hasn't there? NLP? Life coaching? The power of positive thinking? You're going to a job interview, you feel utterly crap, you're completely unsuitable and totally unrecruitable. But you say to yourself, over and over: I'm fantastic, I'm going to boss it, they'd be lucky to get me, who's the daddy? who's the daddy? In the end you believe it, and as soon as *you* believe it, that's what others believe too. You walk into that boardroom and every member of the panel sees the most desirable kick-ass candidate ever to submit a CV. You get hired on the spot.'

Everyone spent a moment or two listening to the whirr of the slide projector fan.

'Sorry,' said the woman.

'This isn't a split brain thing, is it, Donald?' This was from Giulio Tononi, from the same institute as Edelman, but dressed in altogether snappier style.

'Both the corpus callosum and anterior commissure appear entirely normal,' Prof said.

'Ground rules!' I called.

'Sorry,' Prof smiled. 'Giulio was raising the very good point that we should consider what are known as split brain syndromes. It's probable that we each of us have at least two separate and quite distinct selves – left-brain, right-brain – with quite different biases and ways of looking at the world. If the channels of communication between left and right hemispheres are disrupted, the ability of the dominant hemisphere to synthesize the two into a unified self is lost.'

'That's if you believe there *is* such a thing as the unified self!' someone piped up.

'The fascinating thing,' Tononi hurriedly added, 'is that because language is a unilateral function, usually of the left hemisphere, we have no way of communicating with the autonomous right-brain self that's rattling round in these folks' heads.'

'Mickey Gazzaniga managed it, though, didn't he?' said Bushy Beard.

'Yeah, that was really freaky.' Tononi turned to Mick and me. 'Gazzaniga had this split-brain lad with a weeny bit of language in his non-dominant hemisphere as well. They managed to devise a way of communicating exclusively with each side, asked them what ambition they had in life. What an experiment! The kid's left brain wanted to pursue a nice steady career as a draughtsman, just like his dad. His right brain wanted to be a racing car driver!'

There was muted laughter. Edelman patted Tononi on the shoulder.

'Where is Gazza, anyway?' Tononi asked.

'He sends his apologies,' Prof said. 'He's developed an overwhelming fear of flying.'

I'd smoked my cigarette right down. The ash I'd been tapping on to my saucer, but I wasn't sure what to do with the butt. In the end I dipped it into the dregs of my coffee, extinguishing it with a quiet fsszzt. It suddenly occurred to me why Mick was being so quiet. I passed the cup across. He discreetly unburdened himself of a gobful of saliva.

'Speaking as a fellow scientist,' he said. 'I am, of course, fascinated by your conjecture. But you've got to take account of my experience. I *know* I'm a separate person. John and I have utterly different attitudes, beliefs, personalities. We've got absolutely nothing in common. I mean, just look at him. I can't stand the man.'

'Ditto for me,' I said.

A svelte fortyish woman in the far corner suddenly leaned forward in her chair. 'That makes me think of Miguel Ruiz. It's a bit sociological, I'm afraid – I read some, sometimes. He argues that we've got so many contradictory role-possibilities in post-modern cultures. Respectable professional by day, fun-loving family member of an evening, pill-popping party animal at night. He doesn't believe that the unified consciousness can contain all the alter egos, thinks it must inevitably lead to a fracturing of the self. A sort of psychosocial leucotomy, if you like. I'm sure he'd be interested in the case. When he gets out of hospital, that is.'

Prof nodded at Ariadne, who made a note on her clipboard.

'I'd be more persuaded if the McDonalds were female,' Tononi said. 'Women are the ones under the heaviest role pressure. Careers, kids, sex goddesses, culinary queens. I'm sure my wife's self fractured quite some time ago.'

'On the contrary,' the woman replied. 'Our brains have repeatedly been shown to possess superior flexibility. It's you boys who can't manage more than one thing at a time, who don't know whether to be Neanderthals or New Men.'

'Getting back to Ruiz.' This was a bespectacled Steven Rose, from the Open University. 'There is a sound neurobiological basis, isn't there? The phylogenetically ancient limbic system? The Johnny-come-lately prefrontal cortex?'

I gave an extremely loud sigh.

'Sorry,' said Rose. 'I was making the point that we're comprised of evolutionarily disparate parts. The limbic system's been around for donkey's years; it generates our emotional life, all our urges, drives, desires, and fears. The prefrontal cortex is a relatively recent bolt-on, where we do our abstraction and planning, where moral or socialized constraints originate. The two are in a constant tug of war. Left to its own devices, the limbic system would have us all behaving like rutting stags. The prefrontal cortex is perpetually trying to impose a civilized veneer.'

'That's all very well,' said Edelman. 'But the evolutionary trajectory has been towards cortical dominance, hasn't it? What are you arguing? That this is a sort of breakout by the limbic system?'

Rose gave a muffled sort of laugh. 'I'm not trying to argue anything. But that's the basis of Ruiz's thesis, isn't it? That post-modern permissibility allows, in differing circumstances, variable loosening of the prefrontal grip?'

'Well, this has been fascinating,' Prof said, pocketing his laser pointer. 'Very helpful contributions. It's given us a lot to think about.'

'Hang on, hang on,' said Dawkins. 'I can't believe you're all simply *accepting* this. Can nobody see what I can see? I admit, when we started, I thought they were conjoined twins. But look at them now. Look at them in the light of the empirical data.'

Every pair of eyes fixed on us, every forehead wrinkled with concentrated scrutiny. I gave them a little wave. Mick slapped my hand down.

Dawkins got to his feet. 'Come on, people, can't you see what's happening? You go outside, have a look around. It *appears* we live on a flat earth, overhung by an infinite sky. Into which the sun rises each morning and from which it sets each night. When the stars come out, their predictable periodicity seems to impose some kind of order on the random chaos of our lives. That's what it looks like, but is that what you all believe?' He shook his head. 'Of course not. Because objective science has told us how the universe really is. It's exactly the same here. We've got one head, one man, one brain. There is only one McDonald. As soon as you get that concept into your head, you stop perceiving the illusion – however it might be being perpetrated.'

He reached down, grabbed some papers, waved them at Prof. 'These CVs, Donald. We've got Michael John McDonald, bachelor of medicine, bachelor of surgery, member of the Royal College of General Practitioners, full-time GP principal at Beaumont Street Surgery, TV doctor on Channel 5's *Wake Up Britain!*, married to Julia, with whom he has one child – all tangible achievements that can be objectively verified. Then there's this John Michael McDonald. He's apparently a writer of some sort. Hasn't published a thing. Has no qualifications. No intimate relationships. Nothing to substantiate his existence one way or the other.'

Dawkins threw the pile of papers on the desk. 'I'm perfectly prepared to accept the existence of the one – who, I would argue, we can see radiographically imaged before us. As to the other, well, until someone proves the fact of his independent existence, I for one am not prepared to accept the reality of his being. In fact, as I say, I can't see him at all any more.'

He sat back down, folded his arms with an air of finality. Twenty pairs of eyes bored into me. I looked from one to the next dumbfounded face. I could hear our pulse pounding in my neck.

Someone cleared their throat. 'Well, actually, Dawko, now you come to mention it.'

'Yes, by god, I think you're right.'

'Um, yes, me too.'

'One head, definitely.'

'Yep, the beardie's completely disappeared.'

Throughout the collective conversion, Dawkins stared directly at me. Rather provocatively, I'm bound to say. His eyes did appear to have the faraway quality that would come from focusing on the leather-bound volumes stacked on the book-lined wall behind me.

I blew a raspberry at him.

He didn't even blink.

So I head-butted Mick, hard. The crack and his yelped expletive chased each other's echoes round the room.

The senior common room in St Ablart's is wood-panelled, with leather armchairs in nooks and crannies, and the occasional writing table stocked with notepaper headed with the college crest. Heavy velvet curtains drape the windows. The latest editions of every quality daily and serious-minded periodical are available for perusal. On the mantelpiece above the Adams fireplace there is an Olympic rowing gold, displayed next to a Nobel prize medal, both donated by sycophantic alumni who presumably just didn't have the space for any more clutter at home. Mick has dreams of winning the Bafta for best media doc. He fondly imagines they'll put that up there with them.

Prof made his way towards us, weaving between loose confederacies of chatting fellows, three glasses of sherry bunched between his hands.

'Well,' he said, handing one to me, 'that went rather well, I think.'

'I don't get it,' I told him. 'I've just had to sit through the most humiliating repudiation of my very existence, then you come along and give me a drink.' I took a sip. 'For which, thanks, by the way.'

'Oh, I wouldn't take much notice of the Dawk,' Prof

said, smiling. 'He's a brilliant scientist, of course, but he's rather fundamentalist in his empiricism.'

'Meaning?'

'Well, it's just that where he can see something on an x-ray or a scan, he's inclined to assume that's all there is. It's rather reductive, I'm afraid.'

'Surely that *is* all there is, though,' Mick pitched in.

'Patently, no,' said Prof. 'If someone takes you to the Taj Mahal you don't go up to it, have a good peer and say: "Pile of stone, right?"'

'I don't understand,' Mick said. 'Are you saying there's one of us or two?'

'Oh, one head, unquestionably. But I'm also quite certain that both of you exist as well. It's a fantastically tricky problem.'

He chinged his glass against mine. 'Cheers.'

I took a sip of sherry. My whole life I'd been a problem, holding Mick back, interfering with the progression of his career, bringing his marriage to its knees with my insistence on late-night drinking sessions, thinly disguised as literary endeavour. Nevertheless, I was struggling to adjust to the idea of being *this* sort of problem. I think, therefore I am. Or so I thought. Or so I was.

'You took a bit of a gamble, didn't you?' Mick said. 'Leaving the x-ray to the last minute. What if it had showed two heads after all? What if you'd called all those eminent people together to consider a defective MRI?'

Prof shook his head. 'I'm not stupid, Mick. We pulled your films from the John Radcliffe. One of the radiologists is a fellow.'

I sensed the frown in Mick's silence.

'You mean there are x-rays at the hospital that show us with just the one head?'

Prof nodded. 'One neck, anyway. You've only ever had standard chest films.'

'How come no one noticed?' Mick sounded incredulous, a sentiment I have to say I shared.

'You were under the care of the cardiothoracic surgeons, weren't you?' Prof said.

'Of *course*,' said Mick. 'Of course.'

'Why all the theatre, then?' I asked. 'Couldn't you just have brought the old x-rays with you? Saved us a bit of radiation.'

Prof inclined his head a little lower. 'We didn't have your consent, did we?'

I stared at the little half-smile smarming its way on to his face. Like it was a game. Snooping on our confidential medical records. OK if no one finds out, but not something one would parade in public.

'Anyway, nothing short of a full skull x-ray would have satisfied that lot. They're academically rigorous, to a man.'

'They couldn't figure us out, though, could they?' I said.

'There's no obvious explanation, self-evidently.' Prof looked demurely down at the carpet. 'Had there been, I'd have worked it out, I'm sure. This was more of a brainstorming, a gathering of ideas. It's opened up tremendously promising avenues for further research. Gives us material for at least a dozen grant proposals.'

Ariadne, who had needed to apply some powder to her nose, rejoined us. Prof handed her a sherry. Her eyes danced from Mick to me. They glistened with excitement, or desire, or both.

Prof raised his glass. 'The McDonalds. Between you, gentlemen, you should single-handedly treble the research capacity of the department. That's one hell of a lot of RAE points.'

Ariadne and Prof downed hearty mouthfuls. I kept my glass at ease, not because I'd be drinking my own toast, more because I was feeling decidedly nauseous all of a sudden.

'You've made your astounding discovery,' I said. 'Isn't that enough?'

Prof chuckled. Glanced at Ariadne. Who giggled.

'My dear fellow. There's a paper or two in it, I'm sure. But this is a gold rush. Four of the delegates today have already offered to second research fellows. There are so many facets to cover: the neurobiological, the philosophical, the sociological, the psychological. I don't know. This is probably the single most thrilling moment of any of our careers.'

He paused. 'Actually, the elucidation of the mechanism by which cocaine potentiates ethanol-induced excitation in dopaminergic reward neurons in the ventral tegmental area was rather fun, too.' He pursed his lips, shook his head. 'No, even that pales in comparison.'

'Um, Prof.'

Mick's voice was accompanied by a massive surge of adrenaline. I felt our heart scatting like a startling colt. Prof looked at him.

'All this research. That's presumably going to tie up a lot of our time?'

Prof grinned enthusiastically. 'I should cocoa. We'll have you down so many MRIs and PETs and MEGs you won't know you've been born! To say nothing of the *endless* inventory tools the psychologists keep dreaming up.'

'It's just. Well, I don't know how I'd fit it all in around my GP commitments.'

'Ah.' Prof looked thoughtful.

'I mean, I'd love to help. Really. It's the time factor. Plus I don't know how I could continue in practice, not once you start publishing stuff about which, if either, of us exists. Or not.'

'*Publishing*?' I said.

For someone in the public eye, Mick is famously protective of his privacy. He turned down a five-figure sum from *Hello!* for the rights to his and Jules's wedding pics, and knocked them back a second time when they wanted a photoset of the happy family at home after Ellie was born. It's not just his stuff, either. He vetoed overtures made to me by McDonald's (Big Mc), Burger King (Double Whopper) and KFC (2-for-1 offer, last summer). He says no way is he going to be associated with junk food.

'What I'm saying,' Mick said, 'is if you want our cooperation then you're going to have to help us out in return.'

'Help you in what way?'

'Something to get me out of general practice.'

'I see.' Prof sipped carefully at his drink. 'It's out of the question, of course. We can't possibly give money to a research subject. Nothing beyond legitimate expenses, anyway. The MRC would crucify us.'

'But if you gave me a job? A nice little readership, with tenure?'

Prof laughed. Briefly at first, then gathering momentum. Till his face reddened. He turned to Ariadne, who smiled politely, which seemed to fuel his mirth all the more.

'Oh, doctor,' he gasped, eventually. '*Oh, doctor!*'

They do that, the lot of them, whenever they meet Mick. Greet him with a restrained nod and a muttered '*Doc*-tor.' The irony is completely wasted. He so desperately wants to be in the club. He comes across like a prize pooch – much slobbering and wagging of tail and wide-eyed uncritical enthusiasm. And about as intellectual, too, with his brace of bachelor's degrees from a provincial university and not so much as a master's after his name. I hate to see him embarrass himself, but he never listens to a word I say.

'No readership, no pack drill,' Mick said, quietly.

Prof stopped laughing. Took off his specs. Wiped the moisture from his eyes. Was about to say something when the gong sounded for the start of the formal dinner.

During the English Civil War St Ablart's, in common with the rest of the university, was for the king. In fact, for the years of the parliamentarians' vice-free grip on London, Oxford became the site of Charles I's court-in-exile. Now, if you lived with the constant prospect of a bunch of crewcut roundheads bursting in, intent on impaling you on the end of their rapiers, you too would take some precautions. Hence the hidden staircase that leads off the SCR, terminating on the college roof. From here one could make one's distinctly unsteady escape.

These days, of course, there's little mortal danger in being an academic, though congregation did do its best in the Thatcher era when they voted to deny her an honorary doctorate. All the same, if you grew up reading more Enid Blyton than was good for you, the idea of hacking secretively across the rooftops might seem appealing. And when a second identically titchy staircase happens to come out right next to high table in the great hall, it takes not an enormous leap of imagination to decide that this would make a spiffing route to supper.

Every rain-free night the fellows of St Ablart's make their wobbly rooftop journey. The broad gutters are duck-boarded, with chicken-wire wrapped over the wood to give leather soles more purchase. You can peer over the parapet, look down on the orange streetlights of the High below. See the stars in the clear night sky above you. Feel the breeze ruffling what little hair you have.

Prof and Ariadne were a few yards ahead. She's an old enough hand to know not to wear high heels.

'What the fuck are you up to?' I asked Mick, under my breath.

'They're absolutely gagging for it,' he said. 'I don't know what the hell's going on with all the scans and shit, but it does seem you're a genuine enigma. Now you see him, now you don't.'

'And it's definitely me that doesn't exist, is it? You're sure it's not you?'

'Listen, John. This is our chance. They can't do a thing unless we cooperate – there isn't a peer-reviewed journal in the world these days that will take case reports without the express consent of the subject. This is their meal ticket. They'll get invited to so many conferences they'll have to get visiting fellows in to cover their teaching. They're bound to get on telly, too, once they make it public. I'm going to screw them for every last point on the salary scale.'

Mick had a point. For all the condescension with which the academics treated him, they were also biliously jealous. What they wouldn't give for a nice little BBC2 series, or a regular seat beside Tom Paulin on *Newsnight Review*, or even an occasional guest slot on something by Melvyn Bragg. They can't stand the fact that Mick is on the box, week in, week out. Even if it is Channel 5. Even if it is only *Wake Up Britain!*

'You're not seriously suggesting we let them write us up, are you?'

'Think, John! I could get out of medicine. You'd have loads of writing time. Oxford academics don't actually *do* anything, not unless they want to, anyhow. It's the chance of a lifetime.'

'What about Jules? Ellie? What's it going to do to them?'

Mick did his porcine snort. 'As far as I can see, Jules is in the process of shacking up with some bastard she's been knocking off behind our backs for god knows how long. I don't owe her a thing.'

We reached the end of the walkway. Ariadne's back disappeared from view as she entered the narrow stairwell down to the great hall.

'What about me?' I said. 'Don't I have any say in this?'

Mick's hand came up and slapped me firmly on the cheek. Once, twice, thrice.

'You know, John, they're right. For an illusory metaphysical entity, you sure do have a deceptively fleshy feel.'

Mick and I sat with our backs to the ranks of undergraduates eating their suppers at the lamplit tables in the main body of the hall below. From the walls, the portraits of previous college wardens glowered down at the assembled feckless youth. Prof and Ariadne had taken themselves to the other side of high table and, ignoring convention, had seated themselves next to each other. They spent most of the meal in animated conversation, completely oblivious to the fellows on either side. Mick had a visiting professor in nineteenth-century Russian literature from the University of Oslo to talk to. I had an insufferably precocious economics reader who had shot to prominence with his pioneering work on stealth taxation whilst on secondment to HM Treasury.

The meal. Asparagus tips sautéd in garlic butter. Atlantic salmon drizzled with a dill sauce. Raspberry pavlova and cream. The waiters, drawn exclusively from the Indian subcontinent, circulated efficiently, replacing one course with another, recharging depleted glasses. I hardly ate a thing, such was the writhing and squirming in my stomach. I kept replaying that shocking moment when I'd realized there was just the one head. It was exactly how you'd feel if you got up one morning, stumbled into the bathroom for a slash, and while you were emptying your full-to-bursting bladder you took a casual glance in the mirror above the loo and saw *absolutely nothing* there. You look down, there's your plonker merrily splashing urine in the pan; you look up, nothing. I couldn't square it, couldn't even begin to make sense of it. It was frightening, it was revolting, it was embarrassing – all those folks I'd danced and boozed and joshed with in bars and clubs over the years, what would they say when they found out? *Yeah, you know, I always thought there was something odd about him.* You spend your whole life believing in yourself then some fucking scientist comes along and tells you you're sorely mistaken. It just didn't seem possible. I strained against it, I couldn't accept it, I wouldn't accept it. I *knew* I was real. I ate, I drank, I loved, I lost, I lazed and dozed and laughed and worked. I was flesh. And blood. And goatee.

'You leaving that?'

The economist was looking at my pavlova. I pushed it in his direction.

'Not hungry?'

I shook my head. 'I just found out I don't exist.'

'Oh, too bad,' he said, sympathetically. 'That happened to a friend of mine in Cambridge once.' He gave me a rueful look. 'He never got over it.'

I sat glumly watching as he shovelled up his second pudding. The repetitive raising and lowering of the spoon. The mechanical ruminations of his jaw. The bob of the Adam's apple as each mouthful was consigned to its digestive fate. I necked an anticholinergic with a mouthful of wine. Even the habitually excellent vintage from St Ablart's extensive cellars tasted corked tonight. I didn't want to be here, trapped on the side of Mick's head, slowly suffocating. Didn't want to be in this smug, rarefied atmosphere, making polite small talk about the thorny problem of reconciling classical economic theory with the vagaries of actual human behaviour. I longed to be home. Home with Ellie and Jules. My PC, my whisky, my fags. Jules. How would she react to the news? The father of the child growing inside her womb was a non-entity. Would she still want me? Did she want me even now? Or was I as much a figment of her imagination as I seemed to be of Mick's?

But the more I thought about it – the hand beneath the sheet, the butterfly wetness of her labia, those stark blue tramlines on the pregnancy test – the more I became emboldened. That was one tangible thing to which I could cling. Mick had had nothing to do with it, was snoring like a bastard when the moment came. Who's the daddy! Who's the daddy! They could keep their x-rays, stuff their scans. They could tell me what they liked, I wouldn't give in without a fight.

Mick had become embroiled in a one-sided discussion about the works of Dostoevsky, the visiting professor delighted to have discovered a complete ignoramus on whom he could practise his English. I waited patiently, intending to remind Mick about the parlous state of his marriage, the need to get home and make that call. Anything to get us out of this hell hole, back to a world in which I was real. But the Norwegian was droning on and on in his peculiar inflexionless tone. I felt a rising agitation. I could stand it no more.

'Excuse me,' I interrupted. The visiting professor gave me an eager smile, as if encouraging me to enter the discussion.

'Would you mind shutting up?' I said. 'I need to talk to my brother.'

'Of course,' he said, with a polite little bow. 'I bore myself sometimes.'

'What's up?' Mick asked.

'I want to go home.'

'We can't.' He glanced across high table, to where Prof and Ariadne were absorbed in discussion. 'I've got to go to dessert, to close the deal.'

Our heart sank. Dessert. Another hour in a candle-lit side room, fruit and cheese and chocolates, port and cloyingly sweet wines circulating. Then coffee in the SCR. More pointless conversation. More of Mick prostituting himself. More of this intolerable ennui.

I contemplated making myself vomit. Or giving a spontaneous and bawdy rendition of the Cha Cha Slide. Anything to force a resolution to this purgatory.

I didn't have to. At that moment the warden's gavel came down with a sharp crack, signalling the end of the meal. Those who were going for dessert took their napkins in hand. People started to rise, to mill around the table, taking leave of one another. Ariadne came over, smoothed right up to where we were standing behind our chair. Issued a persuasive smile. Over her shoulder I saw Prof hanging back, looking at us. When I met his eyes, he turned away.

Ariadne took the napkin from Mick's hand. Laid it on the table.

'Boys,' she said. 'I am buzzing tonight.'

She rested her fingertips gently on our chest.

'What say we go somewhere quiet? Talk things through. See what kind of understanding we can come up with.'

Ariadne's idea of a peaceful spot in which to conduct negotiations turned out to be Raoul's on Walton Street.

'I love this place!' I bawled approvingly at her, as we stepped inside the dim interior and were hit by a tsunami of sound. Back in our bachelor days Mick and I would come most Saturday nights. Hole up at a table with the rest of the JR posse, limber up for a few hours before hitting the Coven. Junior docs, fit-as-fuck nurses, fun-loving physios. A guy with a pony tail used to work the bar, twirling and tossing bottles like a street performer, sloshing shots into metallic shakers, maraca-ing the cocktails, dispensing them into glasses, frosting the rims with sugar, topping them off with sticks and umbrellas, all as he grooved to the up-tempo house that jumbo jetted the air. He had higgledy-piggledy teeth. His name was Dave. He was cool as fuck.

And he was still here! He caught sight of us as we followed Ariadne through the crowd. Held up a hand as we made it to the bar. Alison Limerick was pumping us down 'Where Love Lives'. My palm connected with Dave's.

'Long time no see!' he shouted. 'How you doing?'

'Yeah, Dave, good.'

Dave had gained some extra piercings. He'd also gained a paunch. His pony tail was striated with grey. Patches of stubble spoke to erratic shaving. The surge of excitement as I'd realized where Ariadne was taking us gave way to disquiet and misgiving. A stark reminder of lost youth. The precipice of responsibility I was on the edge of. How life was turning out.

We ordered cocktails, a Blue Blooded Dragon for me, a Plane Crash for Ariadne. Dave bopped about, but he'd evidently given up spinning bottles, and his hand shook when he came to pour.

'So, exciting day, yes?' Ariadne yelled, once we'd found a seat.

I stared at her. Her flushed complexion. Her dilated pupils. The damp strands of hair over her forehead.

I lit up a fag. Drank some blue dragon's blood.

'Exciting for you. I still don't understand what the hell's going on.' Mick's voice, barking in my ear, surprised me. For a minute, I'd forgotten he was there.

'Neither do we!' Ariadne sounded elated. 'That's what's so fantastic.'

'How *can* there be two of us and one of us at the same time?'

Ariadne shrugged. 'Even the stuff we do know, the nuclei, the neural nets, the neurotransmitters – it's all just mechanics. No one has the faintest idea how any of it translates into qualitative, subjective experience – how it can possibly equate to the Technicolor "I" we all of us feel inside. Brains generate minds, sure, but we lack the concepts even to begin to grasp how. It's like trying to describe Beethoven's Fifth in terms of wave-lengths, or violinists' arm movements, or the amount of spit that drips out of the bassoon.' She grinned. 'We're comfortable with conundrums, absolutely love them. What would we do, otherwise?'

She took her straw between her lips. Her cushion red lips. Eased some cocktail into her mouth. Then leaned forward, the better that we could hear.

'Prof says it's a Copernican moment. Says it'll turn the relationship between matter and imagination on its head. Or at the very least the relationship between imag-ination and perception. He's coming out with ideas and theories left, right and centre. I've never seen him so energized.'

Mick's fingers tapped the table. 'Come on. Matter and imagination are completely different things.'

'That's what everyone thought about mass and energy

once upon a time. You boys might get turned into an equation one day. I equals Mc squared.'

Mick shook his head. 'Prof wants to turn us into a freak show, doesn't he?'

Ariadne shook her head. 'We're all freaks, Mick! The human brain is a freak of nature. There's nothing like it in the known universe. A clump of matter that's capable of self-consciousness? Of understanding the birth of stars, the warping of space time, the evolution of species? Of creating art, of building civilizations, of composing symphonies, of self-destruction, too?'

She glanced around, her eyes sweeping over the Raoul's revellers. People dancing. People flirting. People getting steadily smashed.

'We're animals. We're animals and we're angels. We're moral and immoral. We're altruistic and hedonistic and everything in between. You don't need to worry about helping Prof. There's nothing anyone can say about you boys that's any more bizarre than what we're all trying to deal with every day.'

'Even so,' Mick shouted back over the din. 'There's got to be something in it for us. Life won't ever be the same.'

Ariadne nodded. Drank some more drink. I took the opportunity to do some damage to mine. Then she reached in her bag and took out a sheet of paper. Laid it on the table in front of us.

'It's a standard disclosure form. Sign it and we can have a draft paper with *Nature* by the middle of next week.'

'What do I get?' Mick yelled.

'If this gets off the ground, Prof is making me senior lecturer. I'll have my own team, dealing with the neuro-psychological aspects.'

'And what, I get your research assistantship?'

Ariadne did the straw thing again. The way her lips parted. The way her fingertips rested lightly on it. The way she guided it to her mouth. The way reluctantly she let it go when the drinking was done.

'We'd have to advertise the post. We can't just hand it to you on a plate, not in this day and age.'

'No deal.'

'I'm sure you'd be the best candidate.'

'I'd need a guarantee.'

'We can't put anything in writing.'

Mick pushed the form towards her. 'I'll sign it once I've been appointed.'

She looked directly at him. 'Please. We've got to fast-track the paper before news leaks out.'

I felt him shake his head.

'I'll be very grateful.' Somehow she'd contrived to shout more softly. 'More grateful than you could imagine.'

'This is ridiculous!' I yelped. 'What, you're going to shag him?'

It was so laughable, I laughed.

Ariadne glanced back at Mick.

Who hesitated. Then reached out for the form.

'Let me take a look at that.'

'Well, I'm not fucking signing!' I bellowed, as she handed him a pen.

'It's a tricky area, legally.' Ariadne's voice was barely audible now: the bumping bass, the trumping synths, the seething insistence of the drum box. 'But we're really not sure we need you to.'

Mick was returning to an empty house. To a child's room with its Animal Ark stickers and its Winnie the Pooh light shade and its legions of cuddly teddies and rabbits and penguins and fairy-tale books and what all. To a marital bed with its duck-down duvet and electric blanket and neat little his 'n' hers bedside cabinets and framed photos of the wedding hanging on the wall above the headboard.

But no Jules. And no Ellie.

In any situation, no matter how grave, there is always a silver lining. Some way of looking at things in a positive light. Some crumb of comfort.

I'd had hardly anything to drink, so the trouble he had

coaxing the key into the lock must have been pure nerves. He flicked the light on, then stepped us back. And with a sweep of his arm, ushered Ariadne inside the hall.

The door was barely closed before she was right in front of him. One hand on our chest, the other in the small of our back.

'I'm dying to prove your body map wrong,' she breathed.

His lips and her lips making slippy noises as they kissed. The warmth of her body as it pressed against us, hips to hips. The give of her breasts. The thickening, the swelling, the awakening from slumber. Mick's medial preoptic area blazing like a bush fire.

'Hey! Mick! You can't do this!'

My voice sounded distant, puny.

'What about Jules? Mick! What about Jules and Ellie!'

Nothing.

'She's using you! Can't you see that?'

It was as if I didn't exist.

I could barely look as we climbed the stairs. That wonderful arse right in front of me.

I felt like crying as she unbuttoned her shirt, revealing her braless breasts, her honey-brown nipples. As she stepped out of her skirt. And with a deft flick let her silk French knickers slide down her legs to ripple to a halt around her ankles. And her hands on our belt. And her hands on our fly. And Mick's groan as she found us, and pulled us to her.

Alcohol gives you shit sleep. You might drop like a heifer in an abattoir but come the wee small hours you enter a protracted period of fitful slumber and parched-mouth restlessness. By the time morning has broken it's like you haven't slept a wink and hey ho you've got to face the day.

That morning I came to feeling remarkably refreshed. The sun was bathing the room in brightness, the curtains hanging limply at either side of the window where we'd failed to draw them the night before. Outside there was the sound of bird song. I stared at the ceiling and marvelled at how good – how alert – I was feeling. I made a mental note to go to bed vaguely sober more often. At least once a month, if that wasn't asking too much of myself.

Mick was still asleep, his breathing deep and regular in my ear. I felt a new optimism, a sense that some crisis had passed, that a new day had dawned and with it the tawdry troubles of an unhappy era had been washed away. Somehow, everything was back as it should be.

Ellie was up already. I could hear her pootling about downstairs, chatting away nineteen to the dozen to herself, no doubt recounting the latest narrative involving her imaginary horse, Strawberry Foal. Ah, Ellie. Little beacon of hope, tiny engine of optimism and purpose. And a baby to join her! There was a faint clink and clatter from afar, Jules clearing the dishwasher. Jules. Jules and me. Had she got my email? Is that what had brought her rushing home?

I twisted my head to see the time. Quarter to nine.

Quarter to nine!

A sudden panic, a mental scramble to reorientate myself. Yesterday was Wednesday, today was Thursday, Thursday was a work day, so Mick was late. Hopelessly late. Mick should be in surgery right now, consulting his second patient of the day.

Mick had forgotten to set the alarm.

Mick should be at work, and no one had woken us.

No one had woken us because no one knew we were here.

No one knew we were here because Jules and Ellie were at grandma's.

Jules and Ellie were at grandma's, so Mick had brought Ariadne back to the house.

I strained my neck to look past Mick's oblivious face. Her Timotei hair was draped over the pillow. The bare skin of her shoulder, her back. The hint of her breast below her outstretched arm.

Ariadne was in bed beside us. And Jules and Ellie were downstairs.

No, Ellie was coming *upstairs*. The scimper scamper of her feet, the skippity skip as she came along the landing, passing our door as she made her way to her room. Its Animal Ark stickers, its cuddly toys, its fairy-tales. The pause, the skippity skip coming back this way. The creak as the half-open door swung.

'Uncle John! Daddy!'

The joy and delight on her face. The muffled pluff as she landed on the bed beside me. The smell of her fresh skin and hair. Her neatly ironed nursery uniform.

'Oh, hi, Ellie, darling. Good time at grandma's?'

Mick was stirring now. Sub-cortical auditory apparatus urgently shaking the shoulder of his cortical self. Surfacing into consciousness with a confused groan.

And a long sigh as Ariadne rolled towards us, and opened her pale blue eyes.

'Uncle John!' Ellie giggled. 'Who's that lady?'

Scruples

Jules dropped the Discman in our lap. Then the head-phones she'd retrieved from the computer.

'Put it on,' she told Mick.

'Jules –'

'I need to speak to *John*.'

I watched as he took first one then the other earpiece. His hand was shaking so much he had a real struggle to coax the jack into its socket. Connection finally made, he pressed play. A fizz of snare, a fuzz of synth. The last thing I'd been listening to was Dina Carroll. What I'd have given to have swapped places with him.

Jules sat on the chair by the window, one arm wrapped around herself, pushing the fingers of her other hand through her hair. She was pale. For a second her lips twisted, but she clamped her hand over her mouth, brought them under control. I reached down and turned the volume up to 7, the loudest compatible with Mick's continued auditory health.

'Mum-my!' Ellie bounded into the room. 'Telly's not working!'

Jules got up with a wintery sigh and went downstairs.

'John!' Mick shouted.

I tugged the cable running to his near-side ear. 'Shhh!'

'What are you going to do?' he hissed.

'You're the one who brought her back.'

'I *know*. Please.'

It had been too awful, Jules appearing in the doorway, her face free-falling as she clocked little Ellie on the bed, bouncing up and down on her knees with excitement. And beside her, Uncle John. And beside him, Daddy. And beside *him*, a naked Scandinavian blonde. Who had propped herself up on her elbows, hitched the duvet up around her breasts, and said hello. Jules's face: the confusion, the disbelief, the pain. No matter Mick's erstwhile self-righteous bravado. What price his previous posturing about Jules's supposed affair. This was oh such serious shit. This was the end. The end of home, of love, of family, of companionship. This was the end of everything.

I gave a sigh, handed the squawking earpiece back to him. 'I'll do my best.'

Jules reappeared a moment later, took her seat again.

'I don't know what to say.' Her voice was a tremulous monotone. My guts twisted at the sound of it. Her drawn face. Her perplexed brow. Her slender shoulders, weighted down.

'I got your email. I was *so* happy. I couldn't believe it.' She looked straight at me, her eyes rimmed with tears. 'I thought I'd ruined everything, doing what I did. And then. Then I was late and I thought oh god no, but I was, I was pregnant and I thought what on earth am I going to do. And you weren't even speaking to me and I thought I'd screwed everything up and then you went and sent that email and I thought thank god it's going to be all right after all.'

She shook her head, a bitter curtailed motion. 'You said you'd finished with all this.'

I was acutely conscious of the creased sheets on her side of the bed, cooling still from the heat of Ariadne's body. Ariadne, who had pulled on her skirt and shirt and shoes, and had left clutching her hastily gathered underwear.

'She was the one you went clubbing with, wasn't she?'

I nodded, unable to meet her gaze.

'How *could* you?'

I am not martyr material. I had no objection in principle to dropping Mick from a very great height into a steaming vat of shit. But I am a schmuck, a sleazebag, a deplorable philanderer of the first water. Her husband, in contrast, is the man least likely to. The solid, dependable, trustworthy guy she'd married, the man who would provide for her, for their children, content with what he had, never wanting more, never causing the slightest perturbation to the boat in which we were all afloat. And an absolute putz with women. No way was she going to accept the truth of the matter. Not even if he fessed up himself. Which I doubted he ever would, being as he's as smart as me. I'd had a dream, I had held it like a gossamer-winged mayfly in my hand. Of a family of my own. Of Jules, our baby, Ellie and me. The dream was dead. Long live the dream.

'I'm sorry, Jules. I'm truly sorry. I'd had a really shitty day. It's kind of complicated. We met with all these fucking scientists at this international symposium and they basically told me I don't exist. *Rien*, zilch, *nada*. I guess it freaked me out.'

She let out an exasperated breath. 'There's always some excuse, isn't there, John?'

I nodded dumbly. God, it hurt. Sticking the knife in, ripping it across my belly, watching as my own guts spilled over the floor. But in my stupid wrong-headed calculation I thought we could at least carry on as before.

'What have I done?' Jules asked, her eyes flicking towards Mick.

'Oh, he's just fine,' I said.

'How could I have been so stupid? You know' – she laughed a brittle laugh – 'I always said I'd never marry a doctor. They're so smug and arrogant, think they've got the answer to everything. But Mick seemed different, somehow. Seemed human, and humorous, never too full of himself.'

She bowed her head, squeezed a finger and thumb over shut eyes.

'But time goes by, and we all get lazy and too familiar, and I started to see behind the facade. To see he's just like the others, after all. And I started to realize that what I loved about him was *you*. You never let him get like that, you were always pricking his pomposity, bursting his bubble. Then I started to understand that *who* I loved was you.'

She let her hands fall limply in her lap.

The breath was difficult to get into our lungs. 'You are staying, aren't you? You and Ellie?'

'I don't know.' She stared intently at the valance for a while. 'I don't love him. It would be hypocritical, cruel.'

'Don't be stupid,' I said. 'What happened between you and me, that was nothing, it meant nothing. It was just a shag. We got carried away. He need never know. It wouldn't do any good to tell. He *loves* you.'

Water spilled over the margins of her eyelids. Found its way down her cheeks.

'Do you mean that?'

'He's crazy about you.'

'No, about you and me.'

'Oh, come on, Jules.' I held my hand out expressively. 'Who were we kidding? You and me!'

Dina Carroll had come to the end of a track. I waited till the chunter resumed.

'I know I said some pretty schmaltzy things in that email. But I was pissed. I'm always pissed. I can never communicate with you *unless* I'm pissed.'

Downstairs, the phone rang. The answer machine cut in after two rings. Muriel Redknap echoed up the stairs, wondering if Mick was all right, it's just that they were expecting him in today.

Jules stood. Brushed her hands down her front.

'I've got to take Ellie to nursery.'

'You are coming back?'

A shake of her head.

'What about the baby? What about *our* baby?'

She stared at me for a sad-eyed second. Then turned to go.

'Jules! Wait. Look at me. Look!' I pinched the skin of my cheek, hard. 'I'm not real, see! I don't exist!'

She rolled despairing eyes.

'It's just Mick, there is no John! That's what the scientists said. Stay with him, you need never think of me again.'

Slowly, she shook her head again. 'Goodbye, John.'

Then she was gone. I sat, contemplating the empty chair. How the cushion slowly, imperceptibly regained its shape. Heard her shouting at Ellie to get a move on. And the TV went off. And the door slammed. And the car engine fired.

Then there was just the faint, distorted sound of the CD. Eventually Mick, the realization perhaps dawning that Jules was taking a devilish long time to get back from the loo, switched off the Discman, de-earpieced himself.

'How did it go, big man?'

His voice was cautious. Chastened. Hopeful.

I tried to think how it had gone.

'Not brilliantly,' I told him. 'What did you think of Dina Carroll?'

Downstairs, Mick phoned the practice and spouted some spiel about how I was vomiting and how the pair of us had diarrhoea. The LCD said there were two messages. When he'd finished I hit the play button and we stood there listening as Jules floated out of the speaker, letting us know she and Ellie would be back first thing in the morning. She sounded bright, cheery, completely unconcerned not to find us in.

'Why the change of heart?' he muttered. 'I just don't understand.'

I thought back to how Ariadne had been all over him the minute we were through the door. How we hadn't even gone in the sitting room. How if we had we would have seen a red light winking.

'No,' I told him. 'I don't imagine you do.'

Income tax self assessment

Once upon a Time in the West

After what seemed an eternity, a waistcoated man stepped forward from the crowd and started up the steps to the makeshift stage.

'Thank you, sir!' boomed Slingshot Malone, like the true showman he was. 'Pray, tell, now. What is your target?'

The fellow faltered near the top. But the ranks of spectators had closed tight behind him. Their Sunday bonnets. Their best suits. Their parasols.

He cleared his throat. 'Well, I reckon if you hit the bell in that there tower, that'd be a fine thing.'

From the back of the brightly painted wagon, Mad John and Deputy Mick looked at the church across the street. As did everyone else. The brass bell, suspended in its rectangular aperture, outlined against the blue Nevada sky.

'He's crapping himself,' John chuckled quietly.

'Shhh,' said Deputy Mick, moving the canvas flaps further aside to improve his view.

'Ladies and gentlemen!' Slingshot gestured expansively. 'Stand well back now! The bell in the tower it is!'

He stroked his luxuriant moustache. Then raised his Winchester Repeater, its elaborately carved walnut stock, its blue-grey steel barrel. Worked the action. Bullet in breech, he nestled the butt against his shoulder and peered through the sights. Face still with concentration. And aimed directly at the chest of the slope-shouldered volunteer. Who stood utterly alone at the edge of the stage, the onlookers parting like the Red Sea behind him.

'I take aim –'

He let the rifle sag.

'I am sorry. What is your name, brave sir?'

'Stubbs. Leonard Stubbs.'

'Your occupation?'

'Bank teller.'

Mr Stubbs's voice was wobbling like a highwire artist in a brisk south-westerly.

'I take aim at Mr Stubbs's heart.' Slingshot Malone raised the firearm again, squinted along its barrel.

'Then I pull the trigger.'

His forefinger squeezed. A whipcrack volleyed out. And a puff of smoke. The rifle recoiled.

And – Bong! – the bell tolled.

'And Mr Stubbs is completely unharmed!'

There was a collective shout of amazement. Applause. The clapping gained in volume and vigour.

Mr Stubbs was still standing, trembling visibly but otherwise unharmed. The bong of the bell decayed, became inaudible beneath the whoops and cat calls from the crowd.

'Ladies and gentlemen, you have seen it with your own eyes! I shot Mr Stubbs through the heart! Yet he lives! And the bell tolled!'

Slingshot Malone closed his act with a triumphant flourish and a bow.

Then whipped round and loosed off another shot at the hapless Stubbs.

Bong!

'Sling! ... Shot! ... Malone!' hollered Billy Bucks, bounding on to the stage, clapping his hands energetically above his head. His jowls wobbled their appreciation.

'And let's hear it for his intrepid volunteer, Mr Leonard Stubbs!'

A rousing cheer went up. Billy Bucks steered the now sobbing Stubbs back to the steps.

In the wagon, Deputy Mick let the flaps fall, returning him and Mad John to semi-darkness. 'Shit! How the fuck did he do that?'

John chuckled. 'Magazine full of blanks, accomplice in the bell tower. Don't you know jack shit, lawman!'

Mick looked annoyed. 'But he didn't know he was

going to be asked to shoot the bell, did he? Not till the guy came up.'

'Oh, please!' John said. 'You're not telling me you bought the can-I-have-a-volunteer-from-the-crowd routine!'

Mick's crest fell. 'Right. I see.'

Outside, the audience had finally quietened. You could feel the breathless excitement in the air now, the astounding opening act having won over the most sceptical of onlookers.

Billy Bucks's voice boomed out again. 'And now, for your delight and delectation, Bucking Bucks's Phantasmagorical Travelling Circus is proud to present its latest sense-defying spectacle. Would you please give a very warm welcome to – Mad John McDonald and Deputy Mick!'

'Ready?' John asked.

Mick gave a nod.

And, moving as one, they burst out of the back of the wagon, holding their handcuffed hands aloft as they trotted towards the stage.

There must've been a couple of hundred folks gazing up at them. Mick searched the faces. There she was, off to one side. Doll! Cheering along with the rest, waving enthusiastically. Her dark Spanish ringlets. Her lacy trim. Her plunging embonpoint.

'Is there any among you who would like to earn fifty dollars for a minute's work?'

Billy Bucks allowed his eyes to rove over the forest of raised arms, pointing in the end at a burly fellow in leather chaps and a blue checked shirt.

'You, sir! Would you step up to the stage, please.'

Mick watched as the stranger mounted the stairs, his movements laconic. A pair of pale blue eyes peered out from beneath the brim of his stetson. He was chewing a wad. Spat a thin stream of yellow-brown spittle on the boards as he came.

Billy Bucks brandished a sheaf of bills. 'I have in my hand a grand total of fifty United States dollars. Yours, sir, if you can successfully free these two gentlemen from the handcuffs that bind them! Chose your weapon!'

Mick wasn't convinced about this volunteer-from-the-crowd routine. He was entirely sure he'd never clapped eyes on this man before. The stranger spent a moment considering the implements laid out on the trestle table. Made his selection.

'The axe! An excellent choice!' bellowed Billy Bucks, a sheen of sweat on his face in the midday sun.

The stranger hefted the tool, testing its weight. The curved blade glinted.

'Do you recognize him?' Mick asked, in a stage whisper.

'Nope,' muttered Mad John.

Billy Bucks arranged their wrists either side of the anvil, the red-painted chain of the handcuffs laid across its hot metal. Gave them a poker-faced wink then stepped back.

'If you will, sir!'

The man came over, raised the axe high above his head. His buffalo shoulders. His massive jaw. His stained-toothed grin.

'Aw, shit,' said Mick.

And the axe came down with an explosive CLANG!

Mick opened his eyes. There was no blood spurting. His hand was still attached to his arm. As was John's.

The red chain was intact, stretched across the anvil.

The stranger, face suddenly creased with consternation, lifted the axe to examine it. Touched a finger to the blunt dent slap bang in the centre of the blade.

'Ladies and gentlemen!' Billy Bucks stepped forward, arms lifted in incitement to cheer.

But the stranger cursed, and flung the axe down. Mick felt the thud through his feet. Looked up to see the man drawing his pistol.

'Sir!' Billy Bucks span round.

The stranger cocked the hammer. Applied the end of the barrel to the middle of the chain.

'Shit!' yelled Mick.

BANG!

The acrid cordite stung Mick's eyes. Blinking the water out of them, he squinted through the haze. Saw the splintered hole in the wooden hoarding at the back of the stage. The powder-burn scar in the surface of the anvil. The unbroken chain taut across it.

'You were great, Mick. So self-contained.'

Doll rested her head against Mick's chest, snuggled herself closer in.

Mick buried his face in her hair, breathed in her perfume, the smell of her. Above them, stars twinkled. The campfire blazed, hot on his skin, the flames dancing.

'You were shitting yourself when he pulled his gun!' said John.

Mick felt the cuffs tugging as Mad John rocked with laughter. A whole twelve-month bound to this felon! The hollow pit of his stomach that morning, a year ago to the day, when the disconsolate posse had traipsed back into town, leading the sheriff's stallion by its reins. The sheriff tied belly-down over its saddle. The blood long since drained from his bullet-riddled body. The grieving for his mentor, his beloved sheriff, compounded by the frantic and futile search for the one and only key. The whereabouts of which were known to only one man. Who had met his end in a hail of slugs at more or less the exact same moment Deputy Mick had unwittingly applied the accursed cuffs to his and Mad John's wrists.

Mick sighed. 'I thought for a moment he was going to do it.'

Mad John took a slurp of coffee. 'What d'you want to be free for, lawman?' He clinked the cuffs. 'These are worth a fortune to you, aren't they?'

Mick could feel the money heavy in his breast pocket. Their share of the take, handed over with a hearty slap by a delighted Billy Bucks at the end of the show. A very good wage for a day's work. More than he would have earned in a week as a lawman. But there had to be a way to gain his freedom! Even as he thought it, his spirits faltered. Those increasingly desperate efforts in the early days, when every axe, hacksaw, chisel and mallet in the entire town had been bent to the task. He himself, in tears of frustration, had tried shooting the chain once, blasting six bullets at point blank range. Aside from taking off Mad John's toe, they'd had no discernible effect. Not even Sly Pountney, returning from a stretch in the Pen, had been able to crack it, his caseful of picks and files and master keys useless in the face of the cuffs' devilish lock.

The awkward interview with the state marshal, arriving, not with news of promotion, but to fire him – what use was a hamstrung deputy? How one by one the few friends he'd had had spurned him, tired of Mad

John's lewd interruptions to their every attempt at earnest conversation. And even Julia! How, as the weeks had turned to months, she'd become ever more distant and distressed. Nothing to do with their straitened circumstances, she'd insisted. Everything to do with the horror and confusion of being married to two men. The day she'd finally packed her trunk and left with Fenella aboard the eastbound stage, heading back to Boston and her stuck-up parents.

Mick wrapped his arm around Doll's shoulder, pulled her closer against his body. Thank heavens for Doll! Sweet, musky, raunchy Doll! The one thing that kept him this side of insanity! And thank the lord for Billy Bucks. Whose circus had come to town the day Mick had withdrawn his last cent of savings from the bank. Whose bearded lady had just eloped with the Mule Man in pursuit of hirsute happiness, leaving the cast a couple of acts short of a show.

Mick gazed out beyond the flickering campfire, saw oil lamps illuminating windows in the town they'd just visited. An anonymous frontiersville, the latest in the endless succession of stops the travelling circus would make as it meandered its way across the West. There were men and women cosied up inside those clapboard houses, with real jobs, happy families, settled lives. One or two of them would be the local lawmen. That had been his lot once, with his salary, his pension, his well-bred wife and charming daughter. Julia. Fenella. Now he was to embrace the itinerant life, never sleeping in the same place twice, living footloose and fancy free. It was strangely attractive. Not least because Doll was here by his side. Tired of whoring, but far from tired of making love. Her Latinate passion. Her well-developed thigh abductors. Her mischievous pelvic floor.

His life was edgy, thrilling, invigorating. In a way it hadn't been for years.

What he would give to be free of Mad John, though! These cuffs were their golden egg, the very foundation of this wonderful new existence. But if only he could slip them off when the show was done! To be able to go to the latrine! To be able to ride a horse again! To be left in peace to bury himself in Doll's intoxicating flesh, without encountering an alien hand investigating her every crevice and cranny! She said she didn't mind, said she used to do this sort of thing for a living. Oh, how that lanced him! The thought of her. No. He wanted her to himself. Doll, Doll, Doll.

A horse snickered nervously from the picket. Mick looked up as Slingshot Malone drew near. The old trouper laid his rifle carefully down and squatted on his haunches.

'Nice act you got there, fellas,' he said.

'You too,' said Mick.

'Hey, Slingshot,' called John. 'That Stubbs fella. He do all your stuff, or do you get a new stooge in every town?'

Malone poured himself some chicory coffee from the battered tin pot.

'Truth be told,' he said, easing himself into a more comfortable position. 'I hadn't never set eyes on the fella afore.'

'Sure you had,' said John.

Malone rested his mug down in the dirt. Picked up his Winchester. Stroked his fingers down the cool barrel.

'This here's a magic rifle. Given me by an ole Navaho. Can bend a bullet round corners, even back on itself, if needs be.'

'John was thinking you must've had an accomplice in that bell tower,' Mick said hurriedly.

'That or someone shot the bell for you,' said John.

'Uh, huh,' said Slingshot, nodding thoughtfully.

Suddenly he shouldered the Winchester, aimed it at point blank range right at John's chest.

BANG!

Doll flinched. Panicked horses whinnied behind the wagon. Mick's ears rang with the percussion.

Mad John screamed. Scalding coffee was everywhere, over his hand, his arm, his leg. He tried to jump up, fell down as the cuffs wrenched against Mick's wrist.

'Shit!' John said, shaking his limbs, trying to cool the scorched flesh.

Slingshot was laughing. A deep belly laugh. Mick retrieved Mad John's tin mug, empty now. Held it up the better to see the clean-punched bullet hole through its base.

'Like I said,' Slingshot managed, eventually. 'I hadn't never set eyes on the fella afore.'

Mad John chewed his beef jerky sombrely. Across the other side of camp, Heap Big Rattle was working on a new number. John watched as he stomped and ducked and twisted and weaved, shaking his snakes' tails in rhythmic accompaniment to his incantation. Every now and again one of the reptiles, finding itself dangling invitingly close to a bare brown thigh, would coil and rear. Seemingly without having noticed, Heap would give a deft flick, straightening the snake out like a bull whip. The firelight cast looming shadows on the store wagon's canvas canopy. Feather headdress. Flapping loincloth. Mystical ancient moves.

John sighed. His scalded skin stung like crazy. Slingshot with his weird rifle, sending bullets wherever he intended, regardless of his aim. Ivan Ironjaw, chewing up nickels like they were pieces of candy. Capacious Caprice, who could disappear a whisky bottle in any of three orifices. The Amazing Breasted Man. Messed up kooks, the lot of them. And here he was, as much a freak as the rest.

He glanced at Deputy Mick, leaning back against the wagon wheel, stargazing, Doll snuggled in to his shoulder. Stroking his chest.

He had to get away from them! If he could only worm his hand out of its tight metal hoop! Doll could stick hers in there instead, then the pair of them could canter off into the sunset to whatever future they could carve out for themselves. Good luck to them! But it wasn't his destiny!

Even now he was unclear how it had started. Julia, prim lawman's wife, laughing at his asides, smothering her mirth at his bawdy jokes. Encouraging her daughter to take up his offer of lessons in five card stud. Darning his clothes for him. Taking scissors to trim his goat's beard. Looking at him meaningfully as she laid his plate of beans on the supper table. Rustling her bustle as she walked away. Fuck, it had been so obvious! But so unlikely! Time and again he'd told himself he was mistaken.

The excruciating embarrassment as Mick would take himself off, telling her he was going to look for work, only to walk no further than the saloon. John, sitting on the side of the bed while Doll and the former lawman made their hay. Returning to sweet Julia, sweet unsuspecting Julia, itching to tell her but knowing his word would count for nothing. An outlaw with a bounty on his head, a gunslinger, a train robber, a stagecoach upholder.

And yet. And yet. In the dead of one night, while her treacherous husband snored, how she stole over to his side of the bed. How they found each other. How their hunger had to be tempered by the need for absolute stillness, absolute hush. How he felt both unbearable passion and exquisite tenderness. How he reverenced her. Her slender neck. Her delicate earlobes. Her tapering waist. Her boundless grace, so utterly strange, so utterly wonderful to a rough-born cowpoke like him.

John exhaled deeply. Threw the tail-end of his jerky into the fire, where it combusted in a burst of blue flame. I can't stand it, she'd whispered in his ear, that last night they'd spent clandestinely together. I don't care how you do it. Get shot of him and come join me in Boston. And she'd kissed him. And her fingers had traced a path down him. And she'd gone.

For a bad boy like him to have this scintillating vision, to have her waiting for him back east, with no way of ever holding her again! It was enough to drive a man loco.

'Hey, Slingshot,' John called, suddenly sitting himself forward.

The old trouper looked up from his whittling.

'I guess I owe you an apology.'

Slingshot smiled faintly. 'It does mess with your head, first time you see it.'

'Amen to that,' John breathed.

The embers of the fire were smoking desultorily. The dismantled stage was stacked ready for loading. The horses stood patiently between the wagon shafts as the Nevada sun continued its climb into another cloudless sky.

'You sure about this?' Slingshot asked.

Mad John held his eyes. Nodded.

The rest of the circus stood in a semicircle. Billy Bucks, his bulging belly, his spotty bow tie, shaking his head in puzzlement.

'You're crazy!' he shouted. 'Those cuffs'll make your fortune.'

'He's got a point,' said Mick.

'You don't want to be hitched to me any more than I want to be stuck with you, lawman.'

Mad John's gaze was unwavering. As Slingshot worked the action. Raised the Winchester. Trained it on his chest.

'I take aim at your heart!' Slingshot stage voice boomed across the camp.

The barrel was long, seemed to be reaching out to John, sucking him into its bore. Its dark black bore, going on for ever. Out of which any moment would screech a bullet, a chunk of red hot lead, rending the air.

'Pray, tell, sir! What is your target?'

John held his hand up, dragging Mick's with it. Pulled to tension the chain.

'This!' he shouted. 'The chains that bind us!'

Heap Big Rattle struck up an urgent incantation. The Amazing Breasted Man began to haver.

What was wrong with these people! They must've seen Slingshot in action a thousand times. Seen him bend his bullets hither thither and yon. All right, he himself had been sceptical. But when Malone had shot him in the heart, whanging the coffee mug out of his very own hand at the exact same time, John had believed.

Slingshot's trigger finger tightened.

But what if it had been an elaborate con! What if Slingshot's accomplice had been positioned somewhere in the shadowy camp perimeter, his own firearm trained on John's cup, patiently waiting for the confrontation his master had known might come. John's knees threatened to give way. What if that Winchester was a rifle like any other! To die, here, like this! After all his escapades! His life as a slippery eel no bars could hold!

He stared down the barrel.

If he couldn't have her. If he couldn't have her then he would rather die. Here. Like this.

Slingshot's finger squeezed. The flesh blanching.

Holy Mary, Mother of –

Part Three

I shall not be in the least surprised if in the midst
of the future universal good sense, some
gentleman with an ignoble, or rather a derisive
and reactionary air, springs up suddenly out
of nowhere, puts his arms akimbo and says to all
of us, 'Come on, gentlemen, why shouldn't we
get rid of all this calm reasonableness with one
kick, just so as to send all these algorithms to
the devil and be able to live our own lives at our
own sweet will?'

Fyodor Dostoevsky, *Notes from Underground*

The Main Man

Sundays are *pain au chocolat* mornings. Jules keeps a stock in the freezer, Sainsbury's 'Taste the Difference' range, four per cellophaned pack. One for her, one for Ellie, two for me. When the weather's fine we eat al fresco, out on the patio, with a bloody big cafetière and a jug filled with hot milk, in true French stylee.

I don't know why I baked all four. Ordinarily it would have been a treat. I stared at them, crowded together on the plate. Then I pushed them away, lit a cigarette instead. Took a long cool look at the garden, the primroses prettying the lawn, the daffs nearing their end, a robin hopping round the foot of the bird table.

Mick was wrestling with the *Sunday Times*. Glancing at section after section, before consigning them to the growing pile of unread newsprint on the Cotswold stone slabs. 'Business', 'Culture', 'Style'. Finally even 'Home' was discarded.

'She definitely said there was no one else?' he said.

Five days, not a word from Jules. Grandma's got caller display, so they weren't even answering the phone.

'Definitely. I said to her: So, what, you're off to shack up with your lover now, are you, you scheming little Jezebel? She *swore* there was no one but you.'

He sighed.

'I don't know why you're feeling so sorry for yourself,' I said. 'You got what you wanted.'

OK, that was nasty. But the stupid dumb fuck! You have everything: lovely wife, gorgeous daughter, good job, nice house. Then you go and throw it all away for a naked roll in the snow. I couldn't stand his whingeing, his pathetic self-pity. His moment of lust had cost me everything. And he'd been such a moron! What was he thinking, imagining Ariadne might actually have feelings – any feeling at all! – for him. He'd sold his soul for the most hollow of human experiences, the meaningless fuck.

So she'd already got her signed consent form before she jumped in the sack. So what? Had he learned nothing from the years as my right-hand man! They're all the same. They just want to see what's in our pants. Having straddled it, they go back to their normal, able-bodied lives, giggling about us over a spritzer with the gals, if ever they give us another thought. We're a trophy over the mantelpiece, a dine-out story. None of them actually wants us. None of them except Jules.

'You've had girlfriends back for the night before,' he said.

I took a long drag of my Marlboro. We'd been over this time and again. Somewhere in his heart of hearts he suspected that, while he'd been closeted beneath the earphones, I'd gone and dumped him in it.

'Not since Ellie,' I reminded him. 'You don't understand women. What they put up with when it's just the three of you is absolutely *verboten* when there's kids involved.'

He extracted a fag from my pack, lying open on the table. Popped it in his mouth. Chinged my zippo. Oh, you complete fucking Charlie! It's not like I'm not doing that for you already!

'Do you think I should email her?' he said. 'Tell her I've thrashed it out with you, tell her you've promised you'll never ever bring anyone home again, as long as we both shall live?'

'What about you, though?' I asked.

I sat, listening to the chirp of the robin, sipping my coffee, waiting for him to speak. His mind turning it over. What was he thinking? How he wasn't satisfied. How he regretted his exemplary life. How he could see it all slipping away, the possibility of excitement, of thrill, of adulation. How he wanted, desperately – just once – to be the object of unrestrained female desire. The rejuvenating power of young flesh. The staving off of time. His niggling sense of impending mortality.

'Why hasn't she said anything to *me*?'

He had a point. You leave your husband, traditionally you do at least tell him you're off. Not many folk pass the news on via their brother-in-law.

'Could be a good sign,' I said.

'You think?'

'Yeah.' I stretched a leg out, eased us back in the plastic chair, enjoying being an inscrutable sage. 'Maybe she still thinks it might work. Could be she's just cooling off. Or this might be an artillery bombardment. Once she's softened up the target area sufficiently, she'll come in and finish you off.'

'Doesn't sound too good to me.'

'If she comes back it's very definitely going to be on her own terms, believe me. You might not like it. Neither might I, come to that.'

It was guff, of course; I'd seen the look in her eyes, the finality there. I was just trying to cheer him up. The past days had been awful. Mick moping around much of the time, going on and on about what he'd done. Even worse were the occasions he'd get this ridiculous surge of self-confidence, usually at work, usually after some patient had come in and told him the treatment he'd prescribed had actually made them feel better. As soon as they were out of the consulting room he'd grab the phone and call Ariadne up, invite her over. Like a panting puppy.

I can't, I'm sorry, she'd say, there's this *Nature* paper to write. Maybe when that's been submitted. Having said that, all the contractual stuff with the seconded researchers is going to take a bit of sorting. But perhaps when that's done. Maybe then.

Maybe next time they find they need to put us down a scanner, more likely – *if* he plays hardball. Maybe when hell freezes over. It was all so depressingly predictable. I'd tried to warn him, but he wouldn't listen.

I was the victim in all this. I hadn't wanted any part of it. Christ, I'd even kept my eyes closed during most of the tutorial! Ariadne doing her neurobiological dirty talk: explaining how female sexual arousal is mediated by completely different brain nuclei than in the male. While Mick touched her up: Ooh, yes, that's really getting my ventromedial nucleus going! Telling him how in female primates the ventromedial nucleus produces automatic lordotic display. *Showing* him what lordotic display was. OK, OK, I admit it, I had a peep. I *am* only human. Ariadne, on all fours, exquisite arse in the air, her genitals framed between the perfect globes of her buttocks, for all the world to see.

But thanks to him, Jules was gone. With Ellie. With our baby. The house felt cold and damp without them, no matter the weather outside. Our return from the practice each day was deeply dispiriting. Ellie's rocking horse, motionless in the corner of the lounge, her Barbies wearing the same clothes they'd been dressed in all week. The photos of Jules, beaming at us from various points round the house. Her clothes dangling despondently in the wardrobe. There was no purpose any more; what was Mick doing it for, out all hours of the day, earning all that dosh? Yes, it would come in handy when the Child Support Agency came knocking. But what a joyless existence, in contrast to the light touch of Jules's hand on our back every evening, the bounding bubbly Ellie, there every single day of our lives, the pulsing breathing laughing loving result of all his labours.

I got a takeaway every night, but what little I ate was simply to sate my hunger; I had no relish, not even for Thai. The TV schedules were suddenly filled with parenting programmes – Robert Winston was everywhere. I tried burying myself in work. I kept up the pretence of *Sister Sebastian*. Mick had evidently shed his publicity phobia, but I could still see him having a screaming epi if he knew about the book I was really writing. But even that was hard going. I would sit there, drinking myself into a stupor, Mick long departed for the land of nod, reading and re-reading the same bloody paragraph, unable to add a single word. Till in the end I gave up, gave in, and opened once more the stupid fucking email I got from Jules. Her reply to my declaration of love. Sent in haste before, with a joyful heart, she set about packing so she could bring herself and Ellie home from grandma's first thing the next morning. When, instead of an empty house, she found her lover and her husband in bed with a leggy, naked blonde.

Oh John

I am so happy. Yes, I really do love you.

We have to sort it out. We have to tell Mick. I can't bear to live a lie any longer.

Thank you for emailing, it must have taken a lot of courage. You can still surprise me, you know!

Till tomorrow, Jules/xx

'Come on,' I told him, stubbing out my fag, picking up the plate of untouched *pain au chocolat*. 'We'll be late.'

'Late for what?'

'It's Sunday.'

'You're not going, are you?'

'Sure. Why not?'

'*Why*?' He paused, as if trying to figure out the answer to his own question. 'They've *gone*, John. There isn't any need.'

*

It's funny, but ever since that night with Ariadne, there've been subtle shifts in the balance of power. I don't know. Maybe it has something to do with my having kept on shouting at Mick not to do it. Neither he nor Ariadne took the blindest bit of notice. There can be times now when he acts as though I really wasn't here. Just that morning he'd wanted to scoot down to Newton Road to get himself a Sunday paper. I said no, it was a waste of time, he wouldn't read a word. Usually, I lie doggo and he's stuck in bed till I'm good and ready. But he got us up somehow, and dressed, and out the door and on board the Booster. All the while I kept loosening my limbs, letting everything go floppy, just to show him he couldn't push me around. But it was utterly useless. He ploughed on with his self-determined plan and I found myself incapable of derailing it.

And it cuts both ways. As I got our loafers on, as we made the short walk to St Mark's, I could tell he was trying to resist. It felt a bit like striding through soft sand with a fifty kilo backpack on, but I was exhilarated to discover that for the first time in my life I, too, could impose my own will. This strikes me as a recipe for disaster, one way or another. We may both end up weight-training in an attempt to gain the upper hand.

I sat us in our usual pew. The band was bigging it up for the lord, getting the congregation in the mood before

the service got under way. Come, now is the time to worship! Ellie's little mates were scootling about, playing
horses, doing chasing games. If any of them missed her,
they showed no outward sign. Maybe I should pray, I
told myself. Dear god, what a mess we're in. But I had
only half a pair of hands.

The music finished up and Father Clive appeared
from the vestry. He strode to the front of the sanctuary
and raised the radio mike to lips.

'This is the day that the Lord has made!' he boomed,
ten decibels the wrong side of the sound barrier.

'Let us rejoice and be glad in it!' went the response
from all around.

'What the fuck are we doing here?' Mick hissed in
my ear.

'I don't know. It feels right, that's all.'

What was I hoping for? Some kind of enlightenment?
A sermon from Clive about the way through the moral
maze? What the Bible tells you to do if you happen to be
a conjoined twin who has fallen in love with and
impregnated his brother's wife, the same brother who's
been bedded by a Scandinavian sexbomb by way of
down-payment for his cooperation with an earth-
shattering scientific research project? There is a limit to
the mysteriousness of the ways in which god moves.
What I got instead was Clive going right back to

Genesis, a lengthy discussion about Creationist symbolism in a post-Darwinian world. The tree with the apple. In the garden of Eden. When Tommy Walsh was Adam, and Charlie Dimmock was Eve, and they were a happy-go-lucky pair of limbicly driven ape people frolicking amongst the topiary and the ornamental grasses without so much as a care in the world. Then they spotted the rambling old apple tree, half-hidden behind the tumble-down shed. And Alan Titchmarsh was god and Alan saw what they were thinking and Alan said: oh no you don't, don't eat that fruit, we need to get a move on and knock up this pergola. But Charlie flounced over to Tommy and said: go on, big boy, take a bite. And Tommy did. And Charlie did. And they wasted so much time munching windfalls that the makeover wasn't finished by the time the owners came home. From that moment on they evolved a prefrontal cortex and lo and behold they were just like Alan, moral beings, knowing good from evil, capable of choosing between right and wrong.

Actually, Clive didn't put it quite like that. But that's the gist.

I was clean out of cash. I'm usually clean out of cash. I couldn't get Mick to put anything in the collection basket, try as I might. He wouldn't have behaved like that if Jules were here.

At the end we made our way out through the porch and did the hand-shaking thing with Clive.

'Great sermon,' I told him.

'Yeah, very good,' said Mick.

Clive looked at me. Held on to my hand.

'How's Julia? And Ellie?' he asked.

'Oh, fine, yeah, thanks. They're over with grandma. Short notice thing. Didn't really know they were going till, well, till they had to go. She's not well. Grandma. Not at all well. They had to go.'

Clive relaxed his grip, released my hand.

'I'm sorry to hear that.'

'Yeah, well. She should be better soon.'

'Please God,' said Clive.

'Yeah. Please god.'

Sunday afternoons are utterly crap if you've got no appetite, and you can't concentrate on anything, and if the only person you've got to talk to is a bolshy little self-righteous prick who won't take responsibility for his own actions. All you've got is tired old TV and the prospect of another week about to start its implacably onward grind.

I sat in the chair, pretending to be engrossed in *The Bridge over the River Kwai*. What was Jules doing right then? Was she too staring sightlessly at Alec Guinness and William Holden, wondering how the hell to repair the damage and get us all back together? Was she fuck. She'd be down the park near grandma's, pushing Ellie on the swings, resting a hand on her belly, beginning to plan a future. For her, Ellie, and the wee one. Shaking herself down from the traumas of the past years. No room any longer for her sourpuss hubbie, nor for her terminally fickle lover. Shrugging us off like a rain-sodden cardigan.

'What do you think?' I asked Mick.

'I think it's a bloody good film that genuinely warrants a fifth viewing.'

'No, about us. You 'n' me.' I paused, uncertain of the words. 'What *are* we?'

He gave a heavy sigh. 'I don't know, John. I really don't know.'

This questioning of my existence. It was beginning to make me doubt myself: my memories, the sense I had of myself as a character, a person with a history, a story; a past, present and future. The merest whiff of Irn-Bru would always take me back to my Lanark childhood. But what if it was all a fiction, a comforting confabulation to make sense of my uniquely distressing circumstances. My foundations were being swept away.

'It did all happen, didn't it?' I asked him. 'Mum and Dad, that shitty little prefab, the landfill?'

'Of course it did.'

'Where are all those Milk of Magnesia jars, then? Where did they go?'

'We left them behind when we went to Nottingham.'

'Do you think they kept them?' The memory of our bedroom, every horizontal surface heaving with stoneware.

'I'd imagine the first thing they did was chuck them back on the tip.'

He was right. I could see them doing it. Dad, with his rusty old wheelbarrow, carting load after load. Mum hefting another lot in every time he came back empty.

'Sometimes I wish we'd never left.'

'That's just your inner child talking,' he told me. 'There was nothing for us there.'

'There's not much for us here, either, is there?'

We sat and contemplated for a while. Me, the pyrrhic folly of the single-minded pursuit of wealth, status, private education. He no doubt musing on the palpable shortcomings of a life devoted to ephemeral sensory pleasure. Eventually he stabbed the remote, switching to the grand prix. The swarm of Formula Ones buzzed brainlessly round and round and round.

'What I think,' he said, at last, 'is that we're two heads on one body, always have been, always will be. And all our lives we've been trying to shoehorn ourselves into a monocephalic world.'

'You think I exist, then?'

'Of course you do! So do I! That's the whole point.'

'What about Prof, Ariadne? All that stuff with the scanners and shit. What does that mean?'

'I haven't the faintest idea.' He killed the telly with a single press of the red button. 'But I do have the nasty feeling that some time pretty soon we're going to find out.'

Holy F'Coly!

Aldo appeared at the door to the green room. Burst into a grin at the sight of us. Our made-up faces. Our lippie and liner. Our powder-puff cheeks.

'Miick! Joohn!'

He hurried in, sat himself beside us on the sofa.

'This is going to resuscitate the ratings! The producer is delighted! You couldn't have timed it better!'

'We didn't time it,' Mick muttered.

Aldo fell silent, joined us in watching the monitor, with its live output from that morning's *Wake Up Britain!* Prof's talking head, somewhere inside an anonymous Institute lab back in Oxford. He'd put on a white coat for the occasion. The now familiar MRI and x-ray pictures on a viewing box behind him. In the bottom-left corner of the screen was a still of us culled from the Channel 5 publicity archive, beneath it the scrolling headline, McDONALD SHOCK – TWINS EXPOSED AS ONE.

'They're a likeable enough pair,' Prof was saying. 'An appealing blend of cheeky chappie and sober professional. That's what we all *perceive*, anyhow. What our study shows is that beneath the hullabaloo there is nothing beyond the dull grey and white putty of a standard issue human brain.'

'Just the one?' the interviewer asked.

Prof nodded. 'Just the one.'

'Viewers at home are going to find that very hard to accept. They seem so real.'

Prof gave the camera a sympathetic smile. I could detect the merest hint of a triumphant glint in his eyes.

'Of course they do, that's the fun thing. They *look* just like conjoined twins. *Feel* like they are, too. I haven't touched them, obviously, but my assistant has and she was completely taken in. But sight, touch, sound – taste and smell, even – they're merely the raw materials from which we construct a version of the world in our heads. When you're in a room with the McDonalds you mentally model them as twins even though they're nothing of the sort.'

Shot of interviewer's nodding head. I didn't recognize him. Some new boy fresh off a journalism course.

'And has your study shed any light on how this might be happening?'

'We haven't got a clue, David,' Prof told him. 'Our working hypothesis is that it's some kind of perversion of the theory of mind.'

Shot of David looking blank.

'We perceive other people as thinking, feeling beings,' Prof explained, stooping slightly. 'Oftentimes we even convince ourselves we know *what* they're thinking and feeling. But that's simply a projection of our own experience. We *expect* other people to have minds like us, so we perceive them as such, even though there's no way on earth we can truly know what actually goes on inside another person's head.'

'So you're saying we all have minds like conjoined twins?'

'Oh, look, forget it, David. I found it bedazzling at first. So did the panel of internationally renowned scientists and philosophers who have ratified the findings of our study.' Prof shook his head solemnly. 'What we can say, with some degree of confidence, is that once people are appraised of the hard evidence – when their perceptive biases have been remodelled in light of the new scientific concepts – pretty soon they'll begin to see what's really there. And what isn't.'

'Professor Randall, thank you very much.'

Prof inclined his head again. 'Thank you.'

I took another swig of coffee. Still too hot.

'Do you know, guys.' Aldo was looking at us strangely, almost in alarm. 'I still see the two of you.'

'Thanks, Aldo,' I told him.

'Shh!' said Mick.

They'd cut back to the studio. Hari Ramprakash, Channel 5's chief science correspondent, dressed in a wetsuit, a surf board tucked beneath his arm, was doing his best to do a round-up for Davina. Who was rubbing sunscreen into her arms.

'We spoke this morning to Richard Dawkins, the pre-eminent evolutionary biologist, who was on the panel that Professor Randall referred to there, and *he* told us he's in no doubt there's just a single McDonald. Take a look at this graphic –'

A huge picture of a gorilla appeared in the cloudless sky behind him.

'– now, if you'd suggested to a pre-Darwinian Victorian that this was their great-great-great-great-grandfather, they would as likely as not have challenged you to pistols at dawn. These days, of course, we're more concerned with trying to see the family resemblance. Dawkins told us that the McDonald twinhood is merely the latest in a long line of unfounded human beliefs to fall foul of the relentless march of science.'

'And did he say which McDonald was really there?' asked Davina.

'That's interesting. Yes, we pressed him on that, and what he said was we should look for the one that was least like a monkey.'

'I didn't think the *Nature* paper was out yet,' I said to Mick.

'Someone must have leaked it.'

'That's really fucking freaky, guys,' said Aldo. 'The two of you, talking like that.'

'Can it, Aldo,' Mick told him. 'We're just the same as we've always been. What's on the list for today?'

Aldo usually comes bearing a sheet of the callers to be put through to Dr Mick. His hands were empty, save for an outsize pair of Bermuda shorts.

'The producer's cancelled your slot. He wants you to do an interview with Davina instead.'

Davina has absolutely no stretch marks from any of her pregnancies. And she looks extremely fetching in a red bikini. We eased ourselves on to the vacant sun-lounger next to her, our pallid belly overhanging our waistband.

'Morning, Davina,' we said, in unison.

'I was going to say, "Morning, fellas!" But now I'm really not sure how to address you.'

I smiled politely. Wished Aldo had had some sunglasses for me. This was excruciating.

'It's pretty astounding stuff, what the professor had to say. I mean, how do you respond?'

'Well, we're really not sure how to,' Mick said. 'As far as we're concerned we're thinking feeling entities. We were as shocked as anyone when the scanner showed we're just a brain.'

A member of the production team threw a multi-coloured beach ball. It hit me on the forehead. Bounced off across the sand they'd scattered over the studio floor.

'And are they right? I mean, I'm sitting not two yards from you and as far as I can tell you're still Dr Mick and his conjoined sidekick.'

My vision went a bit misty. Nothing to do with the beach ball. First Aldo, now Davina. There were people out there who felt the same way I did.

'One has to be very careful,' Mick was saying. 'The scientific evidence is persuasive. All John and I would say is, if the viewers believe in us then we'll carry on as best we can.'

'Surely your days are numbered?' Davina said. 'If what we're told is right – and no one has suggested it isn't – it won't be long before people perceive just the one McDonald.' She took a sip of pina colada, smiled a warm smile. 'Not that you look any different to me.'

'That may be right,' Mick said. 'We'll have to see.'

Davina giggled a flirty little giggle. 'I have to ask. Which of you is least like a monkey?'

I imagined Mick's self-deprecating smirk. 'Well, while theoretically possible, no primate has yet typed the complete works of Shakespeare. Nor has one ever gained a medical degree.'

A muscle-bound props assistant, wearing a gold chain and a skimpy pair of Speedos, walked across the set, pausing to kick at a pile of sand. It flew in my face. I blinked the grains out of my eyes, watering all the more now. Behind the camera, Davina's youngest daughter was lying on her back on the padded floor of a playpen, waggling her arms and legs, Aldo gazing adoringly at her through the bars. A baby like I was to have with Jules. Jules! Was she watching this, was she sat down at grandma's, Ellie on her knee? I may never ever see my daughter, my own flesh and blood! Would they do that, in years to come, Ellie and her sister? Sit down in front of the box of a Tuesday morning, the only glimpse of their dads that they ever got?

Davina was asking Mick something else. I was gripped by a sudden, terrifying thought. In Mick and Jules's wedding portraits I am largely expunged, a shadowy half-presence almost totally cropped by the edge of the frame. But in numerous other pictures the whole family is there. Jules, Ellie, Mick and me. And television, too. Mick sets the video on weekly record, can't bear the thought of a *Wake Up Britain!* missing from his posterity archive. Cameras deal in light. Light is a physical entity, just like x-rays, just like magnetism. What was it about pictures that was different? Was I really there? Was I truly in those images? Or did I only see myself because I expected to? Because I expected my *face* to be there?

I have no more than a hazy impression of what a brain actually looks like. You don't hoick a snap out of your wallet, show it to the bloke sitting next to you on the train, tell him: that's a scan of my little girl's neocortex, that is. Looks like butter wouldn't melt in her anterior cingulate. But I tell you, beneath it all she's an impish little amygdala!

You don't pull out a passport-sized x-ray of your wife's skull and say, Look at those perfectly chiselled cheekbones!

But a face! The thing, above everything, that we love! The outward manifestation of the soul! An oh so familiar face, so often stared at in the mirror. So often scrutinized for its handsomeness or beauty, its strengths and its defects, its best side, its symmetry, its character. The faces of others: what they're thinking, how they're feeling, who exactly they are. *My* face, with its wrinkled-eyed grin, its cute little pudgy nose, its disarmingly gappy teeth, its well-groomed goatee! Did I only see myself in photos, on video, because I was expecting to? Did others only perceive me because they, too, believed already that I would be there?

And what of my daughter? Growing up with no knowledge of her parentage. What would she see in the family albums, on the *Wake Up Britain!* screen? Just a void? A nothingness? A father, absent in every sense of the word.

I knew I saw myself. I had to know if everyone else perceived me too.

'Davina!' I interrupted, careless as to what she might have been saying. 'I had this idea. What about a phone-in poll? You know, 0870-263-655-0 if you think Mick exists. 655-1 if you believe in John? Stick a 2 on the end for the both of us?'

Davina looked panicked. Glanced hurriedly at where Aldo was supposed to be. A towel-draped production assistant, heading my way, armed with a Mr Whippy cone, stopped in his tracks. In my earpiece I heard the crackle of static. Then the producer's voice: Davina! Go with it, girl! That's a fantastic idea!

Outside the studio complex the journalists were three deep. Every security guard in the place had been whistled up to try to hold them back.

'John!'

'Mick!'

'John! Over here!'

'Give us a smile, Mick!'

Flashes were strobing left right and centre. As we

stepped on to the pavement the crowd surged forward. The clamour was indescribable. Microphones were thrust in my chops. Dictaphones waved in the air. An overpowered guard thudded against us, his peaked hat tumbling to the ground.

'Fellas!'

'Boys! This way! Boys!'

Somehow we jostled forward. Mick was chanting 'No comment' like a mantra. A leery-faced hack toppled through the cordon, tie skewed beneath his ear.

'John! Who's the monkey! Who's the monkey!'

I took a half-step forward. Could smell the garlic on his breath. His laughing eyes. His flared nostrils. I closed my eyes tight shut and slammed my head forward, giving him everything I'd got.

Strong arms grabbed me, propelled me onwards. Somehow we were bundled into a taxi. The door slamming behind us. A slapped hand on the roof telling the driver to get a move on. Photographers tore alongside as the cab picked up speed. Snap crackle pop!

I put my fingers to my forehead, brought them down to see the blood.

'You all right?' Mick asked, passing his handkerchief.

'Yeah.' I screwed my eyes up, opened them again, things were a bit blurry. 'He was a big fucker. I think I nutted him on the chin.'

The taxi shook the last of them off, sped along the road, London flashing past outside. People shopping, going to work, walking their dogs, idling along. I took a deep breath in, let it out again. Mick did the same.

'Cat's out of the bag now,' he said.

'Tell me about it.'

We sat in silence for a while, me dabbing at my bleeding forehead. I wondered – obsessively, intensely – what the future held in store. Mick had had his shag, now we were well and truly fucked. Public property, our bones to be picked over on the airwaves, in the opinion columns, over pints in every pub in the land. How would the papers come out? *Mirror* for, *Sun* against? *Guardian* on the fence?

'We could do with talking to Max Clifford,' I said.

As we swung into the approach to Paddington I caught the cabbie's eye in the rear view. Braced myself.

'Here. Are you that Dame Edna Everage?'

I shook my head. 'Dr Mick. From *Wake Up Britain!*'

'Course!' he said, slapping the steering wheel. 'My missus is a big fan.'

Safe inside the house I felt the tension drain out of my shoulder. We were alone. Without those we loved, but at the very least we were safe.

The red light was winking in the lounge. Twenty-three messages. *The News of the World*, offering an exclusive.

The Daily Mail, likewise. *The Telegraph*, ditto. Andrew Marr inviting us to *Start the Week*. Sue Lawley would like us to take a break on her desert island. Melvyn Bragg wanted us, *In Our Time*. Paxman fancied a pop. Robert Winston was doing a new series. Trevor McDonald thought it would be peachy if we joined him on *Tonight*. Dimbleby wondered if we would complete the panel on *Any Questions?*

'Robert Winston!' said Mick.

'Forget it,' I said.

No way could either of us do an afternoon surgery. Mick rang in sick. I took us through to the kitchen, tried my hand at cooking. Knocked up some cheese on toast, with a dash of Worcester sauce. Ate one slice, dumped the other in the bin.

The doorbell rang. We froze. Almost certainly the *Oxford Mail*.

'Better get it,' Mick said.

It was Ariadne. Sparkling eyes. Breathless with excitement.

'Mmmm!' She kissed Mick long and hard. Squirmed against us. 'Prof's got me doing the local media, he's covering the nationals. I can't thank you enough!'

She didn't even come in! Peeled away to leave us standing on the doorstep. The *Oxford Mail* photographer, lurking on the pavement, took his shot then tucked his camera back in its bag.

'Here!' I called to Ariadne. 'Aren't you even going to shag him?'

She pretended not to have heard me.

There's something about the way a doorbell rings that communicates the caller's intentions. It's not the length of the press, or the number of times it goes. I don't know; I can't say what it is. At intervals during that afternoon, Mick and me huddled like hunted rabbits at the back of the burrow, the shrill trrring would sound. Each time, I knew it heralded an unwelcome visitor. We would peek guardedly from behind the bedroom nets: a TV crew from BBC South; another from Central News; a reporter from the *Oxford Star*; two Jehovah's witnesses, *Watchtowers* tucked beneath their arms. We would shrink from sight, leave them finally to give up and go away.

But on one occasion I sensed a different kind of presence. Some quality in the bell that said: this is a friend, this is someone who is on your side. Jules! It had to be Jules! She had seen the news, and despite the hurts and the pain she had rushed to be with us again. How I needed to see her. How I suddenly craved the touch of her hand, gliding down our back; the lift in spirit that her unconditional smile would bring. Without further thought I started to head for the hall.

'What are you doing?' Mick asked.

'There's someone at the door.'

'I know! Don't answer it!'

'It's OK,' I told him.

He did the flaccid paralysis thing, but I was stronger. I made it to the door, managed to wriggle my wrist out of his grip long enough to open it. To find Clive waiting on the mat.

'Hello,' he said. 'Can I come in?'

What could we say? We showed him into the living room. I'd been so certain it would be Jules. Jules! Where are you? We stood awkwardly, the three of us, no one seeming to know quite what to say. I hadn't realized Clive even knew our address. I dimly recalled Jules filling in some form, a while after we all began trooping along to St Mark's on a regular basis.

When we were eight, our mum put us forward for our first holy communion. Mick was deemed a tricky problem; you can't take the body of Christ in your mouth then spit it back out. In the end I was the only one to receive the sacrament; Mick had to make do with a sign of the cross traced in chrism on his forehead. The parish priest paid a number of domiciliary visits in the run-up to the service, in an effort to negotiate the solution. I tried to remember what our mother did, how one made a man of the cloth feel welcome in one's home.

'Whisky?'

'Not for me, thanks,' said Clive.

I poured myself one anyway. I couldn't believe I hadn't thought of it before. Clive insisted he'd be fine with tap water.

'I saw the news,' he told us, sitting himself in an armchair. 'I thought I should come round. It must be horrible.'

Clive. His sports jacket. His dog collar. His floppy sandy brown hair.

'Are you all right?' he asked, his gaze shifting to my forehead.

'Just a bump,' I told him. Actually it was an inch-long split in the skin, with a massive amount of swelling and bruising, but you couldn't tell beneath the bandage that Mick and I had somehow managed to fasten round my head.

'Is anyone with you at this time?' he asked.

'Nope. Just us on our lonesome.'

'We can get a rota of parishioners together, if you want. Some support for you in your hour of need.'

The thought of them. Well-meaning but cringe-worthy, rallying round in a crisis.

'We'll be fine,' I said. It had only ever been us, Mick 'n' me against the world. 'Thanks, anyway.'

Clive took a sip of water. Looked at me steadily.

'Julia isn't back, then.'

I shook my head. Gestured towards the window. 'They've been doorstepping us all afternoon. We thought it was best for Ellie if she stayed away.'

'Of course,' said Clive.

What made it so difficult? Why couldn't I just come out with it, say: yep, you guessed it, the marriage is in trouble, our family is disintegrating, I'm scared, I'm lonely, I'd give anything to wind the clock back, I simply don't want this to be the way it's going to be. But I couldn't. It was too complicated. And I would have had to own up to my share of the guilt.

'Clive,' I said.

He glanced up.

'Look at us. Tell me. How many of us do you see?'

He smiled faintly. 'Why do you ask?'

'Why do I *ask*? All day I've had people telling me I don't exist! That I'm just, I'm just some *figment* of Mick's brain!' I paused, calmed myself. 'I need to know whether to believe in myself or not. Whether you think I'm real.'

'Of course I do,' he said. 'I wouldn't be here otherwise.'

'So how come I don't show up on all their scans and stuff? How come some people look at us and only see Mick?'

'I'm afraid I don't have an answer for that.' His rather grave expression yielded up a sudden, bright smile. 'You're in good company, though.'

'There are others like me?'

'I was thinking of the soul. Ever since Descartes suggested it was in the pituitary gland people having been trying to find it, trying to pin it down to a physical location.'

'Pineal,' said Mick.

'Sorry?'

'It was the pineal gland. He thought it was the only unpaired structure in the brain. That's why he decided it was the seat of the soul. Descartes, I mean.'

'Well, whatever. The point is, however hard you try to tie the soul to a particular place, you can't. Some people think that must mean it doesn't exist.' He pushed his tortoiseshell glasses more firmly on to the bridge of his nose. 'I'd say you're in a very exclusive club.'

'But souls don't exist, do they?' said Mick. 'Not any more. We're just brains these days. Just flesh and blood and a staggering amount of neural noise.'

Personally, I wouldn't have suggested to a Church of England vicar that his whole *raison d'être* was a load of hooey. But then I'm not Mick.

Clive gave him a look. 'As Christians we believe the exact opposite. The soul enters the body at the moment of conception, but is never a physical part of it.'

'Yeah?' Mick sounded belligerent, like Clive was suddenly looking like the ideal whipping boy for the traumas of the day. 'How do you explain us, then?

Couple of souls in a neck-and-neck sprint? Not even a photo finish to separate them? So we both hopped aboard and here we are?'

'I never try to explain people.' Clive took a drink, put his glass down on the floor. 'But, yes, identical twins do indeed have a soul each. No one has a problem with that when they've physically separated. The conjoint case is simply a failure of embryological fission, not a proof that two souls cannot become incorporated in the same conceptus.'

Clive read something biological as a first degree, I think, before he got religion. Even so, I'm not sure I'd have tried to out-science Mick. But then I'm definitely not Clive.

'Oh, come on, Father!' Mick's voice was strident now. 'What about stroke, head injury, Alzheimer's? The times I've had relatives say their loved ones have changed – that they've *gone*, even though their bodies are still alive – all because their brains are diseased in some way.'

'The soul certainly manifests itself through the physical body.' Clive's tone was measured, soft. 'If that body is damaged, and that includes the brain, then the manifestation may be affected. But the soul itself is inviolate – it's our spirit, our essence, it's what dictates our response to the world. After all, young children – your little daughter – they have souls, too, yet their expression is filtered through the prism of immaturity. And after death, when the body has completely failed, the soul lives on.'

'Yeah, well, I don't believe all that crap.'

'But that is what it comes down to, isn't it? Belief or otherwise. Jesus was quite clear on the matter – he never offered proof, only faith.'

Actually, I began to wish I was Clive. There's something exhilarating when metaphysics leaves science spinning in the wind, spluttering and fuming at its inability ever to win the argument beyond a shadow of a doubt.

'Did you know,' Mick said, jabbing a finger. 'There's some bit of the brain in religious people, a god spot. I read about it, it's in the temporal lobe somewhere. If you stimulate it with an electrode, it causes intense feelings of spiritual transcendence and the sense of a mystical presence.'

'Meaning?' said Clive.

'Meaning it's all an artefact. Meaning all that stuff is just in your head. Meaning there's nothing out there at all, not really.'

Clive folded his hands together, nodded barely perceptibly. 'But bits of the brain light up whatever we're thinking, or doing, or feeling. When we ache with longing, when we're desperate with grief, when we're consumed by love. You're not suggesting there's no such thing as *love*, are you?'

His gaze was fixed on Mick. Unflinching. The silence went well beyond a pause for thought, got well into the discomfort zone.

'More water?' I said.

Clive shook his head slowly. 'I'd better be going.' He got to his feet. 'I hope I didn't… I mean, I came to offer solidarity.'

'Don't worry about it,' I said, waving a hand in the general direction of Mick's sulkily silent head. 'It was very kind of you.'

'Well, if there's anything I can do.'

'Thanks, Father.'

'Arsehole,' Mick said, when we'd closed the door on Clive.

'He was only trying to help.'

'He was trying to get the lowdown. Creeping round here at the whiff of a scandal. He'll be back down that church office dishing the gossip faster than you can say Jack Robinson.'

'He really got to you, didn't he? All that stuff about souls and love and shit?'

Mick produced a particularly fine snort. 'Don't you fucking start! If it wasn't for you, none of this would have happened. What a fucking mess!'

'Don't try and blame me! Who was it brought Ariadne back, eh? Who's the prat who sent the only person who ever loved us running away as fast as her legs would carry her? With Ellie, too! Your own fucking daughter! That was clever, wasn't it? Well fucking done!'

'Loved *me*. Jules loved *me*, dick brain. She could never fucking stand you, you lecherous fucking bastard.'

The bandage cushioned things somewhat. Certainly for me. The head butt must've hurt him, though, judging by the venom with which he swung his fist into my face the moment after. I responded in kind, felt his nose squash under my knuckles. We stood there, trading round-the-corner blows, each punch loaded with the pent-up fury of a life of insufferable torment.

The phone rang, but we ignored it. Biff! Splat! Kapow!

Dr Day's voice came out of the answer machine. Wanting to let Mick know about an emergency partners' meeting the following evening. They'd decided they needed to discuss his, ahem, future in the practice. After the events of the day and everything.

We stood there, arms hanging loosely by our sides, breathing hard. Listened to what he was saying. To the beep that signalled the end of message recording. Watched as the little red light started to wink once again.

*

I'd been so certain that ring on the doorbell had been Jules. That she would have seen the news, and despite all the hurts and the pain she'd have come rushing to our side once again. I'd been wrong about the bell, but my intuition was bang on. When she came she used her key. Stole into the house unannounced and found us, smashed out of our tiny little minds, sitting at the kitchen table, one whisky bottle empty, the second well on the way. The memories are a bit mussed up. I felt her arms around my neck, heard her saying, John, oh John, how horrible for you, she'd come as soon as she'd got Ellie settled for the night.

I'm fine, really, I mumbled, lurching a little under her weight.

Mick was saying something, his voice hectoring all of a sudden. What about me, he wanted to know. I'm your husband, for fuck's sake. What did she mean, coming in here after days away without a word, crawling all over *him*.

Through the fog of alcohol I could just make out the vague shape of a disaster. With which we appeared to be on a collision course. I tried desperately to marshal my thoughts.

She's upset for me, I slurred. Being told I don't exist. That's all.

Then Jules was speaking. How she didn't love him,

didn't want him, how she was fed up with living a lie. How he was a conceited bastard. And an unfaithful one, too. How once she'd thought it through she'd realized Ariadne had been on *his* side of the bed.

How none of that mattered, anyway, because now she was going to have John's baby.

And John was the man she loved.

I tried laughing it off. Ho ho, nice one, Jules. I disentangled myself, offered her a drink. Sloshed some whisky into my glass and landed it somehow in her hand. Kept up a patter, hoping that if I could just manage to speak for ever then my words would keep us all up in the air and we'd never hit the ground. But in time, I ran out of puff. I sat gazing blearily at her, the confused mix of emotions on her face. Jules, always so full of love, so full of care. She looked lost, alone, standing there. I wanted, suddenly, to hold her.

I held my arm out. Inviting her in.

Mick's fist smashed, full force, one last time. And that was the end.

Income tax self assessment

Once upon a Time in the West

– God!

BANG!

Part Four

Reason cannot comprehend reality, and fantasy cannot manipulate it... Step into the world expecting magic; cause and effect will crush your every expectation. Look at the world objectively, and everything before you turns fantastical and absurd.

Simon Ings, *The Weight of Numbers*

Quite Contrary

Baroness Mary Warnock is one of the country's fore-most moral philosophers and a world authority on the ethics of reproduction. Commissioned by Maggie Thatcher in 1982 to head an enquiry into human fertilization, Mary's subsequent report laid the foundations for the legal framework governing IVF practice in Britain. She's also had a word or two to say about experimentation on human embryos. Her London residence is a charming Georgian townhouse on one of those leafy squares that recall a more genteel era in the capital's history. It has a thirty-foot study on the ground floor, one end of which is lined with floor-to-ceiling book-shelves crammed with innumerable volumes on subjects as diverse as law, philosophy, genetics, embryology, and sociology. If you've ever seen her interviewed on the news you'll recognize the backdrop. At the other end of the room is the 46" plasma screen TV on which she whiles away the hours with her PlayStation.

'How's it going?' I asked. 'Did you ever get anywhere with *Tomb Raider*?'

She shook her head. Looked regretfully at her hands.

'It's this bloody arthritis. Slows me up no end.'

I made a sympathetic noise. Five years since we'd last been here, and time had not been entirely kind. There was still the bright-eyed intellect, that impression of a self-confident mind constantly on the look-out for a moral dust-up. But her posture seemed stiffer. The skin hung more loosely on her neck. And her fingers were noticeably more gnarled.

'You boys have created quite a stir,' she said.

I nodded. Two months since the *Nature* paper and the furore showed little sign of abating. Yes, there'd been the odd high point, but mostly it had been one long low. Mick had been booted out of the practice. Nothing to do with his clinical standards, so they said, everything to do with patients needing to be confident that their doctor was qualified and up to date, as opposed to a monkey. The industrial tribunal is slated for September. The *Wake Up Britain!* money kept us going for a while, but after the initial surge in the ratings, viewing figures once again dipped below the one million mark. The show was axed to make room for *CSI: Murder in the Morning*. I can never bring myself to get out of bed to watch it. Mick badly needs to rouse himself to find another job, but the little fucker is so wrapped up in self-pity he can barely find his toothbrush. We've earned precisely one appearance fee: a handsome sum, but utterly inadequate compensation for the mauling we received at the hands of the team on *Have I Got News For You*. The experience stiffened both our resolves to have nothing more to do with the media. Rent and living costs Mick's been meeting out of fast-dwindling savings. The summer holiday has given temporary respite from Ellie's school fees. I've been forced seriously to contemplate giving up drinking and smoking. Even so, the whole house of cards is teetering. Any day soon it might come crashing down.

All of which was so much worry. There was a glimmer of hope, but I couldn't allow myself to become distracted by thinking about that now. What I'd come to sort out was personal.

'Jules is pregnant again,' I told Mary.

'Oh! Congratulations.'

'Thanks.' I swallowed. 'This time, I'm the daddy.'

She looked from me to Mick, to me. Then to Mick again.

'So he keeps insisting,' Mick said.

Mary sat herself back, folded her hands together. 'I see.'

We all stayed silent for a bit. Mary cogitating. Mick bristling. Me concerned about the erratic gallop of our heart. I was nervous as fuck. Not about Mary, she's a

perfect sweetie. More about what she might say. When
Jules was pregnant with Ellie, the local registrar for
births, deaths and marriages referred the matter to the
Home Secretary, who promptly chucked the steaming
potato at the safest pair of hands he knew. We had a
series of meetings with Mary while she tried to work out
quite what to do.

The problem was which name would go on the birth
certificate as dad. Mick's, obviously, but it wasn't that
simple. Given that we share a single genome and the one
set of genitals, there was no biological basis for determining paternity. In this day and age, the fact that Mick
was actually married to Jules cut no mustard, either.
It all boiled down to intent: which of our *minds* had
been responsible for the conception. Easy-peasy, it was
Mick's. That wasn't the real issue, though. What was
vexing the highest powers in the land were the grounds
on which I could be excused including my own moniker
when we came to register the birth.

Imagine. You've got a bloke bang to rights. Mum's
fingered him as the father, paternity testing confirms her
story. The Child Support Agency takes him to the family
court to get him to pay maintenance. His smarmy pin-
striped brief stands up and says: My client admits he
was present at the moment of conception, he acknowl-
edges that his penis was introduced into the appellant's

vagina, furthermore he does not contest that his genes are to be found in every one of the child's cells, but my client cannot be held to have parental responsibility because he had no *intention* of making this woman pregnant. Then he brandishes the John McDonald precedent in front of the gob-smacked bench. Multiply that case by a couple of hundred thousand others and you've got a full-scale disaster on your hands.

Mary called it an interesting corollary of society's increasingly biocentric view of personhood.

In the end, she decided we'd both have to be named as Ellie's dad. Simultaneously, I would be presented with a specially drafted deed drawn up between me and the Crown, by virtue of which all my parental rights and responsibilities would be formally rescinded. The Queen signs herself Elizabeth R. I put myself as John M.

'Well, we'll just have to do the same thing again, won't we?' Mary said, eventually. She looked rather sad. 'Only this time the other way round.'

I braced myself.

'I'm not signing anything,' Mick told her.

'Ah,' she said.

He may not be able to stop the divorce. In time, he may even be faced with the galling prospect of attending Jules's and my wedding, though I shan't be asking him to be best man. The one way he can get back at me is through the baby. It's shameful, using her as a pawn, but he won't listen to reason.

'I see. Well, that *is* rather complicated,' said Mary. She looked in my direction again. 'You're sure you're the father?'

'Positive.'

Mick issued a derisively drawn-out oink. 'He doesn't even exist.'

Mary made her fingers into a spire, touched them lightly to her lips.

'He does have a point, John, doesn't he? If everything I've been reading is correct, your status as a real entity is beginning to look decidedly shaky.'

'I've got a National Insurance number,' I pointed out. 'And a birth certificate.'

'You've never paid any contributions, have you?' Mick said. 'And, anyway, it's only a short certificate of birth.'

Some enterprising reporter on the *Evening Standard* had been to Myddelton Street, the family records centre formerly known as Somerset House. Sixty-point headline: TWINS REGISTER SHOCK. Apparently the only entry actually to be found in the archive is for a Michael John McDonald. In the concertina file in the bottom drawer of my desk, in which I keep what few personal documents I possess, I have a short certificate of birth for John Michael McDonald. I leaked it to the *Independent*, who obligingly blew it up and reproduced it on their front page. *The Times* tracked down the assistant registrar who transcribed it from the register those thirtysomething years ago. He's got end-stage Lewy body dementia and resides in a nursing home in Dumfries. No one can say whether he used also to be dyslexic.

For what it's worth, my view is he'd simply never met the situation before, had no idea how he should record our arrival as citizens – conjoined births are a perfect rarity, even in the Scottish Borders. In medieval times, having just the one ticker, we'd have been classed as a single person. These days everyone knows the heart is really to be found in the head, so we're seen as two. I reckon he put Mick's name in the actual book, and mine on the copy. I don't suppose he really gave a fuck. I guess he thought he'd remember what he'd done when he came to register our universally anticipated deaths a few months down the line.

'Forget bits of paper,' I said, fixing Mary with my most earnest stare. 'I *know* I'm John McDonald. Have been all my life. I speak like John McDonald, think like John McDonald, feel like John McDonald. I *am* John McDonald. Look at me. You can see that, can't you?'

Mary shook her head, clamped her lips together rue-fully. 'That's no basis for determining identity, though, is it? If we followed that line of reasoning we'd have to empty the asylums. There'd be a couple of thousand Jesus Christs walking the streets, to say nothing of the Devils.'

'Oh, come on,' I said. 'That's entirely different. All I'm saying is, take a common sense view. You're talking to John McDonald, looking at him, thinking about what he has to say. Surely that proves he exists?'

'We've got to take account of the scientists, though,' she told me. 'They've done all the tests, haven't they, and there's just a brain.'

'Yeah, and if they scanned you that's all they'd find too!' I immediately regretted my outburst. She's a love, Mary. I think of her more as an auntie. She sends us a card every Christmas.

She gave a deep sigh. 'I can see you're upset. And I do understand.' She frowned. 'What does Julia say?'

'Oh, she says it's him, all right,' Mick said. 'She loves him, needs him, can't live without him. It makes me sick.'

'What about conciliation?' Mary asked. 'I could fix you up with a good counsellor. You're going to have to come to some sort of agreement, the two of you. I can't see how we can proceed otherwise.'

'The way we can proceed,' Mick said, 'is for him to butt out of my head and my life for once and for all.'

'I'll take that as a no, shall I?' Mary said.

The camaraderie of that *Bridge over the River Kwai* afternoon had long since vanished. These days Mick goes around doing his best to make out I'm simply not there. I know, I know: it's his anger, his self-loathing. He's the one who fucked up the marriage but he has to take it out on someone else. Anyone else. I understand all that, but it doesn't make it any easier. I've tried starving him into submission: if I don't exist, you go and have yourself a curry, then. I keep cracking long before he does, though.

Mary sat forward in her chair.

'Let's meet in a fortnight,' she said. 'I need to take some soundings. And I'd like you two to go away and have some serious discussion. It saddens me. You were such a happy pair, so eminently suited to each other.'

She was right. I thought back wistfully to our previous visits, back when Ellie was a legal non-entity growing in Jules's womb. How thrilled we'd both been. How we kept doing those spontaneous high-fives, his palm slapping on to my palm, complete with a mutual little hop off the ground. Yet my joy for him had been tinged with just the teeniest bit of regret. He'd sensed it. He'd tried to buck me up, reminding me I'd never wanted commitment, never wanted responsibility; telling me how I'd been having such a ball shagging my way through the National Health Service. He was right; I acknowledged it. But, all the same, a tinsy bit of me remained envious. He'd got in first, as he always did. He was the one who'd got married, now he was the one to become a father. There'd be no chance for me to do similarly, even if I did ever meet the right woman – not unless we all moved to Utah. I would have to content myself with being an uncle. The next best thing, sure. But not the same.

Mary showed us to the door. Opened it on to the lovely summer's day. The fumey London heatwave. The little park in the midst of her square. The office workers catching a few rays during lunch.

'That looks nasty,' she said, looking at my forehead.

I touched my hand to the scar. It was healing well, but the lividity would take a while to fade.

'Little altercation with a reporter from *The Tablet*.'

'I should like to bang your heads together,' she said, shaking hers. 'I know there's a lot of pain, but I hate to see you like this.'

'Bye, Mary.' I gave her a peck on the cheek. 'And thanks.'

'Mick?' she said.

He stayed still for a sulky second. Then craned forward, gave her a kiss too. 'Yeah, bye.'

We found a bench beneath the big copper beech. The sun was blistering, the shade a blessing. I loosened our collar and tie.

'Phew! Scorcher, isn't it?' I said.

A pigeon strutted past our feet, eyeing us carefully for

any sign of a packed lunch. Flew off when a girl on roller skates coursed by. I stared across the park, to the white painted facade of Mary's house, its ornate black railings, its original sash windows.

'Good to see Mary again, wasn't it?' I said.

Flip. Whip. Ching. I lit myself a cigarette, loosed off a plume of smoke.

'Come on, Mick, you can't keep this up for ever. We've got the rest of our lives to get through. Serious discussion! You heard the woman.'

As I smoked my way through his stony silence, my good mood began to dissipate. The *Wake Up Britain!* telephone poll results, announced on the final edition of the programme, had been a personal vindication. Only 23 per cent of respondents had voted for Mick alone. A full 70 per cent of viewers believed we both existed. OK, the tally for me on my own was a meagre 7 per cent, and I'd probably skewed the figure with my repeated late-night phoning. Even so, the vast majority of the population seemed unwilling to write me off entirely. I hadn't been confident of Mary, though. Lovely as she is, I couldn't help fearing she'd be swayed by the mocking MRI, by the irrefutable science. Yet she'd come good, had continued to address me as an autonomous thinking being, had refused to discount the possibility of my being a daddy. I could have hugged her.

Now, though. Out on the square. Mick doing his pissed-off Trappist. Was this how it was going to be, for ever and ever amen?

I tried to look at him, twisted myself round as much as my stiff neck would allow. If I could only catch his eye. Appeal to something in him.

It was no good.

An elderly gent, his walking stick topped with a metal dolphin, doddered up to our bench.

'Excuse me,' he said. Despite the heat he had a jacket on, a frayed bow tie. 'I hope I'm not intruding, but I couldn't help wondering: are you Dame Thora Hird?'

I looked at him. His proud deportment. His heavily wrinkled skin. The stains on his shirt front.

'No,' I said. 'She's dead, I'm afraid.'

'Oh. I'm sorry to hear that.'

'Yeah. So am I.'

Happy Families 2

'**M**orning!' Jules said, getting up from the kitchen table, abandoning her dry toast.

Her T-shirt nightie. Her precious, unmade-up face. Her heart-tuggingly unbrushed hair.

'Morning,' I said.

We kissed. The softness of her lips on my lips. It still gave me a massive rush, knowing that those pecks on the cheek were evermore a thing of the past. I encircled her with my arm, pulled her warm body next to mine. Closed my eyes for a second. Savoured the moment. I could feel her belly against me; mine was still the larger, but she was catching up fast, the new life burgeoning inside her womb.

I am ridiculous. Even now I sometimes find myself having to swallow hard to get rid of the constriction that arises unbidden in my throat.

'Sleep well?' she asked.

'Fantastic,' I said. 'You?'

She smiled. 'Still a bit sicky.'

She moved away, her hand lingering briefly on my back. Then, as it always does, her smile began slowly to fade. We both became aware of it, Mick's frosty presence, the icy air on my cheek.

She's not cruel. For ages she's been trying to engage him with hellos, how are you's, even an attempt to apologize for her part in it all, but there are only so many olive branches one person can offer.

'Come on,' I said, seeing her starting to wilt. 'Do you fancy a coffee?'

Out of consideration for her stubbornly persistent morning queasiness I have temporarily ceased to fry. I fixed myself a bowl of Frosties, with a decent sprinkling of extra sugar, and joined her at the table. We ate for a while in silence. I was aching to say something encouraging, but it's so difficult, this poison in our lives. It robs us of every moment, steals from us our rightful joy. And, despite the sheet, it's put the complete kibosh on our love life. We both needed to talk about it, bolster each other, make some concerted plan. But we can't bring ourselves to while he's listening. And the little fucker refuses to put the Discman on, not even if he gets to choose the CD. It's becoming so desperate, I'm seriously contemplating buying him an iPod.

Ellie trotted in from the garden, aka the paddock, where she'd evidently been having an early-morning gambol.

'Neigh!' she whinnied.

'Morning, Strawb!' I called.

She came for a cuddle. Then a cuddle with Daddy.

'Morning, sweetie,' he said, his voice a choked monotone, his hand ruffling her hair.

If there's one person he will speak to then thank god it's Ellie. I can at least give him that. It would be truly awful if he were to take it out on her, too.

After brekkie I grabbed a shower, then settled down to work. No more night writing for me, no siree. Not since the aftermath of the *Nature* paper, in the thick of the media feeding frenzy, when I got the out-of-the-blue call.

Unknown female: John McDonald? It's Candida Lucas-Montefiori, from Dyne, Drewitt literary agency. What are you working on at the moment?

I tried to keep my cool, tried to ignore the sudden lurch in my guts. Candida Lucas-Montefiori! I'd never met her, but how I loved her. The only agent ever to have sent me a personalized rejection letter.

John: Oh, hi. Yes, I took your advice. I've been fiddling with a sort of autobiographical Western.

Candida: Great! Get me three finished chapters as soon as you possibly can. We need to sell it on a partial, while you're still hot property.

John: I'm sorry?

Candida: I'd say there's a four-month window. Miss it and we may struggle to get the advance into six figures. Email me something soonest.

I put the phone down. Stared at it a while, its neat keypad, its matt grey plastic. It looked real enough. Perhaps I hadn't just been dreaming.

'Autobiographical Western?' A rare breach in Mick's impenetrable wall of silence.

'Yeah,' I told him.

'Sister *Sebastian*?'

I shook my puzzled head. 'It's a long story.'

I'm nearly there, I've nearly got the opening fifty pages as good as can be. Since Mick lost the day job I've been keeping regular hours. I bit the bullet, too, and gave up boozing and fagging. It was difficult at first, writing sober. Not least because of Mick's snorts and huffs and sighs every time I brought his lawman alter ego into a scene. Plus the trembly feeling that this might, finally, actually be it. The pressure threatened to derail me for a while. Christ, we need the money! Jules has been taking extra bank work at the John Radcliffe, even though she feels so exhausted. Mick's managed to fix himself some red-eye shifts with the local out-of-hours service, the only medical job it looks like he'll be able to get from here on in. It's practically impossible to see a GP in the middle of the night these days; no one gives a monkey's what kind of doctor rolls up. He gets a car and a driver, and I get some kip, so it's OK. And it gives him a chance to exercise his vocal cords. He still holds out hope that Ariadne will be as good as her word, that there will, after all, be an academic post at the end of the tunnel. She hasn't returned his calls for weeks. Like I said, he's a stupid dumb fuck.

We have so little left in the bank. The holidays are drawing on. Ellie will soon be back at school. Reception this year. An extra thousand a term. Plus the landlord has put the rent up. And the Booster needs a service. And there's the new arrival to think of. I fired up the PC and prepared myself once again to head out West. Six-figure advance! Fuck, did we ever need the money!

Mick has lost all interest in medicine, rarely reads a journal these days. It's been a struggle, but gradually he's found ways to occupy himself during the long hours I spend in front of the computer. His record for the sugar cube tower currently stands at forty-three. Ellie loves the paperclip zoo animals he's become expert at fashioning single-handed. And if the paint on the wall above the desk ever does start to peel, he'll be on to it like a shot.

I don't feel too bad about it. The years of youth I wasted, sat in his room at college while he pored over his textbooks. The sunshine days spent cooped up in dimly lit lecture theatres. The clubbing posses I could never join, Mick doing his inhumane one-in-three rotas as a junior doc.

For days now I've been struggling interminably with the scene where the sheriff's body gets brought back into town. I know Deputy Mick has to have some kind of heartfelt reaction to the loss of his beloved mentor. Try as I might I haven't been able to picture him with any emotions whatsoever; he's as dry as a bone. Then, late morning, I get my breakthrough. In a flash of inspiration, I start to imagine how I'd feel if I lost Jules, Ellie, the baby. If my life were suddenly to be upended, if its precious contents were to be spilled in the dirt, now that I've finally got all I could ever dream of. The desolation. The total emptiness. The desperate, unending internal cry of NO!

That was it. I took those soul-destroying imaginary emotions, transferred them to the star-spangled Deputy faced with the lifeless body of the sheriff and hey presto! the book was suddenly back on track.

Except that Jules came in. With Ellie.

'I've got to go,' she said.

'Oh, shit,' I said, checking the time. She was working

a late up at the John. We can't afford any childcare. It's down to me. Mick and me.

'I've been stuck for ages. I've finally got it going again.'

'I'm sorry.' Jules rested a hand on my shoulder.

I sneaked a guilty glance at Ellie, standing uncertainly by the door. Looking down at her lilac sandals.

'It's OK,' I said, injecting brightness into my voice. 'There's always tomorrow. Hey, Ells, what do you say to a trip to the park?'

She gave me a big grin. 'Hello, trip to the park!'

It swelled my heart.

'No, it's all right. We'll stay here.'

Mick's voice was so unexpected. He'd been shtoom for so long I had genuinely forgotten his existence.

'You fetch some books, honey,' he told Ellie. 'And some jigsaws. We'll see what we can get up to while Uncle John works, eh?'

'But I want to go to the park!'

Her face threatened to cloud over.

'I'll try making you a giraffe,' Mick said.

That got a radiant smile. Ellie skippity skipped off down to the playroom.

Jules looked completely and utterly discombobulated.

'Are you feeling all right?' I asked him.

There was a lengthy pause. Oh, come on, Mick, we've got to move on!

'It's pretty good,' he said, at last. 'Your book.'

I didn't know what to say. The endless barrage of derisive snorts. He hated it. Being as it's our auto/biography.

'I want to see how it works out,' he said. 'The bit with Mick and the dead sheriff. Well, all of it, really.'

Relief came out as laughter. 'All right!' I said. 'Let's fucking do it!'

Jules looks pretty bloody fantastic in her uniform. They wear these sexy blue pyjama things these days. She gave me a full-on goodbye kiss. Then she straightened up. Spent a long time looking down at him, sitting next to me in my executive swivel chair. I stared at her face, her eyes fixed on his. Then I saw her suddenly smile, one of those that's laced with regret and guilt and pity and affection and sadness and just about every other fucking emotion we humans can ever possibly feel. Then she stooped. And I heard the little pwwt as she pecked him on the cheek. And she left.

And it was as if he'd suddenly been let out of jail. For a good couple of hours, while I took Deputy Mick on his frantic but futile search for the handcuff key, Mick played a blinder with Ellie. Pulled off suitably funny accents as he read her *Angelina Ballerina*. Gently encouraged her whenever she ran into problems with the next bit of the *Fimbles* puzzle. Left her in wonder when he pulled off a paperclip rhino, horn and all. He's been so much better with her since he quit all that shit at the practice, but this was a bravura performance.

'Thanks, Mick,' I told him at one point, nodding at the screen. The steadily mounting lines of pure fiction.

'You'd better get a decent whack for it,' he said. 'Otherwise we're really sunk.'

He returned to his kiddie stuff. I plunged back in with renewed vigour. I could save the day, I was sure of it! Candida was talking about foreign rights, newspaper serialization, *Book at Bedtime* – though the language would have to be toned down – even the possibility of a Dreamworks production. And now, with Mick seemingly thawed, back on my side once again, I felt a sudden, terrific current of energy. My mind raced. My fingers flew. Sentence piled on sentence, paragraph on paragraph, page on page. I got to the bit where Deputy Mick, in a moment of sheer panic, draws his Colt and tries to blast the handcuff's chain to smithereens. I felt so well disposed towards him, I decided let him shoot one of Mad John's toes off.

Then Ellie was starting to get a bit restless, needing a change of scene, a breath of fresh air. And I was beginning to feel spent, the extended creative splurge finally exacting its toll. So I saved the file. Backed it up on CD.

'Shall we do the park, then?' I said.

'Oh, yes! Yes!' Ellie leapt up and did a little jig.

'Yeah, why not,' Mick said.

And at that precise moment the doorbell rang.

I forgot, or ignored, or was plain reckless about that sixth sense. The intuition that says whether the person ringing the bell is friend or foe. Trrrring! it went. I felt instantly ill at ease. But instead of obeying instinct, instead of keeping us huddled up there in the study, shhing Ellie so as not to give a clue that anyone was in, I powered down the PC and suggested we'd better see who it was.

To Be or Not to Be

It was hard to imagine what I ever saw in her. All right, she looks bloody attractive. Sculpted face, that ultra-fine blonde hair, her cracking figure. But all that is just so much flesh. Soft, but at the same time hard, unyielding. What of her? The real Ariadne, the stuff that goes on in her head? I hadn't got a fucking clue. Yeah, enamoured with her neuroscience, her way of looking at the world, her way of thinking about people. Besotted with her paragon, Prof. But did she feel? Did she pine, did she love, did she cry at nights sometimes, did she ever do anything for the sheer hell of it?

She adored dancing, I did know that much. Shared the joy I felt at that most evolutionarily inexplicable of human faculties, music. Funk, and uplifting house, specifically.

That wasn't enough, though. Wasn't enough to have thrown away everything I had: Jules, Ellie, now the new baby. Would I really have wasted my life for the sake of her?

Undoubtedly, yes. If it hadn't been for Jules's hand sneaking beneath that sheet, the lifeline she'd extended. Pulling me back from the other side, to a world of warmth, relationship, companionship. Intangible, maybe. Unquantifiable, yes. But enduring. All, perhaps, there really is, when everything else is said and done.

It had been a lucky escape. A narrow squeak. I'd gone within an inch.

What of Mick, though? Was he still hoodwinked by Ariadne's reductive allure? Still attracted by her ready access to unfeasibly expensive bits of hi-tech kit, tools that promised to answer so much, yet revealed the meaning of absolutely nothing? I kept silent throughout his muddle-handed setting up of the video, his popping of Ellie down in front of *Finding Nemo*. Went passively with him as he showed Ariadne through to the kitchen. Offered no help as he knocked up a coffee for her. What would have happened if she'd pitched up when Jules was here? As it was, there was no way we were going to be able to keep Ellie quiet. And just when things looked like they might be sorting themselves out at last.

One Swede in tight linen trousers and a close-fitting fcuk T-shirt. It didn't bear thinking about.

We sat at the table.

'I called, several times,' Mick said.

'I know. I'm sorry.' She was gazing at him frankly. I couldn't decide whether to buy it or not. 'Things have been very busy. Very difficult, too.'

'I'll say,' he said.

This was looking good. He wasn't gushing, like he always used to with the bloody academics.

'Tell me you've brought the contract,' he told her.

Ho, ho! That's it! Ahoy, ahoy, Mick, my boy!

She reached inside her case. Pulled out a sheaf of paper. 'I have, actually.'

Holy fucking shit. She had, too. I watched with increasing alarm as Mick slid it towards us. The jumble of words, the terms and conditions, the endless paragraphs of legalese.

'You'll go straight in at the top of the scale,' she said. 'With tenure.' Her smile was hesitant. 'Everything you asked for.'

Parapsychological rapport. I couldn't speak to him, I couldn't warn him. So I squeezed my eyes shut and willed my thoughts into his head. Don't fuck it up again, you dozy bastard. She's done enough damage, you've only just started to repair it. You've lost Jules, she's mine now. But there's still Ellie. Look how well you're getting on, now you're not knackered out by medicine. And we can rub along, the three of us: you, me 'n' Jules. Different to how it was before, sure. But so much better than nothing. The thought of Ariadne back in our lives. The thought of Mick with another day job. Back to the nocturnal, booze-sodden writing. The smoking. The gulf that would inevitably open up between Jules and me. OK, so he needed some sense of professional purpose, but I was confident there was a market for paperclip animals. Sure, the academic salary would be a life-saver, but at what cost. I could do it, I could do it with my writing. Save the lot of us. Keep the whole fucking ship afloat. I knew I could. We didn't need her. He didn't need her. You don't fucking need her, Mick!

'Thank you,' he told her. 'I'd just about given up hope. I thought you'd dumped on me royally.'

'I'm sorry,' she said. 'It took a while. It's a highly irregular arrangement. The bursar needed a lot of persuading.'

'Doesn't there have to be an interview?'

I could hear the sudden suspicion in his voice. You bet your sweet ass there's a catch, Mick. There has to be a catch.

She shook her head. Gave him a secretive smile.

He took the pen out of our shirt pocket.

No, Mick! Don't do it! Please!

'Where do I sign?'

She flicked to the final page. 'Just there.'

The row of dots waiting for Mick's soul.

He pressed his thumb on the top of the pen. The nib emerged from the barrel. He moved it towards the page.

'There's just one thing I need. Before it's yours.'

His hand stopped. Withdrew.

'I knew it,' he said.

'It's not like that, Mick,' she said. 'Prof's in real trouble. You have to help him.'

'What kind of trouble?'

She reached back in her case, pulled out a glossy journal. *Nature*. Opened it at a page marked with a yellow Post-it. Put it down in front of Mick and me, for us to read.

'He was at the symposium,' Ariadne said, flatly. 'Prof feels so betrayed.'

I won't pretend I followed it all. A long letter, full of polysyllabic scientific words. Published along with what looked like half a dozen other contributions to the ongoing McDonald matter-and-imagination debate. But the implication was obvious, even to a dunce like me. The radiographic evidence Prof had produced had been his and his alone. No one had witnessed the scan or the x-ray being obtained. Until another lab, working independently, came up with the same results, Prof's work had to be considered suspect. Fraudulent, even.

'I need to fly you to Geneva,' Ariadne said. 'Submit you to another scan at. At that bastard's institute.

Otherwise Prof's career is finished.' She averted her eyes. 'Mine, too, in all probability.'

'This is your idea?' Mick said.

Ariadne nodded. 'Prof's completely withdrawn, utterly depressed. Won't even answer the phone.'

'Daddy, I want a drink!'

Ellie was in the doorway. For how long I couldn't be sure.

'Please,' Mick told her.

'*Please*,' said Ellie.

We got to our feet. Fetched her some apple 'n' mango from the fridge. Decanted it into one of her beakers. Popped it in her pudgy little hand.

'Run along, now, darling,' Mick told her.

We sat back down. I felt like crying. Going through it all again. The claustrophobic orifice, us being engulfed by Big Science, the renewed questioning of my very existence.

What if it did show me, though? What if Prof was indeed a tall thin crook? There've been others: scientists who've faked their data, falsified their trials, cooked up unsubstantiated conclusions, all for the sake of fame, advancement, notability. Duping Ariadne would have been the work of but a moment.

What if we went in that scanner and it showed two heads, not one?

What if someone could prove I did exist, after all?

I was a stupid sucker! As bad as the rest of them! I didn't *need* proof. I knew I was real. Nothing that popped out of a MRI could tell me any different.

Mick, though. The pen was hovering. Would it be worth it, Mick? The price we would all have to pay?

He touched the nib to the paper. Started the downstroke of the M. Ariadne eased back in her chair, issued a sigh.

Then Mick retracted the pen.

'We could promise Smarties every day for a month. And a new Barbie,' Mick suggested. He has learned some things from me along the way, after all.

'It's too risky,' I said. 'You just can't trust kids.' I held his eyes in the bathroom mirror. 'We're best to tell her the truth.'

'She'll freak out.'

'She most certainly will not. Yes: if we said nothing and Ellie blabbed. Yes: if you'd actually signed the fucking thing. But not at this.'

'You sure?'

'More than sure. Believe me.'

He looked so puzzled. He thinks about things too much. Always has been completely out of his depth with women. Always will be.

'I thought you *were* going to sign, for a moment,' I said.

He smiled, faintly. 'It wasn't about the job, really. I just wanted to settle it, one way or the other. One head. Two heads. Suddenly there was this chance to know for sure.'

'What stopped you?'

He looked down at the sink. 'I don't know. All sorts of stuff. They weren't ever going to give me that job, not if that letter hadn't appeared. I was so pissed off about that. I thought: you were going to hang me out to dry, you bastards. You try it, see how you like it.'

'I'm proud of you,' I told him. 'Jules will be, too.'

'Yeah,' he said.

Downstairs, Ellie called out for us.

'Sounds like *Nemo*'s finished,' I said.

'Yeah,' he said.

We stared at each other for a moment. Our eyes locked on.

I thought maybe I should tell him I loved him. But I decided against. There'd be time enough, another time. Maybe when the wounds had healed some more. Maybe after he'd agreed to sign Mary Warnock's deed, rescinding his parental rights and responsibilities.

'We'd better go get that girl her tea,' I told him.

'Yeah,' he said, giving me a flash of his old media doc smile. 'We better had.'

Income tax self assessment

Once upon a Time in the West

The smoke from Slingshot's rifle hung in the air, long after the reverberations had ceased to be. The horseshoe of circus folk stood stock still, some with their gazes fixed, horrified, on Slingshot. Others, equally appalled, stared at the body lying prostrate in the red dirt. Its upturned hat. Its pool of blood. Its shattered head.

Slingshot slowly unshouldered the gun. Held it out in front of him. Seemed to be searching it, much as one searches the face of a lover who's just stuck a knife in your guts.

'I don't understand,' he muttered, eventually.

The Amazing Breasted Man sank to his knees. Began openly to cry.

Billy Bucks, sensing that the moment for leadership was nigh, moved swiftly forwards. He grabbed the red-painted chain, all that linked the living and the dead; the one man standing, the other having bitten the dust. Tugged completely ineffectually at it. Like he might be able to achieve what no axe, no saw, no chisel, mallet or bullet had ever done.

'What the hell we gonna do?' he muttered. 'How the hell we gonna *bury* him?'

'Jesus!' said Deputy Mick. Shaking. Spattered in blood bone brain. Bewitched by Mad John. Whose lifeless arm was still wrenched aloft, suspended by the cuffs, as though pointing accusingly even after death.

'Here, let me try.'

Mick looked up. Ivan Ironjaw. Expression grave.

The Russian sent a courteous nod in the direction of John's corpse. Then he grabbed the chain. Bent to meet it. Bared his tombstone teeth. And sank them straight through the metal.

Which cleaved in twain.

John's arm flopped heavily down. Raised a little puff of dust.

Ivan spat out the other end of the chain. Wiped his lips with the back of his hand. Spoke to the dead man: 'You should've asked me first, fella.'

They piled a cairn of stones over the shallow pit. Billy Bucks, finding a last use for the various tools he'd purchased for the handcuff act, knocked up a rough cross from a plank off the stage. Slingshot insisted on hammering it into the ground. His sweat-stained vest. His frantic blows. His desperate need for atonement.

Deputy Mick, composure somewhat reconstituted by a hefty slug of whisky, took a branding iron out of the hastily resurrected campfire and used it to scorch a bald epitaph on the horizontal strut of wood.

Mad John McDonald. Dates unknown. Slippery eel no bars could hold.

Heap Big Rattle provided the percussion as they sang 'Abide With Me', the only hymn any of them knew. It sounded truly awful. They're a phantasmagorical circus, after all, not a male voice choir.

Afterwards, they peeled away in ones and twos, some to the wagons, some to sit gazing out over the infinite range, looking towards the next destination on their endless tour of the West.

Deputy Mick caught up with Doll a few hundred yards beyond the camp perimeter. Grabbed her elbow.

'Where are you going?'

She shook her arm free. Carried on walking.

'Doll!'

'It's over, lawman,' she called over her shoulder.

'What did I do?' he shouted.

'You didn't do nothing! You can't do nothing!' She pulled up short. Turned to face him. 'Those cuffs were our living, shit-for-brains.'

She glared at him for a moment.

'I'm going back to whoring,' she said. 'Least you know where you are with that.'

Then she wheeled around, and continued on her way back to the anonymous frontiersville that had hosted Mick and John's one and only two-man show.

Mick remained where he was, watching her steadily

diminishing figure, the fury in her feet. His fingers rotated the hoop of the cuff, locked for ever around his wrist, its chewed off chain dangling. His own memento of Mad John McDonald.

He felt a hand on his shoulder. Billy Bucks had come alongside.

'Women, huh?' Bucks said.

Mick shook his head. 'I've never understood them.'

'Completely unfathomable,' Bucks agreed.

He clapped a palm heartily on Mick's back.

'So, fella,' Bucks said. 'Fancy learning to juggle? I reckon if we use live mice it'll look pretty fucking freaky.'

The street was one of Boston's finest. Stone-built houses, coach yards out back, plumbing and sanitation. The bare boards were softened by rugs. Paintings on the wall. Gilt-framed mirrors. Carriage clocks. Her parents' fine furniture. Her childhood home.

Julia massaged her temples, trying to ease the headache. Fenella was playing over by the fireplace, a game involving the perfectly carved wooden horses her grandfather had purchased for her the day after they'd pitched up on the eastbound stage those months ago. Julia's parents doted on their granddaughter, her unexpected presence had rejuvenated their tired old lives.

They'd never asked much about what had gone wrong, why Michael was no longer on the scene. Just the odd sympathetic look. Just the sense that she was being handled with kid gloves. They'd never approved of the match. Had always thought she'd been marrying beneath herself. But they were too generous to have tried to stand in her way.

A sudden, unbearable pain pierced her breast. Caused her to gasp for air. She held a hand to her chest, fought to prevent herself crying out. It lasted but a second, then it faded. Fenella was oblivious, was wrapped up in her world of make-believe.

John! It was John! It was the exact same place she always pined for him. The site of her yearning. Her grief at having left him. The pangs she felt of regret.

Something had happened to him. She knew it. Something very, very bad.

John! Oh, John.

'What's the matter, Mommy?'

She opened her eyes to find Fenella standing in front of her, an equine figurine in either hand. Her mouth was slightly open. Her eyes were wide with anxiety.

'Nothing, darling.' Julia fashioned a reassuring smile. 'Mommy's feeling a little sickly, that's all. I'm fine.'

She reached a hand out. Caressed Fenella's smooth-skinned cheek.

'You go back to playing. You were having such a lovely game.'

Oh, God. She felt suddenly helpless. Like there was no control any more. Like life was spiralling down and down. A vertiginous whirlpool. Like she was being sucked into it, her clothing soaked, her hair dishevelled, her limbs flailing, her lungs filling with nothing but ice cold water.

She got to her feet. Steadied herself on the arm of the chair. She must find her mother, get her to sit with Fenella. So she could lie down. So she could still this nauseating wave.

She made it into the hallway, concentrating hard on landing each foot one in front of the other. Was about to call out for assistance when a heavy pounding struck up on the front door.

Something about the knock. In spite of herself, she moved to answer it. The closer she got, the better she began to feel.

Her hand had the barest of tremors as she opened the latch. She pulled the heavy oak slab inwards. Looked with frank incomprehension at the figure standing before her. Gasped, forgetting how she'd planned to retain her dignity should this moment ever come.

'John!'

She stepped forward. Threw herself against him.

'John! Oh, John!'

She felt his arms around her. She hugged him too. He'd lost so much weight. He felt light, impossibly insubstantial. She couldn't help herself. Her vision was wetly blurred when she took a step back, held him at arm's length, the better to see his face, his curving scar, his interestingly barbered beard.

'I told you I'd come,' he said. Face splitting into the hugest grin.

'I can't believe it!' she cried. 'Oh, John! How did you manage it? How did you get free? How are you *here*?'

He reached above his head, upended the stetson, and held it over the place where his heart should have been.

'It wasn't easy, darling. I had to pull off every god-damned trick in the book!'

Epilogue

Main Man 2

'**G**reat sermon,' I told him.

'Yeah, terrific,' Mick said.

Clive beamed at us. Wouldn't release my hand. I'm beginning to think he might be gay.

'I'm so delighted for you all,' he said.

Jules blushed, and looked at her feet. Or she would have done were it not for the bump.

He's been great, Clive. Never asked Jules whether her mother was feeling better. And, though I'm sure he's noticed who's sitting beside who nowadays, he's passed no comment.

'Thanks for everything,' I said.

'Oh, I didn't do anything.'

'No,' I said. 'But you said a lot. And you showed me a lot.'

Ellie was tugging at our trousers.

'Daddy! I want to go home!'

'Thanks,' I told Clive, looking him in the eye.

He nodded. Finally let go.

'Come and talk to me about the christening,' he said, glancing appraisingly at Jules. 'Soon.'

'Sure,' I said.

'Have you thought about godparents?'

I inclined my head, touching Mick on the temple. 'Dr Mick, from *Wake Up Britain!*'

He gave me a broad smile of recognition. 'I thought so!'

It was a warm day. Clive moved off, seeking out the next parishioner to talk to. I stood, enjoying the sunshine for a moment. Jules at my side. Our child in her belly. Ellie, crouching now to examine a ladybird she'd spotted on the path.

I reached my hand up. Gave Mick a brief, brotherly pat on his cheek. I felt the stubble, the slight dampness of perspiration, the warmth of him. Then I brought my fingers to my own face: the bristles of my goatee, the softness of my lips, the shininess of my nose. If anything I felt more real, more substantial than I ever had done before.

I took Jules's hand. Her fingers interlocked with mine. There was comfort in that, the way we fitted together. She called to Ellie, who reluctantly cut short her entomological observations. And then the whole damn lot of us began the short walk home.

It's A Girl!

John McDonald, the conjoined twin, yesterday announced the safe arrival of a baby daughter. The infant's mother, Julia, was formerly McDonald's sister-in-law and their relationship aroused considerable interest in the tabloid press when news of it leaked out last summer. In an extraordinary twist, the labour was of unexpectedly short duration and McDonald's brother, Dr Michael, conducted an uncomplicated delivery in the bath at the family home in Oxford. Both mother and child are said to be doing well.

The birth coincides with the rushed publication of John McDonald's debut novel, *Once upon a Time in the West*, which was itself the subject of much press coverage when it secured a record advance for the UK and Commonwealth rights. McDonald's agent, Candida Lucas-Montefiori, currently negotiating translation rights for the book, wished the couple well at this happy time, but sought to reassure expectant fans that the forthcoming countrywide book tour would be unaffected by the new arrival. McDonald's publisher, Eamon Judge, of Pegasus House, sent his warmest congratulations, and commented that he wished all his authors would take the business of book promotion half as seriously.

Professor Donald Randall, the academic at the centre of the matter-and-imagination controversy that shot the twins to prominence last year, was unavailable for comment. His assistant, Dr Ariadne Vetenskap, conveyed her best wishes, and said her research group at the University of Oxford would be closely monitoring the number of heads on the baby as she grew up.

Names for the little sweetie have yet to be decided.

Acknowledgements

Thanks be to God. Thanks also be to Clara Farmer, Toby Mundy, Emma Grove, and all at Atlantic; and to my agent, Jonny Geller at Curtis Brown. Jason Cowley and Martyn Bedford provided literary encouragement and apposite criticism – I'm deeply grateful. My wife, Lynn, as ever, did that and much more besides – heartfelt thanks.

I am indebted to the Kay Blundell Trust administered by the Society of Authors for financial support during the early stages of the development of this novel.

Who, or what, is John McDonald?
What do you think about *Freak of Nature*?
Have your say.

Join the McDonald debate.

www.philwhitaker.co.uk